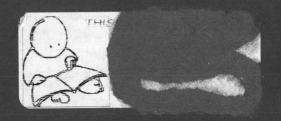

obscene

BODiES

KiM BENABiB

obscene BODiES

a novel

HarperCollins*Publishers*

Grateful acknowledgment is made to Steerforth Press, L. C., for permission to reprint an extract from *The Diaries of Dawn Powell*, copyright © 1995 by The Estate of Dawn Powell. All rights reserved.

HarperCollins books may be purchased for educational, business, or sales promotional use. For information please write: Special Markets Department, HarperCollins Publishers, Inc., 10 East 53rd Street, New York, NY 10022.

FIRST EDITION

Designed by Nina Gaskin

Library of Congress Cataloging-in-Publication Data

Benabib, Kim.
   Obscene bodies : a novel / by Kim Benabib.
     p. cm.
   ISBN 0-06-017437-4
   1. Man-woman relationships—New York (N.Y.)—Fiction. 2. Art museum, curators—New York (N.Y.)—Fiction. 3. SoHo (New York, N.Y.)—Fiction. I. Title.
PS3552.E5358O27   1996
813'.54—dc20   96-45

96 97 98 99 00 ❖/HC 10 9 8 7 6 5 4 3 2 1

For my father,
and in memory of my mother

The artist's two-headed bogey: the hope of being discovered and the fear of being found out.

—Dawn Powell

BLOOD HAD stained the walls of the elevator shaft, and the tenants decided they would have to pay someone to clean it off, grudgingly accepting yet another assessment above and beyond the regular monthly maintenance charges. They might not have gone to such an expense except that the manually operated elevator car was just a metal cage, with gates that opened on two sides, allowing passengers to see right through. It had been built to carry the freight of the last century, and the grease on its gears and cable gave it a quiet, smooth ride even though it creaked with age whenever it landed on a floor. Many of the tenants had been woken by the schizophrenic sirens and strobing lights of emergency vehicles. A few had even seen the body and recognized it. Someone at the board meeting mentioned that the deceased had been more than a frequent visitor to the fourth-floor loft. Another remarked on how four flights was a long way to fall, then wondered to himself, as they all did, what such a deadly accident might do to the value of their property.

Stuart Finley knew the building well, recalling in detail both the first time he visited and the last. Trying to understand his acquaintance with the man who had died there, he considered all that had transpired at that loft during several weeks the previous autumn. He remained surprised at how those events had sucked him in and how fast they had all gone by. There was a time in his life, not long ago, when he would never have imagined even setting foot inside 112 Mercer Street, a place removed from him in so many ways. Of the people who frequented that fourth-floor loft, many were just passing through, others had vested interests, but in some way all of them were accomplices. Stuart wasn't sure exactly what they had done to earn their place in the history of art, but they were there, fitting securely into that great timeline, that slightly false, implausibly tidy story of creativity in which every new movement is cast as a perfectly logical reaction to the one that came before.

one

THERE IS a way of seeing in this city, the hopelessly self-aware way, where every meaningful moment has all the weight of a *New Yorker* cartoon, where everything goes by in an ironic caption, leaving you feeling cheated. The condition becomes more acute during the fall months, moving into the city like so many bits of pollen in allergy season, and seems to worsen with every passing year. I remember attending a party last October where it just got out of hand, a moment when some kind of breakdown in the societal fabric occurred and a bunch of slightly drunk, seemingly respectable adults finally went wacky.

The invitation was a triumph in subtlety, listing only an address on White Street over a photo of wet cobblestones, with the date and time in tiny letters along the edge of the flip side. It was one of those freebie publicity parties, and I was fully aware of how absurd these things could sometimes be, but I never failed to show up, since they were filled with single women. Besides, it was a Tuesday night with nothing going on, and this kind of middle-of-the-week escapism was such low-cost entertainment. It wasn't until I arrived at the

TriBeCa home that I realized my tenuous connection: The woman who owned the place had once hired me to appraise a painting for her. It was a huge space, skillfully renovated, with a thin white spiral staircase that led to a dramatic roof garden. The crowded gathering was built around a show of a photographer's recent work, and many of her framed prints hung on the walls. As I took my time to look at the sharp, textured portraits, each one filled with harsh light to soften its subjects' face, I was introduced to a man named Wendell.

"I know most of them," he said, all bulky under a wrinkled cotton jacket.

"Who?"

"The people in the pictures. They're the photographer's friends mostly."

"Is she here?"

"Not yet," he said.

"Why not?"

"Her plane is late."

"Where from?" I asked him.

"London, she's English." He looked at me. "There's only one reason to go to London, and that's to see the shows before they come over here."

"I don't go in for big musicals," I said.

"Musicals, dramas, whatever. The trick is to see the stuff *before* it comes to Broadway so that when someone tells you they saw it on opening night, you can say you saw it in London. If somebody coyly lets slip how they saw it in previews, you can tell them you saw it in London. It's foolproof."

I struggled to hold a polite smile. "I never thought of it that way, Wendell."

"It's true of everything," he continued. "When I go see a movie, I can't help but think that someone's already been to the premiere, and someone before him got to see a private screening. But it only gets worse, I mean, someone before him could have viewed a rough cut, maybe even one without the sound track, and then there are always the people who got to see the dailies." He shook his head and looked at me. "How can you compete with that?"

"How? It's like holding your hand over a flame," I said. "The trick is to not give a shit."

I hoped he might take offense and leave me alone, but he was only more determined to make me see things his way. "You can't ignore it, that's impossible. There are people in this town who won't read a book unless it's in galleys, who enroll their kids in pre-preschool, who cut work short on Friday just so they can be the first out onto the Long Island Expressway before the weekend rush hour." He looked around and then lowered his voice. "Can't you see the pattern of behavior?"

"I'm not sure."

"Haven't you been listening to the experts? The country's polarizing into a small cognitive elite and a huge underclass." He got closer, right up to my face, a liquor glaze over his eyes. "Don't you understand? That couple leaving work early to beat rush hour is a metaphor. They're out speeding away, with all the benefits of family planning, while everyone else is stuck in tunnel traffic having too many babies."

"What the hell are you drinking," I said.

"A very young Bordeaux." He sniffed the glass. "Could use another ten years in the bottle, easily."

I looked over at several stacks of coffee-table books piled high by the window, all of them brand-new volumes of the photographer's work. "*A Retrospective*," read the words underneath the title. The thick, shiny copies looked heavy and expensive, and every few minutes another person would pick up one of the books and flip through its stiff pages before quietly walking off with it. I kept turning back to check the pile, and each time a little more of that table was revealed. Behind the stacks were a group of nicely framed family photos, and as the books continued to disappear, I saw more and more young nephews, smiling cousins, and friendly uncles. A few people had taken more than one copy, perhaps seeing wonderful gift potential, and I watched one brazen woman fit three of them into her shoulder bag, struggling to draw its leather strings.

"People are taking those books," I said to Wendell. "Are they free?"

"The photographer is supposed to sign them, if she ever gets here. Did I tell you her plane's late? They're gonna ask for a hundred bucks per copy to benefit the Perry Street Shelter, if she ever shows up."

"She'd better get here fast."

Then I heard a woman's voice behind me. "I first suggested they do a book, I mean it was my idea," she said.

Wendell turned around to face her. "I'm sorry," he said, "but I was the one who first conceived of the book. I floated the idea."

"You floated it?"

"I suggested it anonymously, through a back channel."

"You're not even in the acknowledgments," said the woman.

"I asked to be left out," he said.

As they stood there arguing the point, I took the opportunity to scan the rest of the framed pictures. A bit later I sensed that something had changed in the room. People were moving about, gathering their things, grabbing the books from the display, and heading for the exits.

I walked back over to Wendell. "What's going on?" I asked him.

"She had heroin in her Hasselblad."

"What?"

"The photographer, turns out she was arrested by customs at the airport. Word just spread through the place. There won't be any signing, party's over. Everyone's on their way to this thing at 44 Crosby. Good luck getting a cab."

It was that panic-stricken moment of group psychology when people suddenly realize there's a better place to be, a smarter, more happening gathering taking place somewhere else. No one wanted to be left behind, and there was a lot of pushing and shoving going on as it threatened to turn into a frenzy. I watched as people rushed to get their hands on the last few copies of the big glossy book. The table was picked clean; the only things left were the family photos, and I was afraid someone might even go for the nice silver frames.

"I can't remember the last time I had to pay for a book," someone complained bitterly after coming up empty-handed.

"You know my motto," said her companion, "if it's not comp, it's not worth doing."

The book seemed too nice to take, and perhaps simply from my own sense of proportion, I never thought of trying to get one. As I headed for the door I saw that only one of them had been spared. It was sitting open for display on an easel. A young woman walked up to it and looked around as her friends called from the door.

"Claire," they said, "let's go." She looked back at them and then at the beautiful book of photographs on the easel, hesitating. She was attractive, distractingly so, and she and I seemed about the same age. She wore a little gunmetal gray dress, cut low at the top and high at the bottom, the material wrapping its way up her body like a bandage. Its simplicity would have made Mies van der Rohe blush, and it seemed designed to be worn sitting, legs crossed, in a Barcelona chair flanked by a Brancusi sculpture. If there was ever any proof that form never followed function, this was it. Her straight brown hair came down well below the shoulder, and a few of the strands fell to the side of her face as she looked around.

By then it seemed too late to approach her, so I stayed only to see what choice she would make, thinking it would be so much easier to write her off if she took the book. Then I could leave feeling good about having failed to talk to her. But part of me wanted desperately to be proven wrong. "Don't do it," I whispered to myself, "don't do it." She looked over in my direction and noticed me watching her. I quickly focused away, slipping each arm into a dark wool jacket. I tried to hold my discipline and not stare, but there was no way I could leave without knowing if she had walked off with that last copy. So I felt for my wallet, placing my hand against the breast pocket, and finding it safely there, I took one last look at her. She smiled at me, closed the book's cover, and defiantly placed it under her arm before walking off.

Although I don't regret attending, I never did feel fully a part of that affair, occupying instead the middle ground of a bystander and regarding what I witnessed with a combination of wonder and dread.

At work several days later, buried under heavy reference books and tucked away into the sleepy back corridors of the Metropolitan Museum of Art, I could clearly recall that huge apartment on White Street. It was the kind of gem that would provoke intense envy in most New Yorkers the way nothing but real estate does. I filed that memory away in a part of my brain reserved as a storehouse of Manhattan interiors. It was filled with the comparative details of bedrooms, bathrooms, eat-in kitchens, convertible dining areas, ceiling heights, and closet spaces. I had been afflicted with this sickness from an early age—a result of having been raised in this magnifying lamp. But my moment of focus was broken by a phone ringing.

I turned the magnifying lamp off and pushed it away before answering. It was an executive who worked for my landlord, the developer Harry Vogel. Vogel was an old-line name in New York real estate, one of those big families that seemed to own half the airspace over Manhattan. Harry Vogel was the family's silver-haired patriarch. He was famous for his appalling taste in architecture. A few years back he had committed the grossly insensitive sin of demolishing a great old Broadway theater in the middle of the night, just hours before landmark designation. My apartment was in one of the many brownstone walk-ups the family had speculated on during the Great Depression, and it was rent-controlled, making Vogel and me the most natural of adversaries. For years he had been frustrated in his attempts to get the various members of my family who had lived there to leave. But this was different; this sounded like a more determined, more urgent effort.

"A buyout?" I asked.

"Yes," said the young executive. "A one-time lump-sum payment in exchange for moving out."

"What are you offering?"

"What do you want?"

His answer threw me off. "I want fair value," I said. "That's assuming I want anything. I mean, right now I plan to stay."

"We have big plans for that site," he said. "Mr. Vogel is ready to work with you on this. We want you to be happy. Start thinking about where you'd really like to live. You know, a doorman, marble floors, a little more prestige."

Prestige? The guy thought he knew how to get through to me, but he had no idea. I resented his *It's your lucky day!* tone. "I have to go," I said. "Send me something in writing."

city—but even those who move here later in life are doomed to develop it. A trip through this debilitating database could keep me from getting work done, and I had to hang a show that week. There was no time to compare herringbone-pattern hardwood floors with the square parquet variant.

I was an assistant curator of drawings and at twenty-eight easily the youngest member of the department. My office was cramped with the evidence of art scholarship, piles of reference materials, books, and catalogues, their pages marked with little yellow Post-its. I saw this immense, unwieldy beast of a cultural institution as a charmed place to make a career. I had access to all of its great treasures. Well funded, with sprawling wings stealing chunks of Central Park, the Met was where every curator in my field should have wanted to be. But although we had all the technology of the modern age—fax, voice mail, a dazzling Web site, enough X-ray machines and CAT scans to put Sloan-Kettering to shame—the spirit of the place, its politics, its mood and tenor were thoroughly traditional. Hidden among all those back corridors where the public could never browse were the attitudes and mores of another era, a collection of souls that tended to resist the new, and back then I wasn't aware of how much all of it was rubbing off on me.

At that moment I was considering a drawing thought at various times to be by Guercino, the seventeenth-century Italian master. More recent opinions doubted it was from the artist's hand and attributed it to one of his students instead. The small sheet, most likely lifted from a sketchbook, depicted a child and father walking on a road and was drawn in a reddish brown chalk. Its figures evoked intense character even though they were made of just a few short strokes and delicate shading. Concentrating on any tiny marking that might give some clue to its true author, I carefully held the 350-year-old sheet of paper, looking at it through a round

As I hung up I could hear voices outside the open door-way to the office. Harlan Kohlman, chief curator and head of the department, was making his way down the hall with several other people. When he reached my door he said good-bye to the others and came in.

"Big shots," he whispered, closing the door behind him halfway. "They're all lawyers and bureaucrats." He was in his early seventies and spoke with just a hint of a central European accent that gave him an old-world flair.

"Who are they?" I asked.

"It's all so complex, I'll tell you in a moment. How's the work going?"

"I've got this one fairly clean, but any more abrasion would cause damage." I turned the lamp back on and looked through the magnifying glass for dramatic effect. "I would change the attribution. What would you say if I told you I thought this was a Guercino, by the master himself?"

"I'd say you're very wrong. But go ahead, make your case." This was his polite way of giving me the opportunity to explain, but it was also a challenge. He seemed so sure, I began to worry that I had missed something obvious. He had this way of making you feel like an amateur by the cold confidence of his criticism. He knew he was right, and the burden fell on others to prove him wrong. It kept me on my toes and sharpened my developing critical expertise.

"The treatment of the subject and the figure proportioning all seem right. I can't put my finger on it, maybe it's the lines of shading I've seen in so many others of his," I said, feeling the complete inadequacy of my response.

"But Guercino's lines of shading were more severe; the shading here is the right kind, but it's too soft." He looked at the drawing for a moment. "There's one thing that bothers me about this one," he continued. "It lacks Guercino's economy of line. There's a certain thumbnail light-footedness to his sketching that is not at work here. Stop looking at the detail through that damned magnifying glass. By not looking at the whole you miss the overall work."

He was right. I had been looking at this drawing off and on for several days, thinking hard about each line, every corner, running its image through my memory of every similar work I had seen. Then Kohlman, coming from some other engagement, distracted, his head full of other concerns, casually walked in and gave me this crystalline understanding of what he saw before him. His critique was so on-target, as if he had the whole permanent collection memorized and could have delivered this insight no matter what drawing I put before him. Of course he had no such memorization; his only tools were his eyes, his familiarity with the artist, a sense and feeling for the work that came from a long experience handling it. I had the scholarship down, but there was another level of understanding that he operated on, a level that required more years than I had at that point. What we were truly paid to do in that place, more than anything else, was to look and communicate to others what we saw. In a way we were critics, always passing judgment, always placing levels of importance, always operating from the position of skepticism and doubt.

"What's this, carbonated?" he asked, pointing to a bottle of spring water I had on the desk.

"No, just plain," I said when he reached into his pocket and pulled out a bottle of prescription pills. He took one out and swallowed it with some of the water.

"These don't seem to be working anymore."

"Painkillers?"

"It's been so long since the surgery," he said, annoyed. He put the pills back into the pocket of his blazer. Kohlman was a traditionalist, playing the part with a dandy's relish and treating this little corner of the museum as his baronial domain. He was a man who chose his words carefully and had played the politics of academe with finesse. Having arrived in New York after the war in 1945 as a refugee with nothing but his expertise in the Old Masters, he established himself as the dean of the field, writing a coffee table full of books over the years. Despite his legendary reputation, he always remained demure and friendly. "I need you to go to the Carlyle with me tomorrow. Looks like we may be getting some drawings," he said.

"What are they?"

"Important Italians, sixteenth-century. They were donated last year but have been tangled up in this bankruptcy case. I was just in a meeting with all these government lawyers, FDIC, RTC, you get the idea."

"You're kidding," I said. He shook his head and started for the door. "What time?"

"Nine sharp. It's the Carlyle, so wear a jacket," he said on his way out.

"Don't worry, you'll be very proud." I was grateful for the early interest he had shown in me, and now I owed my job in large part to his efforts.

It was at one of his guest lectures at the Institute of Fine Arts that we first met, and he later agreed to shepherd the planning and writing of my thesis. I remember waiting for him as a student the day he arrived for that lecture. Several of us had taken our seats in the former ballroom of an elegant mansion that had been converted into classrooms for the graduate program, its gilt wainscoting and mirrored paneling angrily disapproving of the modern fluorescent lighting and our cheap aluminium folding chairs. Kohlman made his entrance slowly, his old leather briefcase swaying back and forth, white mustache yellowing at the tips, his clothing made of delicate wool. The only thing missing was a monocle. We had all heard of him, read his books, knew his standards, awaited his syllabus with a bit of trepidation. He walked in, stopped halfway, scanned the big ballroom, and said with a straight face, "No one will pass this seminar unless they learn how to waltz." The tension, needless to say, had been relieved, and he had us all thoroughly charmed from then on.

Back then I wanted all his expertise and classic style, his wit and self-assurance. My father had no interest in art. A lawyer, he had use only for the arcane details of the civil code. He could never understand my *diversion* into art history, could never express genuine enthusiasm or even pretend to take part in my interests. But Kohlman was as excited by the Old Masters as I was. "It's all in the work," he used to say. "You stand in front of the canvas or the piece of carved marble and say to yourself, *that's it.* Something just comes through, it simply comes through!" I knew exactly what he meant.

When the time came for me to find work, I didn't have to look far. At first I was made uncomfortable by the suggestion that I had established a relationship closer to him than many twice my age. Kohlman and I never discussed this, and he seemed to think it quite normal. Perhaps this stemmed from his background in Europe, where connections and relationships were as important as merit. Working at my desk that day, in a simple museum office and surrounded by some of the greatest art of the Western tradition, I truly believed that Kohlman might have seen in me something of himself as a young man. But looking back on it now, in the light of how far both of us have come since then, it is difficult for me to have ever had or even now admit such a thought.

By the end of the day my eyes felt the strain of the close work I had been performing. Everyone had gone by then except Jenny, one of the conservators, who was readying herself to leave.

"Stuart, here's another one for our Levy watch," she said smiling. She was holding up the latest issue of *Art in America,* spread open. It was a full-page photograph of the acclaimed painter and conceptual artist Miles Levy, then the subject of much New York media hype.

"Not again," I said.

"It's another profile," she said. "I'll leave it here for you to read." The two of us had started to keep tabs on the artist's press, joking about the dizzying amount of coverage he got. It had moved beyond the art publications and into the mainstream consumer and celebrity monthlies. Miles Levy at home in his kitchen. Miles Levy on the new four-button suits. Miles Levy on the best places to stay in the south of France. Although my amusement had turned to nausea, I still read every profile, still noticed every photograph and scanned every ridiculous Q&A. I was a chronic consumer of this media, and yet I hated its puffery, its total lack of skepticism. For some reason, though, I kept on reading.

"Where are you off to tonight?"

"An opening," said Jenny.

"Of what?"

"God knows."

On my way out I stopped to look at the magazine. Inside was a well-styled photo of the artist posed in his SoHo loft studio, hands on hips, looking out with confidence and full of self-importance. In the background behind his large frame and black hair was a vast space that looked less like a shopworn working studio than an expensively decorated home.

I was familiar with his work. His collage-style painting I considered barely competent, the conceptual sculpture rather workmanlike. Several years earlier an installation piece of his included in the Whitney's biennial exhibition had caused a stir, the vital price of admission to the realm of hype and acclaim. His ideas were slight, political in the most obvious way, yet expressed with a mind-numbing complexity that gave them a certain attraction among critics. "We will begin the bidding at one hundred thousand dollars, thank you," I thought to myself. Those who might want to buy one of his latest paintings had to put their name on a yearlong waiting list, unless they had special pull. His gallery exhibitions were "oversubscribed," meaning every piece had sold before the show even opened. The only way around this was to pay for it ahead of time, sight unseen, an acceptable alternative for those who just had to have *something*.

As I left the museum and headed for home I thought about all those Renaissance and Baroque scholars I worked with, and also I thought of Miles Levy and his loft-to-die-for. The art world was not really one world but a collection of different social spheres in the same orbit. At the center were the artists such as Levy. Beyond were the galleries and museums, the art professionals and schools, the auction houses, collectors, critics, journalists, and various hangers-on. My position as an art historian remained rather removed from the center, not important to answering the question "What's happening now?" but crucial as a provider of legitimacy to the whole order. This was the nature of the long distance that separated Miles and myself, a strange but necessary duality that I had frequently stopped to consider but never fully understood.

What Harry Vogel wanted me to part with was a one-bedroom apartment in a turn-of-the-century five-flight walk-up near Gramercy Park. Unfortunately for him, not only were each of those 850 square feet of space dear to me, having been in the family for decades, but they were also eminently affordable. The place still had its original telephone number, one of the first in the neighborhood. On my answering machine's message I could be heard announcing, "You've reached Gramercy six-one-zero-zero-six . . ." The old area prefix was a piece of nostalgia from a New York now gone, and it appealed to my sensibilities.

I arrived to find an envelope slipped halfway under the front door, and I opened it even before putting my coat down. It was from the Vogel people. They were in a real hurry, I thought, anxious to develop the site before the next recession. The letter contained few details and only the vague promise of cash—the amount, apparently, to be negotiated later.

I took a seat near the bookshelves. The evidence of my education remained crammed into those shelves, from small dog-eared paperbacks to massive art-history books. Greeks, moderns, criticism, *Lives of the Saints* and all that. The moment I finished reading the letter I did not think of the money. I could only picture a wrecking ball crashing through the old plaster, obliterating the crown moldings and the original mantel over my working fireplace. I felt slight sorrow more than anything else. My parents had lived in the place when they were first married. Later my aunt called it home, and with a little luck and impeccable timing, I took over after college.

But then I began to think about the money. What could I get from Vogel? He was rich and powerful, and his plans were always on a huge scale; buying me off was just a small cost, not even a day's interest payments. Playing right into his hands, I thought of the chance to buy a few things I had always wanted, a few master drawings, maybe the small Greek bronze head I had been eyeing in that antiquities shop on Madison. It had been there so long I could probably get it for a song. And how could I ever forget those graduate-school loans? But more than any of this, what I really wanted was to prevent them from ripping the brownstone apart and putting up some tasteless, forty-story, architecturally criminal disaster. That would have been priceless. I liked the thought of holding a rare power over the heavy march of progress. Legally I could refuse to leave, and I hoped there would be others like me in the building. I decided not to respond, to let Vogel sweat it out. As I sat there designing my plan of bad-faith negotiation the phone rang.

"Hello?"

"Stuart?"

"Yes."

"It's Michelle, Michelle White from the Getty Museum."

She was an acquaintance from graduate school who had gone into arts administration, winding up at the Getty in California, a museum famous for its vast resources and a willingness to spend its way to the top of the field. At school I had always wanted to go to bed with her, and we had flirted briefly—at least I thought we had.

The sound of her voice made me recall being next to her in a conservation lab at school. We were wearing clean white lab coats and being shown how to take four hundred years of grime off of oil paint. The instructor handed out pairs of rubber medical gloves for everyone to put on. There is something about rubber gloves. She put hers on like a pro, the rubber snapping loudly against her skin as she stretched them. I was having trouble, though, and she came over to assist me, smiling. I held my hands up the way a surgeon does in the operating room, and she pulled on the end of each glove to fit them on. "Just leave a little tip at the end," she whispered. On several occasions after that I tried to get her to show me more of her technique, but she kept turning me down.

"I love it out here," she said now. "The attitude is totally different. I feel so much healthier. You age more slowly with the sun and the ocean at your door, driving along the PCH with all that natural beauty. My skin's never been better."

"You sound like you haven't changed," I said. She had always seemed like the type who wanted to be a star.

"We've been hearing great things about you, and we know you've learned well from Kohlman." She lowered her voice as if telling a secret. "The trustees are always looking to recruit the emerging talents in the field."

"Is that right?"

"We'll pay for a trip out here. No strings attached, just fly out to visit, rent a car, stay awhile, all on us. I could guarantee you at least twenty percent over your current salary, car allowance, day care, moving expenses, and best of all, an associate curatorship. You know money goes so much further out here."

"Michelle, that's an awful lot, and I'm very flattered, but I don't need day care, really."

"Ah, well, of course not, but would you fly out to see us?" She turned on that sexy, furtive charm. "I'll even book it first-class, if you can keep a secret."

"I don't think I could get the time."

"A weekend is all it takes."

After all we had been through in school, *now you want me?* "I appreciate the attention, but I'm a New Yorker, born and raised. Besides, what about the earthquakes and racial tension? I have a real fear of ignorant jurors and brutal cops."

"I used to be a New Yorker too. But that was another person, not me. I'm new and improved. I don't know how you can do it. Everyone lives like hamsters in those little boxes of apartments. This is the chance to have your own house with a pool and a four-by-four."

"You're forgetting the vacant-faced blonde. Hey, we may need that day care after all." I paused and she said nothing; my remark seemed lost on her.

"You think we're just a bunch of new-money upstarts.

We don't have that stifling eastern-establishment snobbery. You could flourish out here."

"What do you mean? I thrive off that eastern establishment snobbery." Again the words seemed to fly right over her head. She was so lost in her unshakable confidence that I doubted she was even listening to me.

"Trust me, Stuart, once you experience a reserved parking space with your name painted on it, you won't know how you ever lived without one."

"I guess it's the simple things in life that make a difference."

"Look, things are happening out here," she went on. "I could introduce you to all the right people."

All the right people? What was she talking about, the Getty Museum or DreamWorks SKG?

"Michelle," I said, "I'm sorry, but this is the wrong time. Maybe next year." There was no way I was leaving the Met or Kohlman. I considered what I already had to be the best in the world, and I was just trying to get her off the phone. But this was proving to be the day of the hard sell, and she persisted.

"I've never been turned down before. Work with me. I know we could make this happen. I've got fingertips. You know what fingertips are, don't you?"

"What?"

"Instincts, and they're telling me the timing's right for you. Admit it."

"Admit what?"

"Come on, you're ready for this and we want you here. What will it take? Just name it, it's yours."

I let her get that far and then said that I had to go, that I was on my way out to meet someone, which was true.

two

CHRISTINA WAS only two years younger than me, although she and I never had the sibling rivalry that is always assumed. But she had an uncanny talent that I envied, a sixth sense that led her to the most interesting new places to eat in New York. Without fail she would spot the smartest new bars and restaurants that sprang up, often before their phone numbers had been published. I loved having her as a resource, and it was always a challenge to name a place that she hadn't been to. Whenever I would mention a review I had read or a recommendation from a friend, she would politely hint that she was already on to the next place. When she called that night to confirm our dinner plans, she changed the venue on me at the last minute, insisting we go to some new boîte she had been to recently that was just then in fashion. "In another few weeks it's going to peak," she told me. "The buzz is good right now but growing, so you better go soon before it's in *New York* magazine."

"Before?"

"Stuart, when the professional crowd comes, the creative people will flee."

"Oh, then we better go now."

"If you're gonna be like this, then forget it."

"No, no, no. I promise I'll be fine."

"I'm serious."

"I promise, Chrissie."

We met later at the Rizzoli bookstore on West Broadway; she said to look for her where they keep all the imported magazines, and I found her flipping through Italian *Vogue*. I asked her why all the European fashion magazine covers were sexier, bolder, less cluttered than the American ones. The models were the same, but the cover shots just leapt out at you, each one more stunning than the next.

"The Europeans tend to push the envelope," she said. "They don't rely on sales at supermarket checkout counters across America."

"Must be a liberating thing," I said, looking over her shoulder as she flipped the pages. "When you pick up this magazine, it's legitimate. If I pick it up, suddenly it becomes pornography."

"That's because straight men only have one real opinion on hemlines."

"We're for all lengths as long as they're short," I said, and she shook her head.

We walked over to this place on Lafayette, at SoHo's eastern frontier, on one of those blocks where modish storefronts coexist alongside tenement buildings filled with old Italian immigrants. "What's the name again?" I asked.

"Pied Noir."

"Pied Noir? The name of the restaurant is Black Foot?"

"It's the term for a French Algerian," she said. "Some colonial legacy. One of the investors was born and raised there. They call them *pieds-noirs*."

"It doesn't strike me as an appetizing name for a place to eat."

"Look, the food's hearty French peasant stuff with a hint of the American Southwest. Now will you stop?"

"What about the Algerian thing?"

"That's just an *hommage*," she said, sounding like she had no patience for me.

"But I don't see anything here, there's no sign," I said, confused at the apparent lack of any such establishment nearby.

"Right here," she said pointing me to the name spelled out in tiny black letters at the bottom of a window.

"Kind of subtle, don't you think?"

"They're not officially open yet."

The place was bathed in warm glowing light, and its faint yellow walls had a faux plaster finish, complete with veins of hairline cracks. It felt as if we'd barged in on someone's living room. Near the bar was a careful arrangement of little tables, overstuffed chairs, and small rugs, each piece distressed to look secondhand. The young black hostess seemed so skeptical as she scanned her reservation book for our name. She was oppressively stylish, with an attenuated look that was heightened by a pair of towering heels and straightened hair. "So there you are," she said with surprise. But then she sighed and shook her head, all annoyed. "You're an hour late, and I don't have anything right now."

"An hour? The reservation was for eight-thirty," Christina said.

"No, I've got you down for seven-thirty."

"I said eight-thirty on the phone."

The woman had that serious hostess air about her, as if this was some kind of rewarding career, with an overblown sense of importance and a smile that could be made warm or cold depending on what she needed. "Look, there's no way I can do it. I've got all the eight-thirties arriving now and even the early nines demanding tables."

"And now you have us," I said, looking right at her. "I mean it wasn't our mistake."

She took another look at her reservation book. "I'll see if I can squeeze something in."

We walked to the bar, and I tried to get comfortable. "That was kind of rude, I mean you got hot before you needed to," said Christina. "You should never get hot in a cool medium."

"Who are you, Marshall McLuhan? All she needed was a little push." My sister had always been very pretty, with her narrow face and green eyes, and she seemed then to be so much more mature than I had ever considered. I always admired her ability to charm, always respected her social judgment. "Maybe I got Dad's feisty Irish blood after all," I said.

"No, you didn't, I did."

"So then I got Mom's Jewish nerve."

"No, I got that too."

"Then I must have gotten her backbone, that gutsiness."

She shook her head. "Nope, those are all mine too."

"So what's left for me?" I asked.

"You got the rent-controlled apartment. What else do you want?"

For some reason just then I didn't tell her about the offer for my lease, perhaps afraid she would want me to take it. "When Aunt Becky died you were living with what's-his-name at school. I asked you if you wanted the place."

She smiled. "All you got from Mom's side was the guilt," she said.

She was partly right. Our mother was Jewish of the Riverside Drive intelligentsia variety, our father an Irish Catholic from Oyster Bay. I liked how we were mutts, mixed breeds, never easily categorized as *this* or *that*. It allowed us a kind of freedom from young tribal burdens like Hebrew school and sailing lessons. Our parents were young progressives when they met at Columbia in the sixties, marrying right away. She claimed he fell more in love with his job than with her, and by the time they divorced he was no longer the idealistic crusader she had married. But I suspected he found her disappointing as well. She might have still voted Democrat but was no longer the radical free spirit in bed. I had no evidence of this, just a theory that the sex might have been better when there was a war to protest.

"It's so perfect," I told my sister. "Dad went from being a pioneering civil rights advocate to defending corporations against discrimination lawsuits. I mean, that's his specialty now."

"Yeah, well, they hire him for his expertise."

"Don't you find it a little ironic?"

"Stuart, that little irony put us through college."

She had a way of cutting right to the bottom line, always knowing exactly what was at stake, always revealing the subtext when you didn't want to see it.

I had a vivid memory of being on the beach one summer in Martha's Vineyard with my parents. Christina and I were perilously close to the age when vacationing with your family becomes a sign of bad judgment, when no longer was it two adults with two children, but simply four adults. It was on that trip that my father finally lost my mother's respect for good. He would appeal to his kids for an ally. "Will you tell your mother to quit blaming me for the Holocaust?" he would say. I remember my sister sunbathing in a patch of that tall grass you find on the New England coast. She was all contemplative, and reminded me of the woman in Andrew Wyeth's painting *Christina's World*. I took a picture of her lying there, and when she asked me why I told her.

"Stuart, you're hopelessly esoteric," she complained after hearing my reference.

"But it's a great painting," I said, "and how uncanny that the subject is your namesake." She just rolled her eyes and ignored me. That picture I took was still my favorite of her, although I'll admit its similarity to the Wyeth wasn't obvious, and over the years no one had ever made the connection.

"It's a bit cramped, but it's all I've got," said the tall hostess. She dropped two menus on a tiny table and left. I sat with my back to a large party, maybe six or seven against the wall, and felt locked between the edge of our table and the chair behind me. After a half hour one waiter finally approached us, it seemed more out of compassion than a sense of duty. The ordering began with the disheartening experience of having to hear a list of all the dishes they were out of, including the one I wanted and all of the better-sounding alternatives.

"This is like dining in the old Soviet Union," I said, but the waiter failed to see the humor.

Later on I tried to settle down, but all my senses felt strangely invaded. I heard only the boisterous conversation of the large party behind me, smelled only their unbroken stream of cigarette smoke (it was the kind of place that would rather pay fines than ask their beautiful patrons not to smoke), and felt every slight variation in the tension of the chair that was pressing hard against mine.

"You look restless. What's the matter?" asked Christina.

"Nothing."

"Quit looking around at everything so we can toast my new job." She had just become an assistant at the Susan Edelman Agency, a publicity firm noted for its fiercely competitive founder and head. Susan Edelman was famous for her Hollywood client list and the way she would punish journalists she thought had crossed her by denying them access.

Her temper and her army of young and pretty female assistants were legend in the media world. Christina had only been there a few weeks, and already she had horror stories.

"I've never seen so much fear in an office, Stuart. Susan's very demanding, and that doesn't bother me, but we have to speak on the phone in this very rigid way and screen all her calls. Today she screamed at this poor girl for putting a wrong call through. She'll only take calls from a select list, and it's not written down anywhere, you know, like who these people are. You just have to know. If what she calls a *nobody* gets through to her private line, then she'll be all annoyed and take it out on someone. People duck whenever she walks out of her office. The other girls told me to try not to make eye contact when she walks by."

"How charming. What a healthy environment to spend forty hours a week in."

"Forty? Try at least *sixty*, and no overtime."

"Have you learned all the names yet?"

"You don't understand. I had to cut the mastheads out of all the different magazines and memorize them. I'm like ready for a pop quiz on *contributing editors*."

"It's so nice to see you broadening your horizons."

She quickly looked around the room, then leaned in close. "Yesterday Susan had me pick up her dry cleaning and take her stupid little dogs to the vet."

"Is it true she has weight requirements for her assistants? I think I read that somewhere. You know, the way airlines have for stewardesses?"

"During my interview she looked me up and down like you wouldn't believe, but she never came out and actually asked how much I weigh. All she kept asking were these cryptic questions—'What trades do you read? Name five members of the New Establishment. What's the importance of Sun Valley?'—stuff like that."

"Sounds like the job from hell, Chrissie."

"It'll be a good reference at some point."

The group at the table behind us continued to distract me, and the deep loud voice of one member was reverberating inside my head. He seemed the center of attention, sounding so eager to be heard and projecting his words. "Where's Todd?" he kept saying. "I thought Todd would be here tonight. I'm glad the guy didn't show, I'm sick of buying him dinner." The table erupted in sharp laughter every few minutes, rupturing the private space around Christina and me. I made a futile effort to focus on what my sister was saying, to push all the other sounds out.

"So, what brought you to this place?" I asked her, feeling the chair behind me needle its way further into my back.

"A date is what brought me here," she said smiling.

"Who was it? Tell me."

"It was uneventful."

"I didn't ask what happened, just who it was."

"This guy I met last summer at the premiere for the movie of that book, you know, about that political thing."

"Oh, yeah. How was it?"

"It was all right, but I wouldn't order HBO just to see it."

"No, I mean your date, Chrissie. How was it?"

"Fine, I guess. But when we walked into this room, he joked how this is one of those places where you get the feeling that the men and women who eat here actually sleep together."

"I never would have thought of it in those terms."

"Turns out he was right," she said, her grin now twice as large.

"But you said the date was uneventful."

"I wasn't going to tell you, but I couldn't resist just slipping it in there."

Halfway through our meal I was able to establish some kind of equilibrium with the nearby laughter and that projecting voice. There was a certain rhythm to it all, and I learned how to anticipate the crescendos. People kept joining their table, however, and I began to resent every person that was added to the group. I know it was entirely unreasonable, and based on little more than the fact that they were having such a damned good time. Their service was so responsive compared to that of our listless waiter, for one thing. The guy who seemed the center of things, the one who wanted so badly to be noticed—the King of the Banquette, I thought—he kept getting everything he wanted. "Just keep bringing new bottles of the wine whenever you see us getting empty, okay? And I'm gonna need the phone again," he said to the waiter. I wanted to turn around to get a look at him, but I couldn't. My chair was locked in, and all I could do was turn my neck, never getting a clear shot.

I decided then to tell Christina about the offer from Vogel. "You're kidding," she said. "Why didn't you tell me sooner?"

"I only found out today."

"It should have been the first thing out of your mouth. You could realize a lot of money from this. What did he offer you?"

"They didn't talk numbers."

"Stuart, you could get a lot, I mean a real lot. I've heard cases where holdouts made fortunes. But how can Vogel build there? Gramercy Park is a historic district."

"Only part of it. His properties all fall outside the protected zone. But I don't see moving." What were those people behind me smoking, Gauloises? The smoke was now thick, changing the taste of my food, which I had only ordered halfheartedly, since they were out of what I really wanted.

"What do you mean?"

"I don't think I want to leave."

"You mean hold out for a lot of money."

"No, I mean hold out. Period."

"That's insane. Are you insane? Don't you still dream of one day owning that classic six?"

I glanced at the table with the loud man behind me, straining to see him. No luck. People were crowding over him, visitors from other tables stopping by to chat and just kind of hang around. It was a real crowd now, and a waiter had to elbow his way in to announce that a special dish had been prepared by the chef, "something very off-the-menu." Then a woman came by to take several pictures of the man, her blinding flashes bouncing off my plate.

"How about some black and white?" she said.

"Yeah, real contrasty," he said.

The woman began to change her film, placing the little plastic film canisters down on our table, right next to my bread plate, as if I weren't even there. She was so precise with the stage directions. "Good. Now move to your left, no, to *your* left. There. Good, nice, show me some teeth. Now, get closer together. Closer! Great. Perfect." With my back to him, I could only imagine what that pose must have been like. A bit later the chef walked out and asked for praise from all of them, followed by a flurry of telephone calls and more frequent eruptions of laughter thundering over like so many sonic booms.

I like to believe that I could have dealt with a happy, loud, boisterous table, even appreciate the vivacious energy and style such a group might bring to a room, that momentary sensation that this was the place everyone should want to be. But this was turning into a full-blown spectacle. It's not that I couldn't mind my own business. I could, but there was a show going on behind me, a Broadway extravaganza, a Barnum & Bailey roadside attraction. Only the most self-absorbed could have sat there and ignored it in peace. I pretended to ignore it, though, turning to Christina to resume the conversation.

"The Getty Museum wants to fly me out to L.A. to consider a position," I said. "I turned them down, but it's nice to know they're thinking of me."

She put her fork down and looked at me. "First your landlord wants to buy out your lease, then the Getty offers you a job. What's next?"

"Maybe I should be checking my messages."

I tried to keep my composure when the hostess brought even more people to shoehorn into the burgeoning group behind me. She leaned over to me and asked, "Could we just move your table a little this way?" Before we could answer, with my fork still in my mouth, the table was sliding out from under us to make room behind. In order to fit himself at their table one guy had to put one of his legs under ours as if he were sitting with us. I had to say something now, I had to act, if only for my own sanity. I turned to this intruder in a fit of frustration and confidence and said, "Should we do separate checks or just all together?"

That confidence had all the staying power of a briefcase left unattended in the men's room at the Port Authority. All at once they stopped their animated conversation to look at me. Downtown types, every one of them, men and women, part bohemian club creatures, part affluent creativity, and so avant-garde, *so Dada*. They gave off a palpably strong air of sexuality. What was it, gay? Bisexual? Something, anyway, complete liberation for sure. Christina's date hit it right on the money in describing this place. There was a painfully long silence; the Sistine Chapel was cleaned in less time. *What the hell do I do now?* My sister buried her head in her hands; she didn't care to watch.

I tried to look at the loud one, the King of the Banquette, the one I couldn't get a clear shot at. I ducked around to try and catch a glimpse, but I was blocked. "Very funny," he said from behind his curtain of admirers. "But you don't want any part of our tab, trust me."

"I just need a little space, that's all," I said to the phantom-like figure. And maybe a little fresh air would be nice, and I'd like to be able to hear my own conversation, that would be real nice too, I thought.

"Who is this guy, the fucking hall monitor?" They all laughed and then resumed their conversation, as if nothing at all had happened. I turned around, and Christina looked right at me.

"Check?" she asked.

"I'm not leaving. Not now, no way."

"Whatever you want."

I remember cracking the delicate shell of the warm crème brûlée and tasting its burnt sweetness. Christina had broken through hers like an ice fisherman, forming a perfect little hole that grew as she ate. I was too caught up in my test of will with the King of the Banquette to keep mine from shattering crudely. My heart was still beating at an anxious clip when we got up to leave, and I let my sister pass first as we made our way through the tables. What occurred next is a bit of a blur, and I had, to the best of my memory, no intention of taking any action. But there was a glass of ice water near the edge of their table; it was full and cold with condensation. As I squeezed between the chair backs, getting my first good look all evening at the instantly familiar gentleman, my coat brushed against the glass, sending it over the edge and onto his lap. Clearly I had seen the glass, recognized its potential, but to this day I can say only that my subconscious had taken over and whether it was done by accident or intention is still unclear.

It startled him, as it did me. He flinched from the cold of the ice water, and the glass rolled off of him, shattering loudly against the tile floor. Small pieces of glass spread over the floor, and the room fell silent for a beat, quickly filling up again with the familiar sounds of busy consumption. The hostess came over in a rush. She directed a busboy to help clean up the spill, throwing several white cloth napkins on the man's lap. The King of the Banquette and I finally looked at each other, and he seemed calm.

"It was an accident," I said. "I just didn't see it." He remained silent, brushing himself off and looking up at me. I thought he would either get up and hit me or break out laughing again. But he did neither.

"No problem, I'm fine. Just a little water."

The hostess was clearly in a panic. "I'm so sorry, Miles, Are you all right?" she said.

Miles Levy, acclaimed conceptual artist and socialite. Socialite and conceptual artist. Artist and conceptual socialite. The order made no difference as long you got all the operative words in. He looked just like his photos in all the magazine articles, the party pages, the "At Lunch With" profile in the *Times*.

"Something had to go wrong for me tonight," he said.

"Yes, something," I said. Something small and perfectly satisfying, I thought. He laughed again, and I let out a silent sigh of relief.

Christina and I walked out of Pied Noir, emerging from that frenzied realm out into the cool air of a New York autumn. There is something about that season, those ten weeks or so in which all kinds of cultural expression compete fiercely for attention. Miles Levy was in that fray and playing to win. Of course my sister was interested in Levy, asking me about his work and reputation, the price of one of his sculptures and his huge canvases. She and I often played a game of spotting people who were New York famous, little known outside the Manhattan media hamlet. We would each try to top the other in spotting the kind of person who only a few people would recognize—obscure and esoteric. The more so the better. We had our own special scale that awarded its points as the degree of fame narrowed: East Coast, then New York, then Manhattan, then by zip code. Christina always got the best ones. A month before she had recognized the surrogate-court judge who had presided over the battle for Andy Warhol's estate. "I saw Eve Preminger get out of a cab," she told me all excited. To this day I've never figured out how she came to know what the judge even looked like.

Miles Levy would have been worth the full ten points in our little game a decade before. Perhaps five points only a few years earlier. But this seemed to be his moment, and I had to tell Christina that he was now known across the country. We didn't have a category big enough for him, and so I deserved no points for this one.

three

IN THE morning I met Kohlman at his office, and together we made our way over to the Carlyle Hotel in the rain. It was a short walk from the museum, about six blocks south and then one east to Madison Avenue, just far enough to get drenched but too close to justify a taxi. Sheets of rain were coming down in hard, unrelenting waves. I was fighting the wind with my cheap collapsible umbrella, bought one wet day in a panic from one of those street peddlers who materialize in the rain and then disappear when the sun comes out. I tried to step clear of puddles but my progress was graceless, with a look of discomfort on my face worthy of the dentist's chair. Despite the downpour, Kohlman made his way with an elegant gait, each step a careful stride. He wore his usual impeccable attire and seemed to repel water just from the strength of his will. Determined and methodical, as stubborn as he was dry, he carried a large and rigid black umbrella that made mine look like a toy.

"You look like you don't want to know me," I said, trying to keep my umbrella from inverting.

"You're unprepared. One must always have the right tools, Finley."

"That umbrella looks pretty serious," I said. "I don't know if I could live up to it."

"It was a gift," he said. "A friend in London insisted."

I doubted it was a gift, knowing he would rather me believe it was one than know how carefully he had picked it out. Kohlman did everything the same way, approaching all aspects of his life like a connoisseur, right down to the imported blades he shaved with. These things had to pass his strict design and quality standards. But what might have seemed like snobbery was just a guiding principle, a belief held closely, not advertised or talked about in mixed company. The umbrella was meant for himself, not for others to marvel at, and that it perform competently in the rain was all that mattered. Never showy and too tasteful to boast, he operated quietly, his obsession for fine things expressed only within careful boundaries.

We arrived at the hotel and were given directions by the concierge to an apartment on the 17th floor. The Carlyle, a tall and elegant tower, was one of those elemental New York places. In its cafe Bobby Short and his piano had become an institution in the best sense of that word, a gig that was the definition of Upper East Side sophistication, a kind of cliched urban romance for those willing to dress the part.

The privately owned apartments there enjoyed all the services of the hotel and carried the kind of monthly maintenance fees that seemed impossibly high. I knew from what Kohlman had told me that we were on our way to the aftermath of a major cash hemorrhage.

On the way up I tried to dry off, passing my fingers through my hair. I looked at myself in the mirror in the elevator, shoes wet, the cuffs on my pants damp. As a teenager I had always been boyish, seeming a year or two younger than I was, but now my physical presence had caught up to my twenty-eight years. I carried myself differently with the graduate degrees and the curatorship, my confidence as a critic and all that. These things had a way of manifesting themselves physically, so that by now I had achieved the opposite effect, with colleagues taking me for older than I was largely due to the job I held. I felt lucky to be where I was but also somewhat guarded. My situation was unusual. In this field expertise is something you gain with age. A young doctor or lawyer is often assumed to be just an over-achiever, but a youthful-looking museum curator is almost always greeted with skepticism.

The elevator left us at a small landing filled with boxes and wooden crates. The door to the apartment was wide open, the sound of many loud voices in busy discussion streaming out. We walked in from the vestibule, through a long foyer and into the living room. The place was in disarray; boxes of files were stacked high, and all of the paintings had been taken down, the painted sides of the canvases leaned against the walls. Men in dark suits carrying stacks of paper were walking in every direction, ignoring us. I looked through the pantry into the kitchen. Two men were carefully sorting through a garbage bag, their large blue ponchos emblazoned with the letters *FBI*.

It surprised me. I was expecting an urbane apartment finely appointed with art and antiques and filled with a few whispers of polite conversation, as so many of these places were. On similar visits to homes where objects of value were of interest to the museum, one would enter a respectful zone of taste, stepping softly and trying not to offend privacy. But this was not your typical estate appraisal, and the atmosphere resembled more a crime scene than anything else. The man who paid the bills for this apartment, Larry Zolarian, was not in residence at that moment on advice of his lawyers. He had just been served with an indictment from a federal grand jury in the case of his failed savings and loan empire. From the looks of the place, he must have left in a hurry, fleeing to the aid and comfort of Florida's peculiarly generous bankruptcy laws.

One of the government men approached us. We told him who we were, and he directed us to the drawings. "Most of this artwork will be sold by the IRS," he explained.

"We just want to look."

"That's fine, but all documents in this apartment are under subpoena; anything taken would be an obstruction of justice."

We sat at the dining room table to study the contents of a large black portfolio. I opened it carefully, untying each lace. Zolarian had bought drawings for many years, and sixteenth-century Italians were the most well represented in his collection. All the sheets were matted but had been taken out of their frames, apparently to make them easier to move. I removed some tissue paper from the top to reveal a rare Parmigianino landscape of rolling hills and olive trees. What followed were almost two dozen important works by such masters as Tintoretto, Pontormo, Vasari, and Veronese. Kohlman and I were only more impressed as each image appeared, wanting to lift the next mat to see what was there.

There was too much to take in, and after a while I lost track of the time. So many people were coming and going, agents hauling files and computer equipment. They were boxing everything up, even the badly chosen accessories. Everywhere I looked there were groupings of the kind of hideous tchotchkes only an out-of-control decorator could love. I saw random hotel handymen, movers with carpeted dollies, and even other appraisers, a few of whom were inspecting the large canvases that had been strewn around the place. The paintings were all contemporary works: Cy Twombly, Jean Dubuffet, Mark Rothko, a very good Willem de Kooning, and even a big canvas by the primeval tragicomic Jean-Michel Basquiat. Taken together with the old Italian drawings, though, it all seemed such an odd mix.

"What do you think the idea is behind mixing all this stuff?" I asked Kohlman.

"Investment maybe, social entree perhaps. He might have loved the drawings and bought the contemporary work to buy into a certain crowd, a lifestyle. Or maybe it was the other way around. Who knows with these people."

"Maybe he honestly had a passion for both. But it just doesn't balance."

"Apparently that's not all that didn't balance," he said, looking at one of the government investigators. Then Kohlman picked up an auction catalogue that was sitting nearby and began thumbing through it. It was from one of last season's contemporary art sales. "You know," he said, "years ago they would list lots as 'property of a lady' or something tasteful like that." He began reading from the catalogue. "Now they say 'property of the FDIC in receivership of First Federated Savings of Arizona.'"

"Doesn't have quite the same ring to it," I said.

Later Kohlman left to make an appointment, and just as I was about to leave I heard something drop. I looked to where the sound had come from and saw that it was the de Kooning; the canvas had fallen the wrong side down as one of the appraisers was inspecting it. She was trying to pick up the large work, and a colleague helped her. As she rose with the painting, I recognized her. It was the woman I had noticed at that gathering in TriBeCa a week before, that book party that had degenerated into a mad stampede of the cultural elite. She looked at the painting to see if it was damaged, inspecting closely its surface of red and black oil paint. It had wide brush strokes painted in swirls and must have been five feet across. I thought it was a magnificent and moving piece. She looked over at her colleague as if to say, "I won't tell as long as you won't tell."

I could have left soon after that, but I stretched out the time, glancing at her every so often through the double-wide doorway that led into the living room. Running into her again like this, I thought it would be a shame not to make the most of it, but I couldn't decide where to begin exactly. I was stuck weighing options, opening lines, cheap ploys to start a chat when all at once she stopped what she was doing and walked right toward me. She came into the dining room and stood in front of me, placing her hands on her hips, with one leg bent slightly and a heeled shoe turned on its nose.

"Look, if you're going to stare at me like that, then at least you should know my name," she declared, a subtle accent coming through. I was a bit stunned by the brashness of the remark, in fact by the whole way she approached me, determined, unflinching, and I'll admit, altogether intimidating. "Claire Labrouste, how are you?"

I shook her hand and introduced myself.

"Have we met?" she asked. "You seem familiar."

"No, I don't think so."

"I could swear I know you from somewhere, I must."

I shook my head. "I'm sure we've never met."

"You sound too sure."

"I would have remembered you."

"Maybe at some gallery opening?"

"Everybody at an opening always looks familiar," I said.

She paused, then said, "You mean just like the art?" I thought then that she must have known the way to my heart.

I nodded. "It's true, isn't it?"

"Well, sometimes," she said.

"Are you with a dealer or something?" I asked.

"I work for Sotheby's, contemporary art. We're gearing up for the big fall sale, but we always have time to keep track of the bodies."

"The bodies?" I asked.

"You know, the paintings," she said, motioning toward the large canvases in the other room.

"Is the de Kooning going to be sold?"

"Not this year; it's too late to make the catalogue. But it's got real potential. We'll have it next season for sure." She looked at the portfolio containing the drawings. "What are you here for?"

"I work at the Met. Assistant curator in drawings, Old Masters mostly. We also keep track of the bodies, as you put it. I came to see a few Italian drawings, although I never expected to see a Basquiat in the living room."

"It's fairly common to find collectors of the Neo-Expressionists also appreciating the Old Masters. I've seen it before."

"If the drawings are any indication, the guy at least had *some* taste."

"The paintings too," she said. "There's a Levy in the bedroom."

"Miles Levy?" I said way too loud.

"Did I touch a nerve?"

"It's just that this guy squandered people's retirement nest eggs on the craziest stuff," I said. "He thought all this hyped art was a sound investment for his depositors' money." Then I stopped. Maybe I had gone too far, maybe she didn't agree with me.

She shrugged. "People either love Levy or hate him. There's no in-between. I know him fairly well. He's an interesting figure—provocative, I'd say."

"Miles Levy, provocative? I met him the other day."

"The other day?"

"Last night, at a restaurant."

"I'll tell him you said hello."

I had to think about how to proceed. Do I embellish the truth and tell her that we're old pals, that Miles and I both know Pied Noir's private reservation number? Or do I be honest and tell her the real story, blow by humiliating blow. There was, of course, a third option. "That's all right, we hardly know each other. It was one of those chance encounters, friends of friends, that sort of thing." Yes, I thought, how perfectly ambiguous.

"Oh. Well I love Old Master drawings," she said. "I went to a show at the Met a couple of years ago and fell in love with this tiny Rembrandt landscape. The lines were so faint, the figures just specs on the horizon. I remember thinking, how could he evoke so much from so little?"

Rembrandt, I thought, *she likes good old Rembrandt?* Such an old white male bastion, so stuffy, so old news. And, of course, one of my all-time favorites. The rooms at the Met where his stuff hung were among the most poorly attended, compared with, say, the Monet rooms. The crowd-pleasing Impressionists, with all their gimmick-ridden bourgeois accessibility, their show-off technique, their bright colorful pandering (don't get me started), they always drew the big crowds. But highly literate, darkly lit, Old Testament–referencing Rembrandt? Could she really be into the guy?

"If you ever need to see something at the museum or do any research there, you can always use my name." The second I finished saying this I thought how transparent it must have sounded, how obviously interested I must have seemed.

She smiled. "I might take you up on that. It always pays to know the right people." Her manner had turned a bit nervous; she shifted around, fidgeted with things on a table, touched her hair. She leaned against the table, knocking over a round crystal paperweight. All that confidence she had approached me with just a few minutes before had quickly disappeared. "What's the matter with me?" she said. The room was filled with photos and memorabilia, letters from politicians, brass plaques, a bunch of framed "tombstone" advertisements from the financial pages. It looked like a shrine to deregulation.

She picked up the crystal paperweight from the floor and inspected it closely. "Shit, I think it's got a hairline crack."

I walked over to her and looked at it. "That's not hairline," I said. "You put a huge fault right through the thing."

"Why don't I feel guilty?"

"Maybe you've got some deep-seated resentment of crystal."

"Right, abused as a child with Baccarat candlesticks. Look, no one's going to cry over this silly thing," she said.

"They're planning to use everything in this place as evidence."

"What are they going to do, serve it with a subpoena?"

"You dropped the de Kooning, now you cracked this useless thing. You're dangerous," I said.

She smiled. "Hey, wait a minute. Let's just say it hasn't been a lucky morning. There's plenty of time left in the day, though."

"Right, the potential for destruction still looms pretty large."

"So, what do we do about this?" she asked, holding the cracked crystal.

"We? What do you mean, *we*?"

"I wouldn't have broken this if you hadn't forced me to come over here. I mean, you wouldn't stop staring at me."

"Maybe I noticed you staring first."

"Bullshit," she said. "I deal with this all the time. I'm a professional."

"We're gonna have to hide it, put it away somewhere."

"Where?"

"I don't know, but I'm sure the maid does it all the time." I looked around. "How about in here," I said, opening a large desk drawer. She came over and placed the damaged crystal inside.

"Wait," she said as I was about to close it. "What's this he's got stashed away in here?" She pointed inside the drawer to a box for a porn video with the words "Blacks and Blondes" over a picture of various racially mixed body parts.

"Are you familiar with the genre?" she said.

I looked at the offending material and then back at her. "I guess the FBI hasn't checked this room yet."

"I hope they're very thorough," she said. We both laughed, winding down eventually to a slight sigh of humor fatigue. For some reason she wasn't fidgety anymore, but completely calm and motionless, happy and gorgeous. She looked over at her colleagues in the other room, who seemed to be watching us, then turned back toward me. "Well," she said finally, "I guess I should get going. I'm on the job here."

"It's easy to forget sometimes."

"Did you mean what you said about the museum? You know, letting me use those resources sometime?"

"Of course."

"Great," she said, picking up a pen of mine and writing her name and phone number at the top of one of my papers. "Good luck in the saleroom," I said as she started to walk away.

"We'll take whatever we can get." She smiled, then turned, her hair swinging.

"Claire, wait." She stopped and looked back. "I think I remember where we might have seen each other."

"Where?"

"A party last week at Lucy Silverman's place on White Street."

"That's it, you're right," she said. "And you said you were so sure."

"That place of hers is a real gem."

"I'm surprised Lucy didn't introduce us."

"You should mention it to her."

"I just might."

"So will I see you again?"

She smiled, waiting a beat before answering. "I hope so."

four

CLAIRE WASTED no time. Two days later, in the middle of a tedious Friday afternoon at work, she called.

"Surprised?" she asked.

"Surprised that you beat me to it, yes."

"I figured you for someone who might wait."

"What do you mean?"

"You would have waited too long, I can tell."

"You're very perceptive." Her observation made me a bit uneasy, but I was just so glad she had called.

"When can you see me?"

"What do you have in mind?"

"You show me that Rembrandt, and I'll get you into our contemporary sale. You like to go to auctions, don't you?" Her answers came quickly, as if she had lines.

"You'd be getting the better part of the bargain," I said.

"I know."

"Why don't you come to the museum on Monday? The place will be closed to the public, and we can just roam the empty halls, then maybe get a drink some-where."

"I know this place, it's only been open a few weeks, Pied Noir," she said.

"Pied Noir?"

"You know it?

"It's, uh, fine, has a nice room, a real lived-in look."

"You had a bad meal there or something?"

"No, not at all." One of the most memorable meals of the year, I thought, and not because of the food.

"I know, it's a bit of a scene."

"It may not even be happening by next week," I said.

"Right, I hear the chef has already moved on."

I laughed.

"So, were you really going to call?" she asked.

"How badly do you want to know?"

On Monday afternoon Claire met me atop the grand steps to the Met as planned. The weekend had taken much too long to pass. Saturday I tried not to think about it, forcing a casual unconcern, but by Sunday night the panic set in and I began to plan the event in unnecessary detail. I was a bit early, and I sat waiting for several minutes facing Fifth Avenue, my yellow staff ID tag showing out to the world. She also turned out to be early. I spotted her across the avenue, walking briskly. She wore a simple black cotton dress with two stringlike straps that hung over the shoulders and a tiny white T-shirt underneath.

The Met was safe territory for me, and I could navigate it like no one else. "If I had a natural habitat, this would be it," I said as we passed through the magnanimous Great Hall. "I basically grew up here."

"So you were raised in New York."

"And born just a few blocks from here."

"I think raising a child in this city is a little crazy," she said.

"It has its own logic. My mother dragged me to every

gallery and exhibition since I was a toddler. You either start to hate it and rebel, or you make it an education."

"So you did the latter."

"I never understood half of it, but my mother must have known what she was doing when she hung a poster of Picasso's *Guernica* over my crib."

"Must have given you nightmares," she said.

"I can't remember. But I used to roam around this place like Eloise at the Plaza, knowing too much for my own good, pissing people off with my opinions, people much older and wiser."

"My five-year-old niece, Lisbeth, goes to school a few blocks from here," she said. "When I pick her up I see all these adorable little children in cute uniforms holding hands to cross the street. But their conversation is so expressive. They're just like adults, only smaller."

"What's that faint accent of yours I keep hearing?"

"French," she said. "But I went to school over here on and off. The family business kept us going back and forth all the time." She told me how her father used to import wines and spirits for some distributor, and when her family went back to Paris for the last time, she decided to stay here.

"Does it feel like home now?"

"Sometimes it does, and sometimes it doesn't. On a good day it feels like I just got here. On a bad day I start to think I've been here forever."

I looked at a shopping bag she was carrying; it seemed heavy. "You want to drop that in my office?"

She looked around the Great Hall before answering, then said, "I've always wanted to skate in here."

"What?"

"This is a great floor for skating."

"I guess it is."

She held open the bag, inside of which was a pair of Rollerblades. "What do you say?"

"You mean in here? Right now?"

"You said we'd have the place all to ourselves."

"I meant no tourists, no visitors. People still work here, though. The guards have nothing better to do than bust you."

"Oh, come on," she said. "What's the worst that could happen? You won't lose your job."

"I'm not so sure."

"I've been looking forward to this all day, Stuart."

"You're crazy," I said, shaking my head. "You can't use Rollerblades in the museum."

"Says who? I mean, is there a rule?"

"Look, it's a safe assumption. They protect against everything here, even acts of God." I thought about it for a moment. With the museum closed to the public, Monday was a time reserved for visits by the occasional dignitary or big donor. Otherwise it was empty, just a lot of floor waxing going on, and maybe some installation work for special exhibitions. But I was sure this kind of stunt would come under the heading of "frowned-upon," that it was something for which I could get scolded, a mark on my record, a letter in my file. In that moment I imagined the trustees meeting in a big boardroom. "That boy Finley needs a good talking-to," one of them might say. But in the end I gave in only because the last thing I wanted was for Claire to think I was no fun.

"We'll have to be real discreet," I said. "Do these things make noise?"

"You're kidding, right?"

I led her to the Egyptian Wing, which was silent and empty except for the displays. We walked through a long corridor filled with ancient treasures, broken pottery, gold jewelry and all that. "Why don't you put them on," I said. She leaned against a large stone sarcophagus covered with hieroglyphics and changed into the Rollerblades.

"Where should we go?"

"In here," I said, opening a big glass door that led to the Temple of Dendur, an entire Egyptian building saved from the Nile River valley by a misguided museum administrator. The thing had been brought over stone by stone and reassembled in a spacious hangarlike wing at the edge of Central Park. I had always regarded it as an unforgivable waste of space, its only real use as a venue for black-tie parties and benefit dinner dances. It had become less a monument to the ancient Egyptians than one to the late twentieth-century New Yorkers who had paid to have the damn thing brought thousands of miles across the globe and installed right in their own backyard. The temple's address had once been the Valley of the Kings. Now it was 1000 Fifth Avenue, New York, NY 10028. One might even make the case that it had moved up in the world.

Claire skated around the ancient ruin, gaining speed with each lap. "You're so tall on those things," I said, watching her. A group of children playing in Central Park noticed her speeding along and came up to the huge glass wall to take a closer look. They pressed their noses against the square window-panes and seemed jealous of her. "Those kids want to be you," I said. "Look, they're all saying, 'How did she get to do that?'"

"I know the right people," she said. After a few minutes a guard, wearing a jacket two sizes too big, looked at us through the doorway and came inside. I held my breath. "You're not supposed to be in here," he said with an eastern European accent. The only thing I could think to do was hold up my ID card. He told us to go someplace else, unless we wanted to spend the night in there. I led Claire, or she led me, into the American Wing, another big, wide-open courtyard space. From there we went all over (she skated, I walked), winding our way from the musical instruments to the European paintings on the second floor. "Keep up," she kept telling me.

"Maybe you should slow down," I advised. The only time I was faster was up the stairs.

"This is the best way to see a museum," she said. "They should rent skates at the door; I'll bet it would double the attendance overnight."

"I'll be sure to suggest it."

I was glad Claire wanted to see the Dutch painters, since they were my specialty. We entered the first gallery and walked among the Vermeers, their ordered domestic world rendered with such fine clarity. She lingered at the three small pictures of seventeenth-century Dutch life and seemed charmed by them. We moved on to the Rembrandts, stopping at his self-portrait from near the end of his life, his familiar bulbous nose and saddened expression as poignant as ever. I knew this painting well from my childhood, as I did most of these, and more recently I had come by to see it countless times on breaks from work, finding it more moving each time.

"Would have been great to know him," said Claire, rolling back to take it in wide. I stood more closely, inspecting its surface. "What are you looking for?" she asked.

What was I looking for? There were so many ways to answer, but I didn't look back at her, I just kept my eyes on the canvas. "The strokes at the bottom are of a fully loaded brush," I said, "like he painted this with energy, not concerned about being as careful as Vermeer but wanting to get the mood of the moment out on the canvas. Vermeer is crystalline representation; Rembrandt is much more painterly. Precision is great, and I love to look at it, but this kind of emotive honesty is even better."

We continued through the galleries, Claire's Rollerblades making a low spinning sound over the floor, and she asked where I had studied. "The Institute of Fine Arts," I said.

"Oh, the Tute," she said, using the shorthand name for the graduate program, known for its academic rigor and traditionalism. "That couldn't have been too long ago."

"I've been on this accelerated schedule. I work with Harlan Kohlman."

"I've heard the name."

"You probably used his books in school; everyone does. When I first got to know him, I attributed several drawings to their rightful makers. That raised my star very early."

"Something of a wunderkind?"

"I just got lucky."

Claire stopped at a colorful still life of many different flowers in full bloom, all bunched together and fighting for attention. She considered it for a moment, placing her hand on my arm to hold her balance, and remarked how the flowers didn't go together, how they were of all different seasons. I explained that it was painted over a long period to capture each flower in bloom.

She smiled. "I like this, having my own private tour with a resident expert and the whole place to myself."

"You just have to promise to do the same for me, you know, explain some really puzzling performance art down-town or something."

"This place must be important to you," she said.

"This is where my roots are. At least the ones I care about."

"I never had roots like that. I don't mind, though, since it forces me to keep everything in the present, no looking back, no ideal golden age to judge things against."

"You've got to have something," I said. "Some place or memory, some thread to grab on to."

"I do, I mean, my memories growing up are great. But I take so well to new places that I'm able to find something anywhere."

"What about all this?" I said, looking around. "Are you really interested in art? I don't mean just this, I mean any-thing—old, new, whatever."

"To be honest, I kind of fell into it. At the end of the day it's just not that important to me." She looked at me, and I must have seemed puzzled. "Don't get me wrong, what I do is great, it's fun, I love it. Not because of the art, though. I do it because it beats coal mining."

"Sorry?"

"It's a good gig," she said.

"So the art doesn't matter very much."

"It matters in that I have to know about it to do the job, but I'd be lying if I told you it's a passion. At least not a passion like yours."

"So what's important to you, what are you passionate about?"

"Things I try to keep separate from how I make my living. Balzac, Zola, good food, my old dog Duchamp, my dear brother Simon, lots of things. But I make sure they never mix with my ambition."

"Why?"

"There's too much compromising going on, I mean, to be true to your passion. I know this goes against what everyone always tells you, but there should be a wall between your paycheck and whatever you hold dear. I don't go in for this Joseph Campbell 'follow your bliss' bullshit. Nobody likes to talk about work when they get home from it. That's why you have to be so careful." She shook her head and smiled. "It's like this friend I have who's making a film. He used to be passionate about film, but now he can't stand it because he's so immersed in it. He's lost the romantic view of his profession, his art, in order to get the film made, and now it's getting made with all the outward appearances of success. But you can't talk to him about movies, about Hollywood or the industry. He hates it all now. See, it would be easier for him if it were just a hobby and not how he has to make his living. That's what ruins it. I never want that to happen to me."

"So you protect yourself."

"Sort of."

"I guess I'm living in a charmed world. This is a place where I can be true to my passion and collect a paycheck."

"No compromises?"

"Not that I can tell."

She laughed. "There have to be. You're just not looking hard enough." I tried to moderate just the right amount of eye contact, not wanting to make her uncomfortable, but I found it difficult to talk and not stare at the same time. Her pretty face was so distracting. Her complexion was impeccable, her nose sloping down faultlessly, ending just above a pair of full lips. "It's very quiet here right now," she said.

The only sound to break the silence at that moment was the jingle of keys on a ring far away in the distance, and I imagined them to be attached to the belt of a custodian walking down a corridor a half mile from where we stood.

"It can be kind of eerie sometimes, so empty like this."

"I like that."

I managed to guide our stroll up to the roof, where there was an open-air sculpture garden and unobstructed views of Central Park. Claire used the Rodins as a slalom course and then met me at the edge, where we could see several skylines lit red as the sun disappeared. To the left was the Upper East Side, straight ahead was midtown, and to the right were the towers of Central Park West. The avenues that bound Central Park squared it off like great garden walls. I always pictured the museum as tucked into the garden like a bit of sanctuary, protected by Olmsted and Vaux's green jewel and seemingly insulated from the harsh urban reality.

"This is a hell of a spot," said Claire, looking out above the treetops. I wanted to tell her so much that, for me at least, it was the center of the world.

*   *   *

We left her Rollerblades in my office and traveled downtown to go to an opening at a SoHo gallery, one of several taking place that night. It was a mild evening, a flashback to summer, and the sidewalks were filled with people. We stopped first at an espresso bar on Greene Street, where I noticed how every time Claire took a sip of her mocha latte she would turn the cup slightly to catch the foam that had stuck to the sides. I was telling her about the offer to buy out my lease.

"Pretty lucky," she said. "That's a nice position to be in."

"Yeah, I guess." I shook my cup, trying to distribute the sugar at the bottom. "What about your living situation?"

Before she could answer I heard a female voice call my name. I recognized it but could not place it and turned to see who it was. Carleen Moore, an ex-girlfriend with whom I had parted ways almost a year earlier. We had remained friendly but spoke rarely.

"Carleen," I said, standing to greet her. I did a quick introduction. Claire, meet Carleen, Carleen, meet Claire.

"What've you been up to?" she asked me.

"You know, the usual, studying and preserving the art of long-dead white European males."

"Heterosexual males at that."

"Oh, I wouldn't bet on it."

We chatted briefly, catching up. Last time I had seen her she was working as a floater at some theatrical talent agency. Now she had her own clients, mostly soap actresses, she said. She wore a grin as she left us, motioning a good-bye to Claire. It seemed intended toward me, as if to say, "Nice going." Claire looked so good sitting there, spooning for the last bit of foam inside her cup, her legs crossed and a pleasant but smart look on her face. This little encounter with Carleen was the fulfillment of a fantasy I had dreamed the day we broke up. I couldn't have scripted it any better, and I turned back toward Claire, intending to resume the conversation exactly where we had left off, without even remarking. But she spoke first.

"Ex-girlfriend," she said.

"What else. She really eyeballed you, didn't she? Sorry about that."

"It wasn't rude. I mean I would have done it."

A few minutes later a man walked toward us from across the room. He was in his forties, established-looking and well dressed, his hair graying slightly.

"Now it's my turn."

"What do you mean?" I asked. The man came up to our table and kissed Claire on the cheek. She introduced us. He was the owner of a gallery in the Fuller Building on 57th Street, one of the many places she had briefly worked.

"We're going to an opening at Alternative Space," she told him. "I don't know who the work is by, but I've got the invite in my bag."

Then he turned to me. "Don't I know you?"

"I'm not sure."

"We met at that opening."

"I don't recall."

"Yes, it was at the Dia Center in Chelsea, some big interesting sculpture, lots of gauze bandage and mud on these pieces of wood."

"I'm sorry, I seem to have this problem with a lot of people."

"Oh, forget it," he said. "I could be wrong. But have you seen the sculpture I'm talking about? It's a must-see."

"You mean the gauze bandage with the dark brown mud smeared across the plywood?"

"Yeah."

"Sure, I know it. I can't remember whose it was, though."

"Very evocative stuff."

Evocative of what, I thought. Trench warfare? The Somme, 1916? I felt trapped in another *New Yorker* cartoon.

"Uh, right," I said.

"Great texture."

"Yes, brilliant."

We all said good-bye, and I'll never forget his last words to Claire: "Tell Miles I said hello." It was spoken casually, the tone revealing a level of informal familiarity that could only be described as intimate.

"I will," she said.

Claire turned to me. "Was it really brilliant texture?"

"Sometimes you just have to know how to play along." I took a deep breath, then said, "How well do you know Miles Levy?"

"Miles? We're old friends. I got to know him when I worked at Griffin." That was the name of the gallery that handled Levy's work, the place that had discovered and launched him. "He's been generous with me," she said.

"How do you mean?"

"He's introduced me to a lot of people over the years."

"He's big right now. The biggest, brightest star of the moment," I said, regretting having raised the subject.

"He hates being called a star. Really, he's just a normal everyday guy." I doubted then that normal was the right word.

I leaned in close. "I've noticed something about you," I said.

"What?"

"Your eyes stay right on whoever is talking to you, never moving. That's the way it's supposed to be, that's the way they teach you to do it, but no one ever does it anymore. Everyone shifts around, but you lock on."

She looked down, all demure. "I don't mean to."

"It's not a bad thing. It makes people feel like they've got all your attention. Even if I've been boring you this whole time, I mean, all through the museum and everything, at least it feels like you're so interested."

"I do it out of habit," she said. "When I was in school I used to concentrate on what all the other American kids were saying so I could quickly learn how to talk like one of them. I told you, I'm good at fitting in."

"So I shouldn't take it as a sign of interest."

She smiled. "You'll never know."

I led Claire up the steep, creaking stairwell of a building on Broome Street, at the top of which was a large nonprofit space where the crowded opening was under way. She hung on my arm all the way up, slowing me down, laughing, pretending to be out of breath when we got to the top. We took in a group of big canvases about which I can remember nothing. Plastic cups of white wine and club soda were being served, and it seemed as if every third person knew Claire from somewhere. As we walked around I noticed people looking at us, men glancing at Claire and then checking me out as if to see who had won this woman's interest. It made me uneasy.

It wasn't too long before the canvases started to merge with the crowd; people were moving way too slowly, stopping for more contemplation than the pieces seemed to require. We had looked at too much for one day, having skated our way through three thousand years of art at the Met just a few hours before. Claire was still physical, though, still touchy-feely as we sat on a deep windowsill that looked out onto the dark cobblestone street busy with pedestrians and evening traffic.

I began to question why Claire was with me, perhaps feeling that reflexive insecure suspicion at such luck that anyone at least half Jewish is plagued with; that guarded, suspect, *why me* nature. What part of this bargain am I missing, I thought, like old Tevye. But as strong as those suspicions were and as paralyzing as that self-questioning can be, she was giving off enough strong clues with her hands, her eyes, and her body language that I feared letting the moment pass.

We surveyed the crowded room from our perch, and I told her that all the people holding their cups of white wine looked like a bunch of medical patients waiting to turn in their urine samples. That line turned out to be the perfect test, because it really wasn't funny. In fact it was almost vulgar and totally uninspired, but she laughed anyway, a big generous laugh, and I took it as a sign of her happiness with the situation, of her comfort with me. I got the feeling she would have responded well to anything I might have said, not because she had a bad sense of humor or because she was buzzing from the wine, or even that she only cared to please me, but because she was sending a signal. I was betting that she knew perfectly well that it wasn't funny, betting that she knew exactly what she was doing and that her disproportionate laugh, which I clearly didn't deserve, was a kind of green light. And so even though I knew it was a gamble (it always is), I decided then to kiss her anyway. I leaned toward her, bringing my face to hers, and took her upper lip between both of mine, pressing gently. She reciprocated, parting her mouth and moving around mine, tasting, pressing, parting and tasting again. She took a breath. We continued like this for a few minutes, warm and wet, with several variations along this basic theme. The first kiss from Claire came with that familiar feeling of risk and turn of emotion, one moment hesitant, the next deeply involved. Neither one of us could have been so jaded as to escape the shock of the new, an ephemeral and unmistakable thrill of discovery that catches you by surprise every time.

But even at such a moment of raised hair and dilated pupils, even as I lost myself in her, a small residue of insecurity remained. I couldn't get Miles Levy completely out of my mind, and now I wanted to run into him again more than ever. I quickly came to realize that my decisive action had only made me more curious about Claire and more anxious about what the hell she might have been up to with me. I should have never been satisfied with her answer about how well she knew Miles, and I still wonder how much she would have told me had I pressed her just a bit more.

five

Amy Kidd, who lived downstairs from me, stood in my kitchen in the comfort of a well-worn pair of jeans and a big, soft-white cable-knit sweater.

"Run this by me again," I said. "You met with Vogel's people yesterday and struck a deal?"

"My brother is a real estate lawyer, so things moved kind of quickly."

"I'd say so."

"I'll be moving out in a couple of weeks and going uptown into one of his doorman buildings on Second Avenue. It's a good price, and I get the first year free."

"And some cash, right?"

"Yeah, some cash also."

"Don't worry, I won't ask how much."

"Enough," she said, sipping hot tea and leaning against the counter. How much was enough to her? There were so many variables (her age, her career, her love life) that it was impossible to know what would cause her to cash in. She lived in the apartment right below mine, and I was grateful that she never seemed to mind me playing my Miles Davis as loud as I liked. I finally got the figure out of her by being a little disingenuous.

"I have no idea what to ask," I said. "I mean, I'm really lost when it comes to these things. I've been burned before. I need to go in with a target so that—"

"Seventy-five," she interrupted.

"What?" I said.

"Seventy-five thousand dollars. I get the check as soon as I sign the new lease. The papers are being drawn up. I sign them the day after tomorrow." I took a seat at the table. Seventy-five sounded low to me. If her brother was a real estate lawyer then he should have known better. I would have bargained for more cash, since I had no desire for another apartment from Vogel. He owned a lot of those white brick boxes, tragedies from the late fifties and sixties that had spread across Manhattan like terrible murrain. Amy was probably headed for one.

"It just hasn't dawned on me, you know, that this is really happening," I said.

"Cheer up, this is a hell of an opportunity. What are you going to do? Have you met with his people?"

"No, I haven't met anybody. Who else is taking the deal?"

"Everyone. Martha on four, Paul and Katie on the second floor."

"What about that old woman Mrs. Kaplan?" I said. "She's been here forever. She'll never move."

"I wouldn't bet on it. Her kids would love the money, so she probably will." I kept from telling her that I thought they were all being taken for a bad deal. Vogel was surely prepared to go a lot higher if someone forced him. But he was smart, dangling attractive numbers and other apartments in front of people who had been deluded into thinking they were getting generous, once-in-a-lifetime deals. Perhaps it wasn't so difficult to see why Amy had jumped to take an early offer after all. She was older, maybe even feeling pressure to get her life under way. But seventy-five? What was that after taxes? For me there was no harm in waiting.

"I really don't want to move," I said. "There is something about this place, it's perfect. This guy is just going to put the wrecking ball to it the day we move out."

"Don't be a fool, Stuart. I mean, I know how you feel, but you can't sacrifice your own good fortune for some vague urban principle. This is a real windfall. You're young, take the money and buy a mutual fund or something, for Christ's sake. Besides, I'm sure you can find plenty of ways to spend it with your weakness for master drawings and all."

"What I don't like is that it's all happening so quickly and quietly. Everyone seems to be jumping on this like it's found money or something."

"Well it *is* found money," she said, raising her cup in a toast.

My sister called me that night around eleven. Even though it was already Tuesday, I was still reading the sections of last Sunday's *Times* that I hadn't gotten around to. She wanted to tell me that the name Miles Levy had come up at work.

"What about him?"

"Susan asked me to clip all these profiles on him, even small mentions, and to create a file for him. We have a lot of files; we clip everything."

"Why Levy?"

"She says she knows a lot of collectors who might be clients or something like that. She didn't seem to want to talk about it, and she told me not to tell anyone."

"I see you have no loyalty. That's good, Christina. I'll bet it's a very fat file. You must have been clipping away like mad, I mean, this guy's everywhere. It's nauseating." Then she told me about some date she had that went terribly, for the poor guy, that is. She had always been very selective. When I filled her in on my own recent exploits, she got all excited.

"What's her name?" she demanded eagerly.

"Claire," I said.

"Mmm, pretty name. I want to meet her. What's she like? Would I like her?"

"You'd love her. She's smart, very quick, has these snappy answers. She's French, and very cute."

"You said that like it was rehearsed. She must really be on your mind."

"I'm sorry I told you. It's just in the embryonic stages right now."

"I think it's bigger than that, Stuart; I think I can even hear it kicking." I told her that that was enough and to go to bed. I hung up the phone and tried to finish the last few sections of the paper before going to bed myself. By chance I picked up the section that carries all those cookie-cutter wedding announcements and that influential gardening column. I opened to the page of glittering party shots, a spread of black-and-white photographs from various society balls, benefit parties, and hip downtown scenes. While I was scanning the two facing pages with my usual speed and indifference, something caught my eye, and even before I knew quite what it was I felt knots tightening inside my stomach. One of the featured gatherings was an event held at the Griffin Gallery in SoHo in honor of the Wooster Group, an offbeat and sometimes avant-garde theater company, and one of the photos from this stylish happening pictured Miles Levy and Claire, the two of them standing together in a frozen pose of what looked like a standard evening gone by.

Those knots inside my stomach must have been made of piano wire. I felt faintly feverish, as if I had strep, with my forehead getting warm and a lump developing in my throat like a sharply edged cube of steel. I stared at the photo intently, scrutinizing every aspect, the expressions on their faces, the drinks they held, their closeness to each other. The two of them looked the part perfectly, staring out with glee at all those Sunday readers who lacked invitations. I took it personally, as if they were looking right at me, Stuart Finley, that tweedy museum curator who actually believed he might have had a chance with her, poor SOB. The camera, even in this kind of quick paparazzi shot, approved of her. She was a beauty—sincere smile, healthy teeth, and trim silhouette. The simple elements she wore that made her stand out from the crowd: a white shirt with big cuffs that were much longer than the sleeves of her dark jacket, and at her neck an elegant little black velvet choker. Miles was gesturing with one arm as if explaining something, falsely ignoring the camera. His other arm might have been around her waist, but it was too dark to say for sure. They were both identified by a caption, he as the painter and conceptual artist, she only by her name.

Suddenly this frivolous lightweight fare, the trivia that I had always just dismissed with a snicker about the incessant adulteration of serious journalism, suddenly this bit of information conveyed by a grainy black-and-white photo became the most important story of the day, imperative, urgent, a stunning *page-one lead*. For me it was all the news that was crushingly fit to print. I had to admit, they did look good together, a natural pair, happy, well appointed, with both their alcohol and conversation very much under control.

I was so curious about Claire's body. What was she like under those clothes? I tried to picture her with nothing on but that little black choker. I knew those legs quite well from our date, and so my mind had to fill in the rest on up, guessing that her navel was the kind that went in rather than out, with no particular reason except that I wanted it to be that way. I also hoped it wasn't pierced, but I put the chances of this little detail at less than even. Her lean midriff was apparent both from the photo and my memory, as was the slight protrusion of her chest, leading me to imagine a pair of modest, tastefully restrained breasts. My imagination also told of pink nipples that, if encouraged, could take on great definition. This paralyzing case of curiosity only added to my frustrating suspicion that, whatever the reality of Claire's body, the acclaimed artist and socialite Miles Levy was most likely experiencing it at that very moment.

I wondered if my sister had clipped this one for her file, and I considered calling her back and telling her to take a look at it, but now I was in no mood to do so. I turned the lights out and made a futile attempt to go to bed but instead just stared up at the dark ceiling, my eyes wide, my heart still racing, the piano wire inside my stomach finding new octaves of tension. I shut my eyes hard, adjusted the pillows, and turned over, and over and over. I sat up, turned on the TV, did several 76-channel laps until finally, obsessing, I got up. I turned all the lights on and looked at the photo again, this time with my large handy magnifying glass, as if it were a long-lost Old Master drawing. I inspected it like a cold war Kremlinologist analyzing the relative disposition of the aging Soviet leadership as they stood in line to review a May Day parade in Red Square, and of course, just as completely misguided as to the accuracy or usefulness of such information. Along the edge was that familiar photo credit, now magnified into huge block letters: BILL CUNNINGHAM. Feeling now quite childish but proceeding nonetheless, I looked at Levy's arm through the magnifying glass to see if it was around her waist, to see where his hand was exactly, to see, in essence, if I could spot missiles in Cuba. But as I tried to make an educated guess as to whether Claire and the much hyped artist had attended the function together as an item, I finally resigned myself to the fact that there was no way to tell for sure.

six

ONLY BECAME more attracted to Claire as the improbability of a relationship with her increased. It worked like some kind of infallible formula of mathematics: The less familiar the universe she and Miles Levy inhabited, the more intrigued with it I became. Despite this arousal I wanted to appear casual in my interest, and so I waited a couple of days to call her. When we spoke again she asked to see me but not in the usual sense of a date. She said that some afternoons she liked to walk her young niece home from school and asked if I wouldn't mind coming along. I readily agreed, meeting her first at Sotheby's.

I arrived at the auction house and made my way up to a large reception desk on the second level where several women sold catalogues and gave information. The atmosphere there is perfectly welcoming, friendly and open, but as in a fine jewelry store or a luxury-car showroom, there is no avoiding the sense that while everyone may browse, only a few can buy, that sooner or later the men will be separated from the boys and, while they treat everyone with equal respect, they always instantly know which one you are. As I approached the thick glossy auction catalogues that are placed atop the desk for display—English antiques, Latin American painting, watches, clocks, and postage stamps, among others—I got the subtle feeling that I was quickly being sized up by the women on the other side of that desk. What can you afford? I imagined this to be the unspoken question held tightly behind their red painted pursed lips and polite smiles.

They were all expensively dressed and somehow had a way of seeming attractive even if they were not really all that beautiful. It was all in the attitude, the stance, the presumption of power and expertise. I thought, in expertise they're all sheep in front of me, though I was content to conceal this, employing my critical prowess with the restraint of a martial arts master, I told myself, only when provoked. (Of course this conceit was an unfair exaggeration and, if nothing else, a healthy way to deal with my own insecurity at such moments, a convenient and effective defense mechanism for which I could be forgiven in the face of so much oppressive judgment.) And so I figured that I must have failed this test of liquidity in which they looked me up and down. I couldn't have seemed a flush collector or an important dealer because my appearance did not cause them to react with too much energy. After all, I was carrying a pair of Rollerblades, the ones Claire had left in my office. There was a bit of pointless paper shuffling before one of them asked if she could help me. I told her that I was there to see Claire Labrouste and asked if they could ring her extension.

Claire came out to greet me, and there was an awkward moment of hesitation as to whether we would kiss. But she stopped too far away, a full two steps in front of me, and said hello. I had no idea how to read this signal or even whether to regard it as one; I was only disappointed that she had me guessing. "How've you been?" I asked, handing her the skates.

"Great. Look, I hope you don't mind going to get Lisbeth with me. She goes to school over near Fifth," she said looking ready to leave with her coat on and her bag over her shoulder.

"Not at all, I want to meet her."

"She's my older brother's daughter," she explained as we walked west on 72nd Street. She walked quickly, and her heeled shoes made a loud clicking noise against the sidewalk. The arousing sound made her seem important, strong, full of confidence. "Her parents both work late, so I like to spend time with Lisbeth when I can, you know, run errands with her."

"Are they all the family you have over here?"

"Yes. My brother, Simon, is a linguist. He translates at the UN and teaches here and there."

"You miss Paris?"

She shrugged. "Last time I lived there I was fifteen. I think New York is a more forgiving place."

"That's not a word that leaps to mind," I said.

"There are fewer barriers here. Anyone can reinvent themselves, anyone can contribute to the culture and be appreciated. I see it every time we go to visit some new artist's studio. My boss likes to keep up with all the emerging talent, and we make these expeditions downtown to see their latest work."

"Must be nice to see all the loft spaces."

"It always happens the same way," she explained. "We walk around and look at the work and try to be encouraging, and I think to myself that these people are so lucky to be here. In New York it doesn't matter where they came from, what kind of pedigree they've got, who they were ten years ago. No one's raising a bar and forcing them to jump it."

"The barriers are just different. Artists here don't need the approval of the academy anymore, but they still have to pay rent."

"They seem to manage," she said. "Are you nostalgic for the academy?"

"It served a purpose," I said. "It drew the lines between talent and ambition very clearly."

She shook her head. "Are you serious?"

I wanted to backpedal, afraid that I was sounding like some conservative lunatic, some silly close-minded twit, which wasn't exactly what I wanted to put across. "All I'm saying is if I were an artist starting out, I wouldn't move to New York unless money was not a problem. And if that were the case, then my art probably wouldn't be very interesting."

"Do all artists have to have *suffered*?" She sounded way too sober. I began to think we were talking at different tones, at different rhythms. I didn't mean for her to take everything so literally.

She moved her bag to the other shoulder and brushed her hair back with her hand. "What about the pioneers who move into decrepit buildings and old factories to carve out new neighborhoods?" she said as we passed under the green and beige awnings of elegant apartment houses. We walked by uniformed doormen reading the tabloids and workers polishing brass fixtures. I always liked to peer in as I walked by, comparing the various lobbies, some with checkerboard black-and-white marble floors and colorful arrangements of fresh flowers. "We're just waiting to see where the next new area is going to be," she said.

"What, you mean like the next TriBeCa? The next SoHo?"

"Something like that."

"There are no more places to pioneer, we're out of space. There's nothing left on our little island."

She stopped walking and turned toward me. "Real estate seems such a big part of your world view," she said.

"It's pretty simple," I said. "The city goes bankrupt in the seventies, and we get good art. Then the boom of the eighties sets in, and the quality of the art declines."

She looked at me as if I were deranged. "Do you realize how ridiculous that is?"

Now I've really blown it, I thought. Any interest she may have had in going to bed with me was probably fading fast. I panicked and tried to play it off. "I'm half joking."

"But also half serious," she said.

"I like to use sweeping generalizations. They're much more fun. Trying to be fair seems a complete bore." I looked, but no smile registered on her face. I wanted to hang myself on one of those nice apartment-house awnings.

"What about your friend Miles Levy?" I asked, figuring I had nothing to lose now, and still so curious (jealous) about that photo of the two of them.

"Miles?"

"He's had his share of success, hasn't he?"

"Sure, but he's not a good example."

"Why not? He fits the classic pattern."

"Do you believe everything you read?" she said.

"Why, is there more to his story?"

She looked at me, grinning, eyes wide, and seemed then to be so smart, so full of interesting answers. "Come on, Stuart, there's always more."

I wanted her to talk about the glam artist, but we were near the school now and Claire waved to her niece from across the street as we walked toward the girl. She knelt down to kiss her, brushing a few wrinkles from her clothes. I was introduced as a friend, and the little girl shook my hand. "Nice to meet you," she said. I knew the Lycée Français as a school that catered mostly to international students, children of diplomats and all that. Claire had said her brother was a translator, and I was clueless as to how he and his wife could ever afford the girl's steep tuition. All smiles and spirited, Lisbeth and her friends filled the sidewalk in front of the fine Beaux Arts mansion, talking and waiting to be picked up by their parents and au pairs. Before we could leave she had to say good-bye to all of her friends, one by one, as if they would never see each other again, and she seemed to take after her Aunt Claire in the way she drew attention from her male peers. Claire had to pry her away.

"Lisbeth, *dépêche-toi*," said Claire, and the girl came running to us. She walked between us, holding Claire's hand.

"What do you do?" she asked me. I was surprised by the simple directness of the question.

"I work at the Metropolitan Museum. Have you ever been there?"

"Of course I've been there," she said. *What are you, stupid or something?* "I have a painting class there on Thursdays with Mrs. Fenel. Do you know Mrs. Fenel?"

"No, I'm afraid I don't," I said, recalling the children's art class I had taken at the museum when I was her age.

"Why don't you know Mrs. Fenel?"

"It's a very big place. A lot of people work there."

"They have a lot of guards," she said. "Are you a guard?" She laughed at the thought.

"No, I'm a curator. We get to look after the artwork. I study the art, help preserve it and put together shows."

"Sounds boring," she said. Claire scolded her mildly in French, and she became quiet.

"It's sort of like your Aunt Claire's job," I said.

"No it's not. She sells the art." I had to admit the little girl was right about that.

"So, what do you want to be when you're older?"

"I knew you would ask me that," she said. "I want to be an actress. But I want to be in French movies, not American ones."

"But your English is very good, perfect in fact."

"Thanks," she said. "But that's not it. I just think American movies are dumb." Claire looked at me and laughed. The three of us walked several blocks down Madison Avenue to a children's clothing boutique with bright, colorful windows. Lisbeth reached up to ring the bell, her tiny fingers barely touching the small round button. We were buzzed in, and she led Claire around as they looked at different dresses. I was curious what clothing for such little people cost, but there seemed to be no correlation between price and size. When I asked a college-age saleswoman why this was so, she recited something about the number of cuts in a garment. It was the construction, she told me, the stitching, dyes, materials and all that. She said a shirt, large or small, still required all the same parts. "But so do cars," I responded, "and the little ones are cheaper."

"Look," she said in a hushed tone, "it's worth whatever someone is willing to pay for it." Claire seemed uninterested, watching Lisbeth search through a tall pile of folded shirts looking for a particular color. When she got to the bottom the whole stack toppled to the floor into a big mess. Lisbeth stood there knee-high in unfolded shirts looking very guilty.

"*Tu n'as pas de grâce,*" said Claire.

"The pink was all the way at the bottom," her niece responded. The two of them slipped in and out of the languages so easily. Lisbeth seemed to admire Claire like an older sibling and took all her advice, asking what she thought of everything and laughing when Claire laughed, smiling when Claire smiled, disliking whatever Claire disliked. I was quickly bored watching them, though, and I wanted only to kiss Claire. But little Lisbeth would have been witness to us, and I felt somehow that Claire did not want the girl going home and spreading the word.

I began to wonder why she had asked me along; it

seemed an odd proposal from the start. It was not that I minded her niece, she was an entertaining little girl, but I could have suggested a more ideal way for Claire and me to spend time. I couldn't help but think that she wanted some distance, that she had cooled to me and that this was meant as a farewell meeting, a polite hint. But I thought then that she didn't need to see me at all and could have easily avoided my phone call.

Lisbeth lived in one of those anonymous rows of low-rise midblock buildings all the way east by First Avenue. She turned to say good-bye to me after we walked her there. I remember how Claire took out a set of keys to let her inside.

"She's a good girl, isn't she?" said Claire.

I nodded. "She's smart, popular, and I'm sure men will find her attractive one day." Claire looked at me and came closer, taking hold of the lapels on my wool jacket to pull me nearer, and we kissed.

"You're not busy now, are you?"

"I could juggle my schedule," I told her, pleasantly surprised. I was proving to be a terrible judge of signals.

I unlocked the door to my apartment, allowing Claire to enter first. She gave me her coat and walked into the living room looking around with curiosity. "Have a seat," I said. But she just kept silent and slowly circled the room, inspecting each of its different elements, the antique prints I had on the walls, the perfectly aged kilim rug covering part of the hardwood floor, my protomodern chairs. She came upon the shelves and ran her fingertips over the spines of my books, as if by feeling them she might understand what was in them and why I had chosen them. "It's a lot to take in," I said. "Do you want anything to drink? I'm afraid I don't have much, maybe half a bottle of red." Again she did not answer, and so I walked up to her. "Is there something I can help you find?" She looked the place over once again and then looked back at me. "So, what do you think?" I asked. Her answer emerged slowly, her voice soft.

"It's—eclectic."

"Eclectic? That's only slightly better than saying it's merely interesting."

"No, I don't mean it that way. I like eclectic when it's this skillful. You must be a great person to go antiquing with."

"Not really. I just pick up the stuff other people miss."

"Exactly." She looked closely at a small framed picture of Christina. "Who's this?"

"That's my little sister."

"It looks a bit like that Andrew Wyeth painting," she said.

"How did you know?"

"It just does."

"You know how long I've been trying to convince people that the Wyeth was my inspiration? But nobody ever sees it."

Claire leaned against the bookshelves and smiled at me.

"What?" I said.

"Nothing, just that I've been waiting all day for the love scene."

"You? My blood's been rushing since about three this afternoon."

"Poor baby," she moaned. She took me by the hand and pulled me toward the doorway leading to my bedroom.

"Where are we going?"

"To your medicine cabinet."

"Why, what's there?" I asked as we entered the tiled bathroom.

"Your condoms, I hope." She opened the mirrored cabinet, and there they were. I opened the box and took one out, but she looked at me shaking her head. "We'll need more than that," she said taking an entire strip.

Inside my room I watched her from the edge of the bed,

its frame made of polished blond maple. She stood several feet away and took off her shoes, stepping on the back of one to get it off, and then the other. She undid something at the back of her skirt, which loosened it and made it seem held up only by the slight but perfect flair of her hips. She gave it a little push, and it quickly fell to the floor. Then she slid her underwear down toward her ankles, kicking them away with her foot. They traveled far, landing on top of the desk where I kept my bills to pay. She unbuttoned her shirt and allowed that to fall, then dropped her white bra. I thought of that photo of her from Sunday's paper and realized that my imagination had proved astoundingly accurate, right down to a concave belly button stretched thin by the taut skin around her abdomen.

She stepped away from the clothing, which had now formed a small pile on the floor, and sat near me, grabbing my hand and pressing it against the inside of her thigh. We began kissing, but she seemed so much more interested in that hand of mine, which she had a tight grip on and was busy placing between her legs with particular accuracy. I gladly cooperated in this effort, eventually employing fingers from both hands and feeling the sharp strain of repetitive motion. When she noisily finished, I lay there beside her with all of my clothes still on and my arousal in obvious and urgent need of attention. So she got onto the floor and pushed me back, flat on the bed, pulling on the various elements of my clothing until they came loose. She moved along with no hesitation, and I remember most vividly the softness of her lips, the warmth inside her mouth, and the long hair draped lightly over my bare stomach. She came back up and kissed me, her hands gently pressed against the sides of my face, then came around to lie on her back, pulling me with her.

"We were splitting the work so evenly," I whispered.

"Just do your job," she said, her hands trailing along my back, and I obliged. I had a trick of endurance that involved art history I had learned in school: I recited in my head as many of the names, dates, and terms I had been forced to memorize back then, as a kind of mental diversion. It was simple but effective. After she and I fell into a rhythm I began to silently run down a list in my mind that began with the twentieth century: Expressionism, German Expressionism, Abstract Expressionism, Neo-Expressionism. "Mmm, I like that," she said.

Minimalism, Modernism, Post-Modernism, Pop Art, Photo-Realism, Surrealism, Naive art, Art Nouveau. "Mmm, yeah," she said.

Bauhaus, Cubism, Futurism, Cubo-Futurism, Fauvism, De Stijl, Dada, Neo-Dada. "Oh, that's good too," she added.

I moved on to names and dates: Duchamp, born 1887, died 1968. Kandinsky, born 1866, died 1944. Gauguin, born 1848, died 1903, and so on. Then I tried only those whose names began with the letter *W*: Watteau, West, Whistler, et cetera. This one is difficult, and I used to challenge anyone to quickly reel off more than ten. Somewhere between Warhol and Wegman I noticed the perspiration forming between our bodies, all warm and clinging, and as Claire passed her hands from my shoulders to the small of my back, the tips of her fingers glided sublimely along my pores. After I felt myself reaching a sort of half-life, she began to make some noise and I tried women Impressionist painters, Pre-Raphaelites, Dutch and Flemish masters. She was getting much more expressive now and seemed well on her way, her breaths becoming shorter. I felt her tense as I began to date the great marble works of Bernini, and finally, on *The Ecstasy of Saint Teresa,* begun 1645 and completed 1652, the moment ended perfectly.

Now I no longer cared about that photo of Claire and

Miles Levy; my curiosity had been thoroughly pacified. I realized then that this was the only activity that could have effectively banished the thought of that photo from my consciousness. I rolled to her side, and she looked at me, beaming brilliant red.

"I was wrong about you," she said, leaning against me.

"What do you mean?"

"I mean, up until just now I thought you were only an art expert, you know, just some Old Masters scholar. I was afraid there for a minute that that was all you were good at. But you've turned out to know a few other tricks, wonderful tricks." She smiled. "I guess what I really mean is, I'm just glad there's more to you than art history."

seven

OF COURSE I did not imagine that I would be among the most welcome repeat customers at Pied Noir. Despite this I went there again on Claire's rather animated insistence. Those tables had become an even more sought-after commodity in the short time since I first visited, that fateful night of bad treatment and spilled ice water. There was no denying this place was the spot of the moment for a particular crowd of creative types, a vaguely defined group that straddled the worlds of art, fashion, independent film, magazine journalism, and all that. I arrived to find several parties waiting for tables at the front near the door; they had squeezed inside to seek relief from an early fall chill. I looked among them for Claire, but she was not there, nor did she seem to be mixed in with the deep pack at the bar. That stylishly attenuated black hostess was again on duty, and I asked her if a young woman of Claire's general height and build had come by looking for someone.

"Oh, you must be Claire's friend," she said.

"Yes, that's right."

"They're already sitting. Follow me." She led me into the

buzzing room, winding through tables and chairs, her shoes making her so tall I thought she might take out two or three parties if she toppled over. I followed her to one of the well-placed banquettes, where I found Claire sitting squeezed between two men along the wall. Two other guests faced inward, and an empty chair seemed reserved for me. Claire introduced me to everyone as I took the seat. I reached around the table shaking hands and paying close attention due to my unfortunate tendency to forget names the moment I hear them, but to my surprise most of these proved to be names I already knew. Next to me sat David Lieberthal, owner of the Griffin Gallery, a powerful and well-connected dealer whom I had seen before and read much about. To his left was the publicist Susan Edelman, Christina's manic employer. Across the table from me, next to Claire, sat Miles Levy. His assistant, Todd Bryce, sat to Claire's other side. I was always curious what one of these artist's assistants really does: apparently enough to warrant bringing him to dinner.

"Have we met?" asked Levy.

"Yes, a couple of weeks ago, right here in this room. There was a terrible accident, I believe it involved a glass of ice water."

He smiled. "That's right, you soaked me. I remember going home to change that night." There was an awkward handsomeness about him; his face was strangely unsymmetrical, almost as if he had been in an auto accident—one that left him not disfigured but just mildly different, a little more interesting. It was an angular face, chiseled thin and weathered. He wore his thick black hair parted and was still addicted to those harsh French cigarettes. Todd was closer to my age, well built and also good-looking. With Claire flanked by these two bookends, I felt a bit inadequate, notwithstanding my performance the other day. The two of them only made me want to be nearer to her. After the introductions came the de rigueur expressions of interest in my area of scholarship.

"Oh, you must work with Harlan Kohlman. How's that old man doing?" asked David.

"He's doing well," I said.

"He's still active? Still writing?"

"Still alive?" Miles rang out, smirking.

"Yes, working as hard as ever." Miles took the last sip of a drink and then asked my age. "Twenty-eight," I said. "And you?"

"Like a good stock, I fluctuate somewhere in the mid-forties," he said.

"Let us know when we should sell."

He took a deep drag of his cigarette as I said this and seemed impatient with the process of exhaling. As he struggled to quickly clear the pipes one would have felt impolite not to have waited silently for his reply, as if he had a tough piece of steak to swallow. "Dump everything, the stock is going to shit," he said as soon as he could get enough clean oxygen to the brain to operate the motor skills of speech.

"You sound more like a stockbroker than an aesthete," I said.

"What's an artist supposed to sound like?"

"I wouldn't know. Most of the artists I deal with died long before the invention of sound recording."

"I bet a lot of them spoke the language of the streets, the vernacular. I mean, I don't think they were all so genteel."

"You're probably right," I said. Then David emptied his wineglass before weighing in.

"This stockbroker analogy is interesting. Artists are risk takers, thrill seekers, they court danger. I mean, hell, Caravaggio fled Rome on charges of manslaughter."

"I never knew that," said Susan, sounding falsely interested and looking around the room. Did someone like her know anything more about Caravaggio than his famous name?

"Well it's true," said the dealer. "He painted his best stuff as a fugitive."

"He had a problem with authority—the first real bohemian," I pointed out.

"He also died young, didn't he?" said David.

"1610, of malaria. That would have made him thirty-eight," I quickly added with all the confidence my expertise could muster.

"Dying young isn't all that bad," said Miles, "as long as your legend lives."

Looking back on it now, I can hardly believe the prescience of this little exchange. I now marvel at how well they knew their historical models, their precedents. They had all the right references, and they didn't even know it yet.

"Was it really malaria?" asked Todd from across the table. I nodded. "It's like AIDS killing off young creativity," he said. "All the destruction it's caused the artistic community, the unfulfilled potential. I could list the names we've all heard of, but there are so many that had yet to make their mark." His words sounded genuine, heartfelt, and I agreed with him, but it wasn't something I wanted to talk about as I contemplated ordering a twenty-dollar serving of cassoulet without knowing who would be picking up the tab.

Claire looked at Todd. "I wouldn't draw parallels between lives in the seventeenth century and those at the end of the twentieth," she said. The same thought had gone through my mind just then, and I wanted to tell her how right I thought she was, but I never got a chance. All I could do was look at her.

"People are resorting to extremes," Todd went on. "Just last week one of the drug companies had a bomb scare. People want faster drug approval."

"That won't change anything," I said. "The public will just regard it as criminal."

"But most of them haven't been through the disease," he said. "They don't know what it's like to have friends taken by it."

"Exactly," I said.

"Exactly what?" asked Miles.

"Most people don't know what it's like firsthand, they have the advantage of removal. Their view isn't clouded by the emotion they would have if they were involved. It's better to come at it objectively, rationally."

Miles looked up from his glass. "You sound a bit old-fashioned. I mean, truth, objective knowledge, these things have become obsolete. Claire was right to say we shouldn't compare the centuries. The world has become a more relative, subjective place. There's almost no point in giving opinions anymore. Your right is always someone else's wrong."

"Right and wrong still exist," I said.

"Look," said David, "in the end what really matters is that your opinion wins out, that it survives."

"That's right," added Susan, breaking the seal formed by her pale-colored lipstick. "We shouldn't be afraid to offend."

"No one's ever accused you of having a timid mouth," said David, referring to her reputation, and she laughed. Then the dealer turned to me. "You know that Susan has her own P.R. firm." I nodded. "She gives good spin," he said smiling, and I thought then that they must be sleeping together.

"I still say everything is relative," Miles said. "Opinions, discussion, texts—all communication is relative."

"Then it would all be meaningless," said Claire.

"Well, no fixed meanings anyway." Miles sounded like an overeager student regurgitating hip phrases from a handbook of poststructuralist theory. He must have believed those ideas were still somehow fashionable, I thought, but in struggling to understand them he had lost his way and given up to glib sound bites and half-formed allusions. I wanted to tell him that Foucault and Derrida were old news, but I couldn't figure out how to make it sound polite.

Later I asked Susan about one of her employees, my sister, and she was surprised. "The girl's doing well. She had a rough time of it in the beginning but seems to have picked up the essentials. I'm even considering her for a special project."

"What kind of project?" I asked, but she changed the subject.

"I find that everything at the firm runs better when I have an office full of terrified young assistants. It's really one of the keys to my success," she said, laughing.

When we ordered, Susan asked our attractive waitress her opinion on every dish. "Is it good?" she kept asking. "Is the fish fresh? You know fish has to be fresh." I imagined what her reaction might have been had the waitress said with a straight face, "Yes, we have an odiously rancid salmon served in a velvety *beurre blanc* sauce. Twenty-two fifty."

The kitchen had run out of a few dishes just as they had the last time I was there, and even Miles had to change his order. "This place is inconsistent," he said.

"But you're consistently here," I remarked.

"Yes, always at this table, it's what they call a set reservation. This place is like my own Cedar Tavern, the old Cedar Tavern. Come to think of it, the food was never any good."

"But I thought good and bad were subjective terms, obsolete notions to you," I said. "There are supposed to be no absolute truths, right?"

"You're just so much smarter than us." Then he looked at Claire as if to ask, What's with this guy?

"Just giving you a hard time," I said.

"You like to mine irony, don't you, Finley?" Miles kept calling me Finley throughout the night, and it made me a bit uneasy. Harlan Kohlman was the only other person who ever presumed to call me by my last name like that, but this seemed intentionally impolite.

"It's the ability to recognize irony that separates us from all other animals," I said to him.

"I always thought it was that we can make love facing each other," said Claire.

"You're both wrong," said Miles. "It's that we're able to make love facing each other but often choose otherwise." He wore a slight but irritating smile when he said this, as if he knew all about my interest in Claire. I kept noticing how close he got to her, often whispering something in her ear or eating off of her plate. He was trying to establish some kind of private conversation with her at the expense of the rest of the table, and she kept resisting. They spoke to each other in low voices, and I couldn't quite follow what it was about, perhaps the continuation of some previous argument, I thought.

"When are you going to tell Simon he has to stop this?" he said to her, placing his hand on her forearm.

"We'll talk about it later, Miles."

"You brought the whole thing up before we left the house tonight."

"I just wanted you to give me a straight answer."

"I told you I would. That should do."

I noticed Claire gently move her arm away from his hand. "I'm sick of your conditions," she said.

"You want me to just give you a blank check?"

"Not now, Miles. Can't we just—"

"Fine."

Not wanting to appear too curious at this bit of tension, I struck up a conversation with David Lieberthal. A thin, middle-aged man, he looked fit, tan, well rested, and casual in a chambray shirt and a blazer. He asked where I had gone to school and then told me how he got his start in college selling Pop Art prints to his friends' parents during the sixties. Now he employed dozens of people at his gallery, which was a large operation comprising offices in New York (with space in SoHo and on 57th Street), Los Angeles, Tokyo, and an affiliate in Paris. "I was just like you," he said to me, "no one could believe how young I was."

I remember Miles turning to Susan and asking, "Have you seen the Avedon shot?"

"Yes," she said. "You were broken by the frame."

"What's that?" I asked David.

"Miles was photographed by Avedon with about six or seven other hot artists, and you know how his group portraits are several frames long? Well, Miles got split in half," he explained, laughing.

"It's much better to be the one cut off by the frame," said Miles. "It gives more status."

I looked around the crowded room and was struck by the fact that I had managed, somehow, to join the very table that had so annoyed me only a week before, when my sister had dragged me to this red-hot corner of the world and asked me not to appear so unaccustomed. It's too bad she's not here to witness this, I thought. "This place is doing well," I said to Miles.

"I'm a ghost investor," he said. "It's only been three weeks, and already we're losing our chef. No one's worried. We've got a couple of barely legal Mexicans in the kitchen who've already learned how to make everything. Look, it doesn't matter what you feed fashion models, since most of them are planning to throw it up before the night's out."

At some point I noticed that the banquette adjacent to ours was filled with people who knew Miles. After a while I realized they were his groupies, part of his entourage; some I even recognized from the night I had been there with Christina. They all had lots of flair, stylish nocturnal types with pale white skin and mostly black clothes. After our entrees had been cleared away, the artist got up to do a round of table hopping. He took Claire by the hand and walked around the room with her, stopping at several tables to chat. The people he approached were delighted by the attention, and the room had the kind of busy energy that made such a move seem natural. I watched Miles put his arm around Claire's waist, his hand gripping and rubbing and squeezing. She didn't pull away the whole time, and it drove me crazy. They went on like this, stopping for a word with the hostess before returning.

"So, Finley," Miles said to me later over coffee, "you're really a museum curator?" I nodded. "Then tell us your opinion on deaccessioning."

"I'm all for it if it's done to improve a collection," I said and then quickly realized that his question was not meant to be serious. He grinned and I took a sip of my coffee. "Look," I said, "let's just all agree that you will always be more interesting than me; that way it'll no longer be a point worth making."

He shrugged and said, "How do you and Claire know each other? I mean, did you put an ad in the *New York Review of Books* or something?" He liked to laugh at his own jokes. I looked at Claire to try to gauge her comfort in this area. But she just stared back blankly without a hint of what she may have wanted me to say.

"We met at the Carlyle Hotel," I said.

"Any special occasion?"

"An estate appraisal. They're usually pretty routine, but this was the home of Larry Zolarian."

"He was just indicted," said David.

"Right, the apartment was filled with all these government investigators when I arrived, you know, FBI, IRS, and all that. I was there to see some master drawings that he had. Claire was looking at these big contemporary paintings, I remember one in particular, a fantastic de Kooning."

"A real beauty," said Claire. "I predict it'll be the star of next season."

"So the two of us got to talking, realized we had a common friend and so forth."

"Stuart gave me a very private tour of the Met on Monday," she added.

"Very private?"

"Miles, the place is closed on Mondays," she said.

"Oh, I see, I guess membership has its privileges." He laughed again and then lit a cigarette. "God, I haven't been up there in years," he said, blowing smoke.

It was not until later that night, shortly after we arrived at a party given for the anniversary of some glossy arts magazine, that I was able to talk to Claire alone. The crowded gathering was held in a vast photo studio in the West Village called Industria, where during the daylight hours one would normally find models, fashion editors, and photo assistants. David Lieberthal subsidized the thick monthly with his advertising, much of it for Miles Levy's work. In return the publication provided a friendly editorial environment, and it was no surprise that the artist and his dealer were the real stars of the event. Every so often a camera flash would go off in one corner or another, lending a bit of glitter to the packed party.

The place smelled of fresh paint. Everything was intensely white: the floor, the walls, the radiator pipes and ceiling sprinklers. Drifting around, I ran into several people with whom I was mildly acquainted. Some I had known in graduate school, others from galleries and foundations I dealt with at work. Those familiar cartoonlike captions were once again filling the air. "Hey, didn't we meet last summer at that party at the Rubell house?" asked one.

"I don't think so," I said.

"Yes, I'm sure of it," he insisted. "We argued about the Guild Hall show, remember?"

"It's been dry for a few summers now," said another.

Nearby I saw Claire gravitating between clusters of conversation. Our eyes met, and I excused myself from the informed talk around me. My timing was perfect; I had bailed out just as one fairly bright young woman, sporting a very conspicuous choker of small fine white pearls, began to discuss her lifelong identification with Frida Kahlo.

"What do you want to drink?" Claire asked me.

"WHAT?" The music was loud, some kind of revivalist disco/soul hybrid.

"What do you WANT TO DRINK?" I told her, and she returned a few minutes later with two sweet vodka gimlets. I held my glass close and took several sips in a row, then looked at her for a moment. She was a dark beauty, her eyes almost the color of dirty copper, the very tops of her irises hidden by the eyelids. Those eyelids seemed heavy, sometimes giving her an intense, world-weary look. Her brown hair fell with shape and curve against a stretch satin T-shirt. The little top allowed a midriff peek every time she raised her glass. I was becoming convinced she could pull off anything she pleased. As I considered the space between the top edge of her jeans and the bottom of that tiny shirt, I wondered how many times Miles Levy had gotten his hands in there.

"You're very quiet, Stuart. What's wrong?" she asked.

"What's wrong? Nothing except that you and Miles seem attached at the hip."

She shrugged. "He and I have been friends for a long time."

"I thought he was a real jerk there toward the end of dinner."

"You're new to him, and he just gets kind of protective."

"Of you?"

"I guess."

"Why, are you two together? I mean that might explain certain behavior, don't you think?"

"We're not together."

Now *I* was the one to shrug and look around.

"Don't be so sensitive to this stuff," she said. "We've only known each other for all of two weeks."

I took another gulp of my drink, this time turning the glass up too far and causing a bit of spillover. I dabbed it up with a damp cocktail napkin and blinked as another camera flash went off.

"Claire, let me ask you something. Where do you live?"

"What?"

"Yes, where do you live? What I mean is, with whom do you live?"

"It has nothing to do with—"

"Every time I've asked you this we seem to get interrupted by something or the subject suddenly changes."

"I live with Miles, all right? Is that what you want to know?"

"You live with Miles Levy," I said, slow and emphatic. "You live together, in his grand loft, no doubt. Not that it makes any difference where, but just that you live with him."

"It's not that at all, like we 'live together.'"

"I don't understand."

"I just rent a room from him, it's a huge place, almost public really. A lot of people shack up there. There are always people coming and going."

"So why be so evasive?" I asked. "I mean, if it's no big deal."

"Evasive? Look, Miles and I have an unconventional relationship. It's not easy to understand."

"Tell me about it."

"We have this history. We were together for a long time, and then it was kind of on-and-off. Now it's off for good. He lets me live at his place cheap, real cheap; you can appreciate that." She looked at me, and I let a small smile creep in. "Before, it just seemed too complicated and unnecessary to explain. It doesn't matter is what I'm trying to say."

"So then leave with me now," I said to her with a touch of hopefulness in my voice. "Come over, we'll go uptown together, and you can stay with me."

"Not tonight." She looked away toward another group of people, her arms folded.

"Why not?"

"I can't."

"Why?"

"Because I promised Miles I would stay here with him. This is an important night with the art press and all these clients. I said I would stay." I nodded and looked into my empty glass.

"Fine," I said. "That's fine. If that's what you need to do, then, you know, of course, do what you want. Have fun. I'm just not in the mood for this. I can't have one more conversation about how Damien Hirst is the new Jeff Koons, so I'm gonna call it a night, if you don't mind." I put my hand in my jacket pocket and felt for the coat-check tickets. "Here, you'll need this," I said, handing her one of them.

"Stuart," she said to me. I began to walk toward the large steel door. "You're being such a baby." She followed me over to the coat check. "Oh, I should go home with you now, just like that? How fucking immature is that? Come on, there were never any conditions when I brought you out with us."

"Claire, honestly, I don't expect you to go home with me, not at all. But I'm not going to stay here all night just to prove that to you. You'll have to take my word for it." I slipped on a long wool coat, and we looked at each other.

"I take your word," she said. "I'm not sure why, but I do. Look, I'm sorry about Miles. This just didn't go the way I thought it would."

"How did you think it would go? I mean, why did you ever pick this night to see me?"

She paused, then said, "I don't know."

eight

I WAS NEVER the type to wake up early on a Sunday morning to go out to get the paper and bagels. While I enjoyed the elements of that ritual as much as anyone, I always felt there was no reason to do it at eight when it could be done closer to noon. Christina, by contrast, was religious in her Sunday-morning ways, claiming her copy of the thick Sunday paper around dawn near her building in West Chelsea. When we were growing up together, she would only let me read the sections she was finished with. If I could get her permission to see a few sections of the paper she hadn't read, they would have to be kept neat—no backward folds or unaligned loose pages—and had to be put back in the rigid order in which she always placed them. There was a certain logic to that order, she maintained, but it was too complicated to explain. I used to fear that her life would be thrown into chaos if the *Times* introduced a new section.

So when my phone rang at three minutes to nine on Sunday, I was asleep, dreaming that I was at a flea market and had come across a seventeenth-century Dutch landscape drawing in some cheap plastic frame, forgotten about and misidentified. The owner was asking only twenty-five dollars for it. It was a recurring dream of mine and always a frustrating one because I never quite made it to the point of possessing the fine drawing before waking up.

"Stuart, are you up?" asked the voice at the other end. It was Christina.

"I am now."

"Have you been out yet?"

"No, Chrissie, you just woke me from that dream."

"Which dream? The one where you inherit that classic six off Park? And you always wake up screaming and in a cold sweat because at the very end of the dream you can't afford to give the doormen their Christmas money?"

"No, not that one. The other one."

"Don't you still want that classic six?"

"What are you, a broker? Forget it. What's up?"

"Nothing, I just wanted to say hello to the new man-about-town."

"What?"

"Stuart, don't be so modest. This is one hell of a debut. I mean, you even look pretty good standing there next to this very glam woman."

"I don't know what you're talking about, Chrissie. I'm going to put the phone down now, but you're welcome to keep talking while I get a bit more sleep."

"Don't you have the paper yet?"

"No, why?"

"Oh my God. Stuart, you're in it."

"What do you mean?" I said, now fully awake. I sat up at attention, pulling on my comforter and propping up the pillows behind me.

"There's a picture of you and a woman at a party on the Evening Hours page, above the fold, no less. It says it was a party to celebrate the five-year anniversary of *New Arts* magazine."

Good God. "Are you joking?"

"No, it's definitely a picture of you."

"Is there a caption?"

"Yeah, it says, 'Claire Labrouste and Stuart Finley were among the guests celebrating at Industria Superstudio.'"

"Where did they get my name?"

"I don't know, but they got it," she said. Then she lowered her voice. "This Claire, is she there? I mean, is she with you now?"

"No. This thing was on Wednesday night. I haven't spoken to her since."

"Too bad."

"I know. Well, how do we look?"

She waited a beat. "Unlikely," she said.

"What do you mean?" I asked, all defensive.

"You make an unlikely couple, I mean, only because I know you so well. You look good, don't get me wrong, but she looks totally glam. Maybe it's just that she seems to have, like, two whole inches on you."

"She's kind of aggressive with her heels."

"Must be."

"Yeah, well, we're not a couple anyway. We were actually having a little disagreement when they must have snapped the picture. Do we seem unhappy?"

"Not at all. You have your glass of Stoli in your hand, and you're talking to her, while she's got this blissful smile on and is looking into your eyes like she adores you."

"That's not the way I remember it."

"That's the way it looks. You should really go out and get yourself a copy."

"Why don't you just become my publicist? At the end of each month you can compile a folder of my clips so that I won't have to bother."

"It will cost you."

"How much?"

"Say five percent of your earnings for the first year."

"Speaking of publicists, hours before that party last week I was at dinner with your boss."

"Susan? Why don't you ever call to tell me these things?"

"I've been meaning to."

"What was she like?"

"Everything you said and more. I almost lost my appetite."

"Was she with David Lieberthal?"

"Yes, and Miles Levy too. She said she's giving you some special project?"

Suddenly her tone became serious. "Stuart, are you on cordless?"

"No, why?"

"Miles Levy has just become Susan's secret client."

"Secret client?"

"You know, it's *déclassé* for an artist to have P.R. people. Nobody is supposed to know. She's got me working on the account, and there's all this clandestine procedure I have to follow. We have to feed his items to the columnists very carefully."

"So why don't you ever call to tell me this stuff?" I asked.

It quickly became a morning of unexpected phone calls. Jenny from the museum phoned to say that Harlan Kohlman was feeling fatigued and had elected to take the week off. She said he wanted me to retrieve some papers and books from his office on Monday and bring them to his apartment so he could continue with his writings. He figured that I was the only one who knew exactly what to get and where to find it in his wildly disheveled office. Besides, Jenny reminded me, I was the only one in the department whom he ever let have a key to the place.

The phone rang again at ten. "Hello?"

"Finley?"

"Yes."

"It's Miles."

I swallowed. "Miles, how are you?"

"I've been meaning to call you, Finley."

"Is that right?"

"Yes, look, I'm sorry about the other night. I know I might have been a bit, what's the word, awkward with you over dinner. I didn't mean anything by it, and I want to make it up to you."

"Dinner was fine. You don't need to make anything up to me. Did Claire ask you to do this?"

"Claire? Well, she did give me your number. Look, what are you doing today?"

"What am I doing? I'm on my way out to an estate appraisal, why?"

"On Sunday? Bullshit. You're not doing anything of the sort. You must come over for brunch. It's a Miles Levy ritual."

"Brunch? At your loft?"

"Yes, it's catered. And I want to show you my work."

"That's all right, really, you don't have to have me over. I'm just going to—"

"I insist," he said. I thought about it for a moment. I wanted very much to see Claire.

"What should I bring?" I asked him.

"I have everything. Just bring yourself."

The Mercer Street building was a perfect example of its day, with its cast iron facade and factory-size windows. I pressed the button for Levy's loft, and the front door buzzed right open, no one ever asking who it was. The elevator required some intuition. I stepped inside the cage and looked for buttons, but there were none, only a manual lever that turned like the helm of a warship. I shut the inner gate tightly and brought the lever back toward me. Wrong direction. The elevator dropped below street level, so I put it in neutral and it jerked to a stop, its cables snapping against each other in the shaft above me. I looked up, seeing right through to the heavy swaying cables, and considered taking the stairs, but an aborted sortie might look bad, and the stairs would have me arriving, if not out of breath, at least slightly flush. I moved the lever forward this time, and the car abruptly began to rise. The ride itself was smooth and quiet, it was the stops and starts I knew I would have trouble with. As I approached the fourth floor, I began to realize that I would have to throw the thing into neutral exactly at the landing. I missed by two feet, so I put it in reverse and missed again, this time four feet below where I wanted to land. Every time the car jerked to a stop I felt sure they could hear me from inside the loft. I tried again and heard a few loud sparks. Now the lever did nothing. I was stuck. All I heard was the loud clicking of an electrical relay whenever I tried to go up or down. Before too long the large steel door with a red painted 4 on it opened, and I was greeted by Miles.

"Finley, what's up?" he yelled down.

"Hey, Miles. I was just trying to make an even landing here."

"It breaks down all the time. Here, open the gate and give me your hand," he said, looking down at me. It seemed a little daring. What if the car started moving while I was climbing out? I knew it wasn't supposed to work that way, but after seeing Miles swing open his door with the car midway between floors like that, I was beginning to second-guess the safety of this contraption. I held my breath, and he pulled me up into the loft.

"There are people in this building who would rather pay off city inspectors than fix anything." He had a look of

Sunday leisure, greeting me in an old pair of canvas boat shoes, no socks, a pair of badly fraying twill trousers that stopped too high on his ankles, and a faded sweatshirt that draped over his broad shoulders in lots of folds. His hair didn't seem just-washed but was still clean, nicely out of place and perfectly thick. How did he manage to affect such informal morning comfort? Such a look would have taken me hours to manufacture and then would only seem too studied, too thought-over. It made me want to excuse myself, go to the mirror in his bathroom and mess up my hair, wrinkle my shirt, untie one of my shoes, do *something*.

"Let me show you around," he said.

The space was vast, covering the entire fourth and fifth floors, he told me. The entrance and work space were on the lower level, and the private living areas were all upstairs. The lower level was spare and painted white. Across from the elevator was parked a vintage Triumph motorcycle, lit from above like a piece of sculpture. It was restored and in perfect condition, the chrome polished, the paint waxed, and the seat upholstered with distressed leather.

"This can't be legal, keeping it in here like this."

"It's a violation of just about every fire code I can think of," he said. It seemed he was just waiting for me to remark on how wonderfully eccentric this was, but I refused.

"It's kind of a shame. I mean, it doesn't look like you use it much."

"I would, but the whole bike scene is so beat. Every asshole has one now."

He walked me around a corner to reveal a large but neatly kept work space. The worktables were covered with dried-up drops of paint that made them look like Jackson Pollock canvases. There were shelves packed with jars, tubes, brushes, cans of paint, tins of acetone and other toxic chemicals. Along one wall was a storage rack built of unfinished two-by-fours and plywood. It rose all the way up to the double-high ceiling and was filled with dozens of canvases leaned against one another. "You produce a lot of work," I said, surveying the inventory.

"You think there's something wrong with so much output?"

"No, no, it's not a criticism," I said, noticing his sensitivity to the subject. "I guess it's a sign of real discipline."

"I may seem too productive, but I guarantee you, it doesn't come easy. I struggle to produce my work. I struggle mentally, physically. I know some of my critics think it's a bad sign, disparaging the amount of work and the speed with which I make it. To them this makes it less valid somehow, but it's hard labor for me." He smiled and said, "You know, sometimes I envy the Colombian boy who delivers my groceries. He has it easy in ways he doesn't even realize."

"Come on," I said.

"I know it sounds ridiculous, but some days I wake up and feel like I'd rather go and deliver groceries than face a freshly primed canvas. Sometimes I want to throw off the burden and work for tips like that boy." He laughed. "But that's just what this stuff does to you. You lose your perspective."

We stepped along the creaking wood floor, and he seemed to be leading me toward two paintings that had been placed out for display. Miles Levy was primarily known for two things, his collagelike paintings and his conceptual sculpture and installations. One of the latter was included in the Whitney Museum's 1993 Biennial exhibition and was the star of the show. It was titled *The Right to Bear Arms* and was a small dark room into which the viewer entered alone and put his or her eye up to the scope of a rifle. What one observed through the crosshairs was a fast-moving series of photographs of dozens of innocent victims of random gun violence in America. But cleverly mixed in among these photos was a video image of the viewer himself as the "target." In all his sculptures and installations politics was the crucial aesthetic element, and it helped establish his reputation with a particular group of avant-garde critics and editors from two or three small-circulation but important career-making art magazines.

His paintings, by contrast, were where he made his money, perfectly designed to appeal to the young, hip collectors and the interior decorators who bought for the rich. They used images from advertising, product design and packaging such as candy wrappers, cookie boxes, cigarette packages, old postcards, and cigar bands. These elements were not actually applied to the canvas but simply painted to look like they were, painstakingly illustrated to seem pasted on. For those in on the joke it was a whimsical play on traditional collage.

"I want your opinion, Finley," he said. "I want to know what you think of my work. These are my latest. No one has seen them yet."

I looked uncomfortably at the two canvases he had leaning against a table and said nothing for a moment.

"Don't think too hard," he said.

These were similar to the others I was familiar with, except that the elements were parking tickets, traffic summonses, income-tax forms, and other government printed matter skillfully arranged and obscured by washes of white, gray, and blue paint.

"There is a real expressive energy," I said finally. "The colors are moving."

He looked at me. "Come on, you can do better than that."

"Are you sure you want me to?"

"I want you to be honest."

"What do you care what I think, anyway? I'm just a historian, a scholar of the distant past, a preserver of old objects."

"I don't know. I guess I want your approval, I want you to place this in the great timeline of art-historical context."

"Whatever that means. Look, I wouldn't know where to

begin. You have an audience for this work right now, a public. No one will ever know how to truly assess your work until its time has passed. That's true of all work."

"You have an audience too. What you do is measured in terms of public reaction and museum attendance."

"I don't have an audience, I have a set of standards."

He laughed. "What allows you to say that one work of art is better than another? What is it, Finley, that allows you to say good here, bad there?"

Here it was. This was the heart of the matter, the question of the century, at the end of the century. Between Levy and me, this is what everything came down to, besides Claire.

"My opinion," I answered. "My personal response to the work."

"Your personal response? What gives your particular personal response the right to influence anyone else?"

"We all have the right. It's a constant process. It can't be stopped just because one day you might find yourself on the losing side."

"Sorry?"

"You can't call the whole premise into question just because it fails you."

"But the premise isn't failing me," he said. "It's actually doing pretty well by me."

I looked around at the expensive square footage we were standing in. "You're right," I said. "It's been treating you very well."

"Are you hungry?"

"What?"

"Brunch. Don't you want to eat?" he asked.

The eating was done upstairs. There was a lot of nicely worn-in old country furniture around up there—large bureaus, French chairs, tall cupboards, and a long table, all of it painted in soft summery pastel colors. Spread along the table was an enormous assortment of food from the nearby Dean & DeLuca gourmet shop—smoked fish, prosciutto, croissants, pâté, and cheeses. It seemed enough to feed all of SoHo, TriBeCa, and the East Village. Claire came over to say hello when she saw me.

"Who's all the food for?"

"The usual suspects," she said. They began arriving almost as soon as she said it, a bunch of Levy's friends, groupies, other artists, Todd, and of course David Lieberthal and their new best friend, Susan Edelman. There were about two dozen people standing around picking at the pink strips of fish and dipping into the spreads like guilty raccoons. I remember asking Todd why he wasn't eating as I spread a bagel.

"I've already had my early meal for the day," he said. There was a laziness to the way his words came out, a kind of unfocused fuzzy ease. He started into a whole speech about why the food on that table was bad for me. He told me all the ritual elements of his lean diet and how it was designed to add, on average, ten years to his life expectancy. But there was another reason why he wasn't thinking about food. He came close and said quietly, "Right now it's called Daydreamer, but they're always changing the name."

"What?"

"It's a very pure heroin. Over on Fourth Street you ask for Daydreamer. Last month they were calling it Black Magic. No sticking needles, you just inhale it."

"You don't betray any signs," I said.

"You can operate fine. I'll bet you could do it at work, at the museum, and no one would know."

"I don't doubt it," I said, thinking that one could get very fucked up at the Metropolitan in complete silence and relative safety. Everyone already believed the paintings talked to them. Drugs might just bring the mummies back to life.

"I've got more downstairs."

"No, that's all right. I'm strung out on cream cheese right now, but thanks."

He smiled. "Let me know if you change your mind."

Later I looked out one of the big sun-filled windows with Claire. Mercer Street was busy with Sunday strollers. More than a few carried shopping bags I was sure they would save when they got home, the ones that come from stylish stores, with thick black rope for handles. "I was going to call you," she said in a soft voice.

"But you didn't."

"Last week was a bad time for me."

"I've been wanting to see you."

"It's the same with me."

"You could have," I said.

"Miles and I had a big blowout after you left that party."

"What for?"

"Over you," she said.

"What happened?"

"He said he wanted me to move out. He said that if I was going to keep seeing you, then I should leave."

"You surprised?"

"Yes I'm surprised. He and I aren't together. He's been letting me live here since we broke up months ago. He has no claim to me, no right to keep me from seeing you. He wants to give me a hard time, I mean, give us a hard time." I liked the way she rephrased that last line. It sent a little chill up the spine.

"What happened between you two?"

"I dated him when I worked at David's gallery. It was a long time ago. He had me move in. But things went bad, and after a while I left him."

"You broke up, but you didn't actually leave him. I mean, you stayed here."

"Yes, but look at this place, it's like a hotel. I basically took a room. Todd lives here, a lot of different people have lived here at times. We made an arrangement."

"And now he wants you to leave if you keep seeing me."

"It's got nothing to do with you specifically, it would be the same with anyone."

"Look, just leave. I mean, screw him."

"I'm afraid to burn a bridge. He could make my life difficult. He could make my career difficult."

"How?"

"You see what goes on, the people around him, the collectors and the dealers. These are all people I have to work with every day. I've been trading on his name for two years, and he knows it. He could make me *persona non grata* overnight. Stuart, sometimes I wish I had never chosen such a tiny, incestuous corner of the world to make my way in."

"Don't let it control your life, Claire."

"It's like payback time for all of those favors I got. You know those breaks you get because you're fortunate enough to be able to connect a few dots? Well, you take those breaks, and you know way in the back of your mind that you're giving up a little bit of your freedom."

"But this is ridiculous, Claire. Eventually you'll have to break the tie."

"Eventually."

"Look, you're smart, you don't need crutches like this. You were never given anything you didn't deserve, you're more than qualified. I mean, there was never any lack of merit, right?"

"No, but you know it takes more than merit. You have to be smart, work hard, *and* get lucky. After you show that you deserve something, you also need to have people on your side." I thought about Harlan Kohlman when she said this. Miles Levy had been her Harlan Kohlman, only now the guy was prepared to take it all away from her. She looked at me, and I took her hand in mine.

"So what do we do?" I said.

nine

DAVID LIEBERTHAL stood triumphant in the middle of the killing room, boasting about what it takes to be a great dealer. "It isn't just the ability to sell, you also have to know where all of the bodies are buried." He had just finished selling one of Miles Levy's paintings to a very eager member of the New Establishment when he made this remark with the kind of casual self-satisfaction you find among successful salesmen. His client had already departed when David looked at me for a reaction. But something about this proud moment made me not want to seem so impressed, something made me not want to give him the kind of obvious, almost reflexive praise I knew he expected.

When brunch at the Levy Factory had ended earlier that day, David asked me if I wanted to watch what he said would be a typical sale, and I agreed to tag along. On the short walk over to his gallery on Wooster Street he seemed his characteristic calm, and told me how he didn't work on Sundays as a rule, but this important prospect, this guy who had expressed such interest in Miles's genius, was leaving town that night to fly back to Redwood City, California, and so rules could be broken for about $150,000. I was curious about the interested party and thought, who really buys this stuff anymore?

"Where's the money these days, David? I mean, the eighties are long gone."

He smiled. "I don't think in those terms. I refuse to be a victim of economic cycles. You have to keep reinventing the wheel. The money didn't dry up. It just moved around, changed hands."

"So who's got it now?"

"Hollywood and Silicon Valley," he said. "Anything to do with software, entertainment, technology. Any kind of intellectual property." He looked into the window of a sleek furniture store. "The power is with the content providers," he said, admiring a small neo-Biedermeier foyer table. "The shift has been going on for years." He paused, still fixed on the table. "You know, I've been eyeing that table. What do you think? You like it?"

"It has a certain competence."

He looked at me. "What does that mean?"

"It means I like it."

He grinned. "Anyway, take this guy we're going to meet right now. He's exactly what I'm talking about." He went on to tell me about James Nickolas, a computer whiz who had written the crucial code for some software that lets you navigate the World Wide Web. A "killer app," in David's words. He dropped out of Stanford to help found something called an Internet access provider. The company went public in a frenzy of high-tech speculation, and now, on paper at least, he could afford to collect *cool* art. "A nice chunk of the nation's wealth was transferred to him *overnight*," said the dealer. "And as far as the eighties being over," he went on, "well, they might be, but there's no shortage of ambitious people out there. Trust me. The glitz might be gone. I know taste and discretion are the buzzwords, but that's just window dressing, just style. What happened during that decade was never really rejected, never rolled back, and the world was made safe for the ambitious," he said as if telling me the happy ending of a fairy tale before bedtime. He admitted that there were fewer people participating in this economy of "intellectual property." But he didn't seem to care.

"How many content providers could there be out there?" I said. "It seems a rarefied group on which to base all this optimism."

"I don't need a lot of buyers, just a few reliables."

"And their friends."

"Right," he said. "And throw in a couple of able-bodied wannabes for good measure, and business will always be good."

I wasn't familiar enough with the details of his business back then to know if he was in a state of denial or if this was actually true, that sales were still robust, effortless. In some way it might have been in his interest to perpetuate the myth that sales had dried up, that money had tightened, because then he would seem all the more skillful for having survived. At that moment I decided to take him, temporarily, at his word. I would have to wait to find out whether his pop sociology was at all sound.

We arrived to find the street-level gallery marred by hip vandals. Its front was a sleek garage door made up of square frosted-glass panels sectioned off by unpainted strips of aluminum. Breaking up these modernist lines, however, was a poster of protest from a feminist art group famous for its guerilla tactics. David had been criticized for not representing enough women artists, and his gallery was often the target of such actions. "They're a bunch of asexual children who claim to speak for women artists," he said as he tried to peel off the offending poster. "These crybabies come here in the middle of the night and paste their propaganda all over my property." He gave up trying to unstick the paper as it only tore off in little pieces. "Besides," he said, "it's not even true that we only have male artists. What about Karen Nivens?"

"She's dead," I pointed out.

"Yeah, but we still handle her estate."

There was a real simple beauty to the stark, antiseptic space. I had been there to see many shows over the years, never failing to be impressed by how utterly barren it all was. Among the few esthetic elements were the ultrawhite walls, a smooth gray floor made of rubberized concrete, and a tall reception desk completely free of objects. Several young women sat behind the desk, allowing the most subtle of smiles as soon as it became clear that I was a guest of David's.

The gallery's current show was a single monumental sculpture by one of his other artists, a huge construction of steel I beams, twisted and rusting. I walked around and gazed up at it while we waited. "It would never fit inside my house," I said, my words echoing around the sky-lit space.

"It costs more than your house," said the dealer.

"How much?"

"I sold it last week to a big Venezuelan bank. It's customary not to divulge the price once the piece has been sold."

"Of course," I said. Then I asked him about Miles's work. "I thought there was a waiting list for a Levy."

"There is. His last show here was oversubscribed; every piece sold before the opening."

"So what are you going to sell this guy today?"

"A piece I sold last year. It was about to go to auction in a distress sale, but I convinced the owner to place it through us instead."

"Why?"

"It's too soon to test the secondary market. I don't like auctions, they're too public. If these guys don't buy it today, then I'll buy it and keep it off the market for at least five years. You have to be careful when you choose to resurface. If people think it looks familiar, you'll get burned."

Just then another assistant entered the gallery carrying a large bag from Dean & DeLuca. He seemed just out of school, but somehow already cynical, disappointed with life. He walked up to the others sitting at the reception desk, looking stone-faced. None of them looked like they wanted to be there, and I figured that this Sunday duty was a rare burden for special occasions like this.

"What took so long?" said one.

"There was an ambulance on Broadway and a big crowd out front," he said.

"What happened?"

"Who knows. Some schmuck must have choked on their focaccia," he said. "So who's got the sun-dried tomatoes and mozzarella?"

As they dealt out the sandwiches and settled the bill I noticed that one of them had ordered only a bran muffin while the rest had baguettes stuffed with various delicacies and beverages that came in small imported bottles. She ate the muffin quickly and then wrapped up her crumbs in a napkin. I supposed then that she was, like most normal young people in New York, on a budget, and that ordering ten-dollar sandwiches every day was not possible on her gallery-assistant salary. But rather than let the others know her situation, rather than not take part in this SoHo ritual of an "ordered in" art-gallery lunch, she simply used the excuse that she wasn't usually hungry at that hour and grinned politely while the others gorged themselves on portobello mushrooms, roasted peppers, and stuffed grape leaves.

The Silicon Valley content provider still hadn't arrived, and Lieberthal quizzed these underpaid art groupies to find out whether they had heard anything. They hadn't. As we were waiting, two men walked into the gallery, one with a small video camera held up to his eye. "Oh no, not these guys," said David. He quickly ran up to them and placed his hand over the lens. "Sorry, but we're closed today. There's no shooting allowed in here."

"We're from 'Art Access,' the public-access cable show; maybe you've heard of us."

"I know who you are, but you can't just barge in here and take pictures without permission."

"Hey, get your hands off me," said the one with the video camera. The dealer began to push them out the door. "What are you trying to hide? Look, man, this is free publicity."

"I don't care. Now get the hell out."

"You're on camera, buddy, and it ain't flattering. This will go out to all of Manhattan."

David locked the door after they left. Then he turned to me. "Maybe I was too hard on them. Shit, now they have me on camera being a real prick."

"Don't worry. How many people will see it?"

"Everyone watches public access. I'm just so anxious about Nickolas. Where the hell is he?" It was the first time I had seen Lieberthal get unsettled. He always seemed such a model of control.

A minute later James Nickolas arrived. Not the pocket-protected hacker I had imagined, he was thinly bearded as if his name were Fabrizio, his hair strangely unnatural, as if chemically relaxed. He wore a dark, double-breasted suit and a dark shirt underneath buttoned to the top, no tie, and a very forward pair of black shoes with buckles that screamed: *I'm not a sissy*. He must have had a strong sense of himself, the kind of guy who had others make his introductions and sign for his bills, I figured. This wasn't what I had expected. Somewhere underneath all that merino wool was a techy, a computer engineer, and I knew this look of his had to be brand-new, bought and paid for with the ones and zeros of code, Fortran, Machine Language. I would have killed just then to have had a copy of his high school yearbook picture. There was only one word for this new look: *revenge*.

He came with four others: an art consultant, the consultant's assistant, an older man—perhaps a financial advisor of some sort—and a girlfriend. His *first* and *only* girlfriend, I thought. A petite young woman with well-tanned, slightly freckled skin, she was heavily laden with shopping bags and seemed, by the grin on her face, to be thrilled with all the new places she was going, all the new people she was meeting. But she stayed close to her beau, almost protective of him. I imagined her as the only one who really knew him as the guy who chewed on pens in the back of class, the only one who could reveal the ugly past. When David offered them something to drink, I saw the one dead giveaway for Nickolas's true style, the one bit of evidence that could never be covered up by his girlfriend's smart taste. He had bandages wrapped tightly around his wrists and hands, and she had to help him open a bottle of mineral water. Carpal tunnel syndrome was a small price to pay for being a pioneer of the information age.

For a few minutes they eagerly thumbed through the Miles Levy press kit, a burgeoning folder of carefully photocopied articles, interviews, and critical essays. As they perused the mass of clippings David did his best to connect with Nickolas. "Nice going on the IPO," he said. "I heard anyone who bought in after the first fifteen minutes of trading was a sucker."

Nickolas looked up from the folder, smiling. "They told

me I'm prohibited from talking about it for sixty days," he said, sounding falsely naive.

"Sure. A man doesn't *have* to talk after he scores like that. The stock was at a hundred dollars faster than you can say *plug and play*." I figured this was David's way of making friends, of making everyone comfortable by referencing the guy's success in such an insiderish way. It seemed he wanted Nickolas to know that he was one of them, that he understood them right from the minute they shook hands. It was a real *people-like-us* kind of moment. The hot initial public offering was the perfect metaphor for the new economy David had described earlier. The only people who could really benefit were the hypersmart, the overachievers, the insiders. IPOs gave everyone else—the suckers—the false hope of opportunity, like the gushing wildcat oil rigs of a century ago. Nobody doubted that Microsoft was now the new Standard Oil, but only a few understood how the real power of a monopoly was derived from the legend of the free market, the *two-dropouts-in-a-garage* myth.

When they all got into a small elevator, crowding next to one another, David looked at me.

"Get in," he said.

"It's too small, maybe I better walk up."

"Come on, Stuart, get in."

"I don't mind walking, really."

"There's plenty of room."

I acquiesced. "I don't like elevators," I said as the door managed to close. We were all pushing up against one another when the art consultant, a middle-aged woman with dark frizzy hair who seemed fidgety and had impatiently pushed the DOOR CLOSE button, turned to David. "We're only here to see the latest work. We're not interested in bottom feeding," she said in an obvious attempt to assert herself, but David was unmoved.

"Of course," he said. "I wouldn't waste your time."

"We just came from Paula Cooper," she explained, as if to make her point clear.

"Oh, yes," said David, "They're showing some hot new discovery over there." I could already sense that the consultant was going to be no match for him.

Just then the elevator door opened to a private viewing space known as the killing room, presumably because that is where the killer deals were made. One of Miles's canvases hung on a wall. Beneath it was a single white bench. This painting was just like all the others I had ever seen, an amalgam of disparate elements painted to appear like a collage, with shadows to suggest that the pieces had been pasted on in relief. Miles had filled it with a lot of women's makeup packaging, little bottles and compacts, powder brushes and lipstick tubes. Behind it all was a female figure rendered in the bland 1950s commercial image of a smiling housewife. She was naked except for her checkered apron and a pair of yellow oven mitts.

Nickolas and his entourage inspected the big canvas, looking at it from afar, close up, from the left, from the right. David let them get comfortable before moving in on them. While they silently observed the painting I noticed how he watched their eyes make contact with one another, their body language and the way they shifted their weight around as they stood. After a while they conferred briefly in hushed tones.

Lieberthal walked up to the painting and stood in front of it. "I'm in love with this one," he said. "I tried to convince Miles to paint more like it, but he refused. This is the last of the series, there won't be any more painted collage fallacies of this type. Miles is afraid of repeating himself." This was a lie—Miles had shown me two brand-new ones sitting in his loft just a few hours before. But they all seemed more interested after hearing this.

"Are you sure?" said one of them.

"It's the culmination of the series; they've all been sold," said the dealer. "But try to forget about that. That's not what's important. Just tell me what you see. I want your gut reactions."

"I like it," said Nickolas, "but I'm not sure it's the best one I've seen."

"Let me ask you something," said David. "What comes to mind when you think of Miles Levy?"

"What comes to mind?"

"Yes. I don't mean the man. I mean the work. Forget about this canvas we're looking at here. Just forget about it, and tell me what you perceive as the hallmarks of his painting."

"Pop references, a lot of pale colors, oddly drawn women, mostly without clothes, bent over, legs spread, that sort of thing." He shrugged. "That's it, really."

"Good," said David. "Now look at this one again, and you'll see why it's one of Miles's best."

"I'm not sure I follow," said the well-groomed hacker.

"Look," said David, "you're probably only going to own two or three Levys in your collection, right?" The art consultant nodded. "So, in that case, they all have to *say* Miles Levy. They have to be real signature pieces. You should be able to take one quick look at it and know why it's typical of him. The ideal is to build a collection where every piece has that quality."

"It's true," said the consultant.

Nickolas looked at her, then turned back toward David. "Right. I only want signature pieces," he concluded.

"Think of all the great collections you're competing with," said David. "If you own one Warhol, it should be a Jackie, a Marilyn, a Mao, a Brillo box. If you own one Jasper Johns, it should be one of his American flags. You follow me? Frank Lloyd Wright built a lot of good houses, but the best ones are in the suburbs of Chicago. Everyone knows that. And everyone will know which of Miles's paintings are the *right* ones to own."

I couldn't believe David was on the level with this. The whole concept of placing value only on the easily recognizable types was so anathema to everything I stood for as a curator, as an art historian. And besides, Wright's best houses were *not* the ones near Chicago. There were some pretty good ones in Pennsylvania, Wisconsin, California. But then I realized that it didn't matter. David's words were tailored to his audience.

He walked back over to the big canvas and looked up at it. "Your collection will be glaringly incomplete without one of Miles's painted collage fallacies. These are his signature pieces. And remember, this is the last of the series. There aren't going to be any more like it."

At that point they might have understood what David was saying, they might have accepted this reasoning, but it wasn't clear yet that they had been infused with the desire to possess this particular painting. By the looks on their faces they didn't seem excited, they weren't exactly desperate for it. The consultant began to ask a barrage of skeptical questions: When, exactly, was it painted? Had it been photographed or written about? Had it appeared on any catalogue covers? Had it been exhibited anywhere notable? Were there any previous states, false starts, or preparatory sketches that could be obtained? It seemed she was just trying to earn her keep, trying to seem necessary, relevant, like a doctor who pokes her head into your hospital room for sixty seconds only to justify her visitation fee.

Then Nickolas said suddenly, almost disappointed, "To be honest, there was one at Christie's a couple of seasons ago with these big red stripes running vertically down the canvas. I wanted something like that. That's really what I had in mind."

After hearing this I figured all was lost, that Nickolas now had no intention of buying this one, and that he was looking for a polite way to say good-bye. He even glanced at his watch.

Lieberthal must have sensed as much. He tried telling them how important this painting was in an effort to keep them from walking off his used-car lot. "This is an example of what the critic Henry Geldzahler called *making it new*," he said. Of course that was Geldzahler quoting Ezra Pound, but I wasn't about to interrupt, I only wanted to be invisible. David brought a book of Miles's work from another room. "I wish there was some way you could let me know what you want out of the painting, what you expect from it," he said. "Maybe this will help." The dealer put his foot up on the bench and rested the book, a Griffin Gallery–produced catalogue, on his knee. He flipped the pages of color plates until Nickolas told him to stop.

"Tell me about this one," he said.

"Nice. One of my favorites. It's in Japan." David turned the page.

"What about this one?"

"Yes. What about it?"

"Who owns it?"

"I believe it's in a private collection in Greenwich."

"Who?" said Nickolas.

"This guy, he develops planned communities." David turned more pages, and Nickolas kept asking him not about the works but about the owners. One was in the MoMA collection, one was in the Saatchi collection, one was at the Dia Center.

He didn't care about the museums; he wasn't responding to them the same way he was to the private owners. Then I realized David knew exactly where this was going when he opened to two of Miles's canvases on facing pages. "This one is the Steve Martin," he said. "That one on the right is the Dennis Hopper."

Nickolas froze, looking intently at the pages, then turned to look at the canvas hanging in the room, realizing, as everyone else now did, that they were almost the same. "That's funny," he said. "They're pretty similar. I mean, all the colors, the imagery. They must be from the same series."

David nodded. "The L.A. collectors are on the cutting edge right now. They're buying up all the best stuff. I just got a call from someone out there looking for any more of these. Word of mouth is really driving this business right now."

"Who called you?"

"I'm not free to say. When you can tell me about all that stock, I'll tell you the name." Nickolas smiled. "Put it this way," said David, "when they come out with those power lists, he's always near the top." It proved enough to turn the tide. Nickolas was now much more interested, and although there were still details to be worked out, the fact that he was ultimately going to walk out of David's gallery owning this painting had been decided, whether he knew it or not, at that moment. This was what it had come down to: who else owned Miles's stuff. At first I was surprised that there hadn't been any of the mind-numbing language I had come to expect in connection with so much contemporary art, the hip references and impenetrable talk of meaning and signs, of appropriated corporeal representations, of recontextualized myth and metaphor. But then it made sense. David hadn't used any artspeak because these weren't intellectuals, these weren't a bunch of critics from *Artforum*. David knew he could skip the theory—the nice five-dollar words—and still get them to *believe*.

And so here we were, the legendary dealer and myself standing in the middle of the killing room, alone, and his remark to me about the bodies was lingering like secondhand smoke. Nickolas and his group had left after a session of deal making that could only be described as protracted. I could tell David was waiting for my reaction, and I didn't want to seem too impressed. I looked at him. "What do you mean?" I asked.

"This one came out of an obscure collection. I know all the collections, where to find the pieces, where to find work that will sell. But now it's all about star value. Everyone secretly wants to be a movie star. You saw it. His eyes lit up at the mention of Hollywood. Silicon Valley is in love with Hollywood. Hollywood is in love with Silicon Valley."

"Great. I'm ready for my close-up," I said.

"Look, I know you think it's obscene what goes on up here, peddling the bodies and everything."

"I believe anything is worth what someone will pay for it."

"A sucker born every minute, right? Or maybe it's just a case of the emperor's clothes?"

"No. You would like me to say that, wouldn't you? You need me to say it's a case of the emperor's clothes because you sort of define yourself in opposition to those who would say that."

"What do you mean?"

"You expect me to play my role, to play the philistine, the conservative critic, the shocked viewer. You brought me here expecting to get some abhorrent reaction. Or maybe it was just straight praise. I don't know," I told him, shaking my head.

"You really believe that?"

"You must think I'm one of those tweedy overeducated curators who fell romantic for the Old Masters while he was on his Grand Tour."

"That's bullshit. I've got real respect for you."

"In a strange way you kind of need me."

He shrugged. "Hey, I was just asking to see if you had a

good time observing it all. I brought you here because I thought you might get a kick out of it, that's all."

I found his tone so disarming, as if he had told me to take it easy, that it was no big deal, and I immediately felt badly for having spoken my mind. Even then I wasn't sure what had caused my outburst. Selling was sport to him, and all he had wanted, apparently, was someone to savor the moment with.

ten

THERE WAS a good Greek coffee shop up on Madison Avenue where I met Claire before work one morning. I knew it well, having stopped there most days on my way to school until the seventh or eighth grade. I loved its absurdly large menu and the heavy coffee cups with worn, chalky edges. I would always order a piece of marble cake, and I remember how they kept each slice wrapped in plastic, imparting a not unsubtle aroma of Saran Wrap to the entire experience.

"I'd really like a piece of that marble cake," I told the waiter. Claire gave me a funny look. "On second thought, just a toasted bagel."

She smiled. "Get whatever you want."

"No, you were clearly passing judgment there."

"Sorry. It just seems a bit heavy for this hour."

I thought about it. "You're right," I said. "All those years I never realized what an awful breakfast that made."

"What?"

"See those kids at the counter?" I said.

She nodded.

"I used to stop here before school," I told her. There was

a group of kids of various ages near the front of the place buying muffins and making change for the crowded bus that would take them straining up the avenue's slight hill. A few of them had on junior varsity jackets with the names of their schools written along the back: Browning, Spence, Dalton.

"Did you have one of those jackets?" she asked.

"I was never into that whole physical-exertion thing. While all my friends were on the soccer team, I was busy taking pictures for the yearbook."

"Any regrets?"

I shook my head. "Who wants to run up and down the Great Lawn kicking up dust? It was in bad taste, a bunch of prep-school kids using homeless encampments as goalposts. Besides, someone had to get those live action shots. It's just too bad I was such an incompetent photographer—nothing came out, they were all blurry. I had to make excuses about how my pictures were 'artistic,' since the school had spent so much money to have all that film developed."

"Tell me about an old girlfriend," she said, smiling.

"Kathy Cushman. Tenth grade, we got high at some scholarship fund-raiser. I think it was at the James Burden mansion up on Ninety-first. Smoked a joint and got laid in the butler's pantry."

"Nice," said Claire. "So where's Kathy Cushman these days?"

"Last I heard she was a buyer for Bergdorf's. I guess at some point she acquired taste."

Claire placed her hand on mine. "Maybe she's always had good taste." She seemed so excited and happy just then, full of energy. All morning she never stopped staring at me, smiling at me, touching me. She said she wanted to stay over that night, and the next night, and the night after that. "And what are you doing this weekend?" she asked, and I had to laugh.

"What's with you?"

"Is he addicted?"

"I'm not sure. He stops for long periods just to kind of est himself. But he also drinks a lot, so you can never be ure when he's on it, or what he's been mixing. He doesn't ven know what he's doing. It makes him kind of hostile, npredictable."

"So you have a problem with *the way* he does his drugs."

"I don't care what he does. Sometimes he can be brilliant, ther times he's a fool. If I can go on living my life and only ave to deal with him when he's brilliant, then that's okay."

"Does he charge you much rent?"

"It's a token. He refuses to take more. Look, the place is aid for, it's not like he's got cash-flow problems."

"Even so, why would he do you the favor? He just likes aving you around?"

"Who knows. I'm not going to start asking questions."

"You're right," I said. "Why fuck with it? It's one hell of setup." I decided to stop questioning it. I didn't want to sk scaring her off by seeming like I couldn't deal with the tuation.

She had to run to work then, and she made me promise call her there. "Make a reservation somewhere," she said, aching into her bag for a tip as we got up to leave.

"Where?"

"I don't care where," she said, and we kissed.

ovanni Battista Tiepolo. Italian, Venetian, 1696–1770. When u visit the Metropolitan Museum of Art, walking in through e main entrance, then cutting across the Great Hall and mbing the monumental stairs that lead to the rooms of iropean paintings, you are greeted at the top of those steps a gigantic Tiepolo known as *The Triumph of Marius,* a ntastical scene of the Roman general riding home after vic- ry and being cheered on by a bunch of strange characters

"Nothing," she said. "Just be available."

"I'm right here."

"I know."

I reached over to fix an out-of-place strand o
hair. "Is the loft not a pleasant place for some
could tell she didn't want to talk about Miles, b
so curious about their arrangement.

"Did I tell you that Todd offered me heroin
over there on Sunday?"

"I wonder what took him so long." She t
Todd had Miles using the stuff now. His drug
the fashion perfectly, she said. "There's somethi
way he uses the stuff that's so him, so Miles Le

"What do you mean?"

"He's late to them. He started using cok
eighties. But when it fell out of fashion he was re
since he had become hooked. So he started s
cigarettes, which was a little more discreet,
respectable, except the cigarettes stink from
chemicals used to refine the stuff. It's like the s
ing plastic. You can pick it out at bars. But no
come back in a big way, and so of course Miles
on. It's really Todd's drug, though."

"What does Todd do, anyway?"

"He keeps himself busy. Basically he makes
get paid and the dry cleaning gets picked up.
for Miles, gets him his fix. But it's so typical that
shoot his heroin. He inhales it."

"That's common," I said.

"I know, but with Miles it's like he'd *nev*
know what I mean? He'd never put a needle
wouldn't touch the stuff if he had to. He ref
hands dirty. He's very bourgeois about it. E
sanitized."

1 2 1

poking their heads into the frame of the tall painting from all directions. From there you can turn around to admire the view under the limestone arch back down the stairs and across the Great Hall. It is a trick of all those correctly proportioned classical details that you're surprised not to feel fatigued after climbing those steps. They appear much more imposing than they really are.

After seeing Claire that morning I took this exact path to work. I never liked to use the employee side entrance or even take shortcuts. The hall of Tiepolos seemed the best way to reintroduce myself to work every morning. I glanced at the oversized painting, which was really a panel taken from a wall recess in a Venetian *salone*, and then, since there was still time, made my almost ritualistic stop at the Rembrandt self-portrait several rooms away. The Tiepolo is huge in scale, the Rembrandt much smaller and more intimate. You could be close friends with both, but you wouldn't think of inviting them to the same dinner party.

Before going into Kohlman's office to get the various notes and articles he had asked for, I stopped at my desk to try to solve a puzzle. I had been passed a rare French Renaissance drawing, a red chalk study of a partially draped kneeling woman done in a kind of mannerist, exaggerated style. The drawing was a recent donation, and certain details of its provenance were missing from the record. While several of us worked as a team to fill in these pieces, my specialty was the Baroque—the seventeenth century in Europe—and so it was left to someone else with a better background in the French Renaissance to find the specific project this sketch might have been made for. I was asked, instead, to identify a small marking in the lower right corner left by some unknown previous owner. The tiny marking could have almost been mistaken for a blemish, a small stain, or the brownish spots that develop on aging paper. At one time it was customary for collectors to put their initials or some personal symbol on works on paper, like writing your name and the date in elegant script on the frontispiece of every book in your library. Later the practice was frowned upon, and now it is unheard-of. But these almost insensitive stains of vanity provide useful information when reconstructing the life of a given work.

Under magnification the marking looked like a palm tree in an oval, but such a symbol was not in any of the reference books we used to identify these things. No one in the department had ever seen it before, not even Kohlman. My best guess was that it must have been some colonial type, some merchant who had made his fortune in the tropics. The week before, I had drawn a half-competent sketch of the symbol and faxed it, along with a polite letter, to a specialist at the Courtauld Institute in London who I thought might help us out, even though I would have liked to discover it on my own somehow. So much of our work involved simply studying closely the drawings in silence, learning the peculiarities of an artist's hand, understanding the choices artists made and why they made them. I wanted to get to a point where I could recognize the tiniest stroke, the faintest line, and say, with some confidence, whose work it was. Even though this day's specific task was less about art than detective work, I sensed Kohlman's absence. He would have discussed the marking with me, he would have debated the merits of my guess, challenged what we thought we saw. Only a few people could convey that kind of passion and devotion, making you feel they would be there doing the work whether they were getting paid or not. Instead of dreading work, I thrived on it, and I realized then how much Kohlman was responsible for that. I wanted to get over to his apartment and see how he looked, I wanted to make sure he would be coming back soon.

Just as I was giving up on this one, the reply came through. I turned off the magnifying lamp and then heard the fax machine heating up. The specialist I had contacted knew the marking, and it turned out I had guessed correctly. It was used by some eighteenth-century collector who had imported sugar from Haiti. The papers relating to his collection were in the Louvre, according to the brief note, and I would now have to contact Paris to have them loaned to us.

These tasks were typical, almost mundane, but I wouldn't have given them up for anything at that point. The idea was to keep breaking new ground, to add, even in small ways, to the general understanding of the art. These were the little pleasures of the job, and they were what we used to measure our success in a place where not everything was for sale, a place where art and commerce didn't need to be constantly reconciled.

But then maybe I was wrong about this place, maybe there were more subtle pressures of commerce that I needed to own up to. When I locked the door to Kohlman's office I was stopped by a guy who worked in the museum's office of publications. Chester, famous for his carefully parted straight hair, pressed khakis, and Knickerbocker-like nasal honk. I switched an armful of Kohlman's papers to my left side so I could shake his hand. We chatted politely about nothing, and then he lowered his voice. "Your request on the Raphael book for next spring was accepted, but they're cutting the number of plates. And the Italians are just too expensive. This printer in the Philippines came in with a lower bid." He was talking about a catalogue that would accompany a major exhibition of Raphael drawings scheduled for the following year.

"We always print in Italy," I said. "They do the best work."

"Sorry. The feeling is, people won't care. I mean, it's not exactly Monet's water lilies," he smirked.

Preppy jerk, I thought. The goddamned Impressionists, that's all anybody wanted now, that's all the big crowds would show up for. Every gift-shop card and poster had to be a pleasing summery scene that only made me want to throw up.

"You're right, Chester, they're definitely *not* Monet's water lilies."

When I arrived at Kohlman's apartment house on East 71st Street by about midday, the doorman called up to announce me. But the respected and aging art expert declined to have me up and instead came down to take a walk in the park with me. "They told me I'm supposed to stay in bed, but I need fresh air," he said when he got down. I was relieved to see him in good spirits, breaking the rules and cursing his doctors. I thought he would look pale, but he had good color and even had a little white handkerchief peering out of a breast pocket. Those little details were his joy. He left the papers I had brought from his office with the doorman and led me across the avenue into Central Park. He had lived in that building almost as long as I had been alive, and I was sure that whatever he had paid for the apartment wouldn't even get you a midsize luxury car now. Even so, he did well for himself, penning a standard college art-history textbook in the early sixties that was still widely used. It had been revised over the years and reprinted so many times that its royalties must have easily covered his expenses.

"Have you been seeing this woman long?" he asked me. We were circling the boat pond, which had been drained for the winter, and I was telling him about Claire.

"No, not at all. She thinks Miles Levy will sink her career or something. She's afraid to antagonize him. I don't know if she'll take the risk of getting closed out of his world."

"Don't worry about it."

"Why?"

"See her without him knowing. After a while she'll know if it's worth it."

"She lives in his loft. It's huge, two whole floors. I was there over the weekend, and Miles showed me some of his work."

"All that tiresome political art," he said. "They're preaching to the converted. The impact of subtlety has been lost on these people."

"I was at Griffin too, a guest of David Lieberthal. I was even inside the killing room."

He stopped walking to look at me, his thick mustache almost completely white. "Miles Levy, the Griffin Gallery," he said. "None of this seems like you at all."

I just shrugged. "By the way," I said, "Chester from publications told me to cut the number of plates in the Raphael book. And they won't use your Italian printer."

"I'm not surprised," he said.

We sat on a bench in the sun, and he told me how he used to reject early proofs of book photos if they weren't close enough to the original works, how he used to demand thick paper and special binding methods. "But I'm too old to fight those battles anymore," he said. I asked him about his days as a young man when he first came to the United States, something he rarely discussed. He told me how lucky he was to find a teaching position at the New School right after the war. "There were many of us refugee scholars looking for work at that time," he said. I imagined that he had left behind memories, family and friends, and I wanted to ask him about them, but he looked uncomfortable trying to remember it all.

I shouldn't have been surprised to see a tall truck parked outside my building with the name Moishe's Moving and

Storage painted on its side. That afternoon several of the strong-looking Israeli Army reservists were busy hauling furniture and boxes from inside the old brownstone and rushing to beat the departing sunlight. I recognized some of the furniture as Mrs. Kaplan's old colonial revival pieces. Amy Kidd was moving out the next day, and most of the others would soon follow. I didn't want to think about the building being empty, about Vogel's inadequate offer and his vile plans. I didn't want to know about his development schemes and his tax abatements, about his zoning variances and his co-op conversions. All I wanted was that little apartment, where Claire and I would spend each night of the rest of that week, in bed. She told me that being able to look up at the intricate crown moldings during sex heightened her pleasure. For this one reason alone those original hand-carved details had to be worth at least seventy-five grand. I kept ignoring calls from Vogel's people, kept hanging up on them or insisting they had the wrong number. No, I was doing just fine where I was, thank you.

eleven

I RAN INTO Todd Bryce at my sister's office. I had gone there to pay her a long-promised visit, and by chance he showed up to run some errand for Miles. When Claire had told me that all Todd did was pick up dry cleaning and open mail, I never thought to question her. Perhaps it was because I had assumed right from the beginning that he was just a fixture, just another vacant-faced hanger-on. I remember first meeting him at Pied Noir and being mindful only of the potential competition. What I had missed that night were certain clues, one of them his age. He was the only one my age besides Claire. David was in his early fifties. Both Miles and Susan were forty-something, but Todd was my peer. And so even though our paths couldn't have been more different, in some strange way we had both found ourselves at the same place with the same people at the same point in our lives. I wanted to like Todd, I wanted to be able to get along with him because we seemed such opposites, and life sometimes feels like it's just one long struggle to become well-rounded. But I had turned down his early overture, and now I wasn't sure I was going to get a second chance.

Susan's boutique firm was in a building on lower Fifth Avenue in the Flatiron district, an area home to a lot of creative industries and served by minimalist coffee bars and halogen-lit stores filled with cool, unsensible shoes. I got into an elevator with several people, each one dressed with flair and carrying black portfolios of varying sizes. Christina had once remarked that all you ran into in the neighborhood were creative directors, stylists, and graphic designers. "Makes it hard to meet straight men," she complained.

She showed me into an open space filled with six or seven desks. "This is like our war room," she said. Along one wall was Susan's large glassed-in office. The publicist was pacing back and forth on the phone, nervously twirling its long cord and looking out at her troops.

The Susan Edelman Agency was just that: Susan and her dozen or so assistants. Respected by those who required her services and dreaded by those who needed access to her clients, she was an immensely successful woman. I remember how Christina had dug up every article ever written about her before she interviewed to get the job. Nothing in all that absurd research proved so revealing as this one fact: She had never married. Even past the age of forty she was known to show up at big parties without a date so she could be free to *work the room*.

"So what exactly goes on here?" I asked my sister. She wore her neat brown hair short, the ends coming down to rest near the sides of her adorable, softly featured face.

"This is a factory of carefully controlled information. Sometimes the client wants coverage. Sometimes they don't. It all depends." She leaned her chair forward a bit and lowered her voice. "With Susan, every journalist is assumed to be an adversary, so she negotiates the tone and terms of all coverage."

"The terms?"

130

"Every detail is argued over," she said. There were strict rules for hotel-room junket interviews and endless haggling with late-night talk-show producers. "Susan demands the first guest spot, and she loathes Friday-night bookings because no one's home to watch."

"Millions are still watching."

"Sure, but it's a much less desirable group." Print was another story entirely, she said, since there's so much more to negotiate, to argue over. "And I don't mean just checking a reporter's quotes."

She explained the various degrees of coverage. A few clients were big enough for a magazine cover, while most could get just a feature with no cover. Still others might have to settle for a little front-of-the-book piece. And who's the writer? Could they agree on the photographer? They also might try to place a gossip item. But where to place it? In one of the daily papers or a weekly? And which columnist was in favor that week, which one did they need to reward, which one did they need to punish? Did they want to use names, or were they engineering a *blind item*? "This is all fairly standard stuff," she said.

"Let's say you want to start a rumor," I said, "but you can't have your fingerprints all over it. How do you do it?"

"That's a whole different level." She explained the existence of a bicoastal network of people through which a chain of buzz could be started by placing just a few well-chosen phone calls. They had to be careful with this method, though, because they could lose control over the chain, and the rate at which it expands could sometimes reach the speed of a Malibu brushfire. It worked by reaching a few key people they called *feeders*—an editor, a studio executive, a restauranteur—and Susan could be sure that each would begin working the item through his or her circle at once. "When it works well it's like ballet, it's beautiful to watch," she said.

Like all the other assistants, Christina had to answer the

phones, handling them with real dexterity. It was like watching her put out fires. At one point she had six different lines on hold and she checked several clipboards that held lists of names as the phone's lighted buttons blinked away. Sometimes she would look at a board where perhaps two dozen magazine mastheads had been tacked up for quick reference. I wondered if the people at the other ends of those lines knew they were being subjected to this little test. They must have suspected something, since a check of the hierarchy was now such standard treatment.

As Christina dealt with that hyperactive phone I looked at a memo from Susan on her desk titled PROHIBITED ANGLES. It was a list of points, the first reading: *"No process-revealing articles! No fly-on-the-wall pieces!"* Then I looked more closely at two of the clipboards. One was a list of names at the top of which the words PUFF GUYS were written in black marker; the other list was headed TOUGH GUYS. She told me that the *puff guys* were *approved* magazine journalists— writers who could be counted on to portray the client in glowing terms, since most of them had become style and entertainment journalists simply to get on comp lists. "They may not make much money, but they lead enviable lives," she said. Staying in favor was more important to them than getting a good story, and they tended to pitch articles about their friends or, more likely, people they *hoped* to become friendly *with*. "It's not about how many Pulitzers you have, it's about how often you get comped." The *tough guys* were prohibited writers known to be uncooperative. It was filled with the names of anyone who had either criticized, satirized, or been generally negative toward any of their clients. "Basically anyone who wrote for the old *Spy*," said Christina.

"What are you working on now?" I asked.

"I'm trying to get this woman Juliet Wilcox into that new magazine *Traffic*." She showed me a few photos of the attractive young woman. "She'd be great for their 'Breaking Out' section."

"What's that, a feature on acne?"

"No. It's like their up-and-comers."

"Is she an actress or a model?"

"It's hard to say exactly. She's just *known*."

"But what's she known for?"

"Stuart, you have to learn not to think of people's careers in such conventional terms—like *what they do*."

I smiled. "You're right. How unreasonable of me."

"Forget it," she said, putting the photos away. "You don't have the sensibility for this stuff. You can't be skeptical in this place. There's no room for that. Cynics, yes. Skeptics, no."

"Which one are you?"

"I don't know. Last night I had door duty at this premiere party Susan threw. You should've seen me, I had on a headset and was checking names off a list." She looked at me. "There's no turning back now."

Just then Todd walked into the office and went straight in to see Susan. Closing the door, he recognizing me through the glass and waved a quick hello.

"Todd Bryce," said my sister as if announcing a dinner guest. "Velvet boy-toy."

"Velvet what?"

"He's been linked with people."

"*Linked* with people?" I shook my head. "You should really hear yourself talk. You speak a whole different language now."

She shrugged. "You've met Todd."

"Yeah, so?"

"Don't you find him a little too good-looking, a little too glamorous? He works out at my gym. I've watched him spend ten minutes in front of the mirror just looking over his own body."

"It must have pained you to watch," I said.

"When you're on the StairMaster you've got to look at *something*."

I could see Todd and Susan through the glass. He pulled an envelope containing photos out of his bag, and Susan went through them quickly. They were all of Miles. She discarded some and held up others as he nodded or shook his head. They seemed to have settled on one of them when he placed a call from her phone, putting it on speaker so she could talk. It must have been David or Miles at the other end, I thought. Todd got up to leave a bit later, swinging his bag over his shoulder, and walked over to say hello to us. I was sure he didn't care to admit that Miles was now Susan's client, but the careful secret seemed so obvious to me that I had to play with it.

"What brings you here?" I asked, all bright-eyed.

"Just doing a favor," he said quickly.

"What's Miles working on these days?" I was trying to stay on-topic.

Todd hesitated. "He's doing a new series of paintings based on bureaucracy. You know, red tape. The absurdity of government."

"Yes, I saw one of the canvases at the loft."

"We're also doing a poster for PETA."

"That's People for the Ethical Treatment of Animals," said Christina.

I turned to her. "I know what it is."

"Sorry. You looked a little nonplussed," she said.

Todd told me the inspiration for the poster was a famous painting by Goya. He gave me his ideas about it, showing a real understanding of the great Spanish realist's work, and I thought my sister must have been wrong about him. If he did spend ten minutes looking at himself in the mirror at the gym, then he must have also spent a good deal of time reading and developing his ideas. He was a much more eloquent defender of Miles's work than the artist himself. His point of view was at least interesting, while Miles didn't even have one, as far as I could tell.

I asked where he had gone to school, and he said he was largely self-educated. He had grown up near Pensacola, Florida, and left at eighteen to become a model in New York. Instead, he found himself working at some hip hotel on West 44th where his job interview was like a casting call, and it was there that he met people in art and media. He started to paint and show his slides around endlessly before landing his job with Miles, stretching canvases for the artist and picking up the loft's weekly supply of mineral water. "I never planned to do what I'm doing now," he said, "but I couldn't be happier. Miles has been very generous. We're like partners."

Todd Bryce might have been admirably self-made, well read, and full of interesting ideas, but there was still something shallow about him. He was too eager, too starstruck by the fortunate string of events in his life, and I figured that somewhere along the way he must have lost his perspective, lost his reference point back to reality. Just as my sister had said, it wasn't how good you were that mattered, it was how often you got comped, how many words, how many party shots, how many quotes. It must have been hard not to start believing that these were the only ways in which to determine whether a particular life was a success or a failure.

I remember what a fast talker Susan was. She left the security of her glass-enclosed warren and came over to greet us. "Can't talk," she said. "I'm on my way to lunch. I just got Juliet Wilcox into the February *Traffic*. Seven hundred fifty words and a head shot."

"What did it take?" asked Christina.

"A little trade," she said, walking to the door. "I gave the editor my table at Pied Noir for tomorrow night, which is okay, since I won't be using it. I'm so late. If Zach Phillips calls, tell him not to run his piece until March. And tell that *E.T.* producer he can have fifteen minutes with Eileen at her hotel. Fifteen and *that's it!*"

"Where's Eileen staying?"

Susan had to answer from down the hall. "The Chateau Marmont."

I decided then that I was no longer having fun. I had to go back to the museum and get some real work done.

"Leaving?" asked Christina.

"Yes, before this healthy skepticism of mine turns into a dark nihilism."

"Better hurry."

I was at home with Claire that night, the two of us lying on top of my still-made bed and deciding whether or not to have a late drink somewhere when, almost out of nowhere, she told me that she was, sexually speaking, a submissive. Taking in this information, I realized that I always had a way of gaining people's trust after knowing them for short periods of time. I remained puzzled as to why people I sat next to on airplanes were telling me about their analyst before we would even reach cruising altitude. I don't believe they are all so vulnerably open. Instead, I've come to think that it's something about me, maybe the way I listen, or perhaps something I'm not even aware of.

"I think I've seen enough of you now to trust you," she said. Her desire to be dominated was more along the lines of nuance, she told me. She wasn't into the gimmicks, the gear, or the heavy role playing, all that Lower East Side kind of stuff. Instead it was a much more subtle way she hoped I might be with her.

She sat up, which I took as an indication that she was

serious. "I like to feel a little helpless. I need to be, like, over-come." She must have sensed the need to elaborate, since I said nothing. "It would be kind of cool," she said, "if you could lose some of that sensitivity. What I mean is, you don't need to be so light to the touch, so to speak."

"How do you mean?"

"Pick me up, throw me around, pull my hair," she said. "I want to feel *pinned.* I like to feel a little trapped some-times. I need to be *handled.* Don't worry, just put me the way you want. You know, flip a leg back if you need to."

The first time we made love I could have been forgiven for thinking everything had gone well, but she said that in the back of her mind was a little bit of worry.

"Worry about what?" I asked.

"I wasn't sure you had it in you, you know, to mistreat me. I don't think you have one ounce of jerk in you."

"I never perceived it as a shortcoming."

She smiled. "Stuart, you look so puzzled right now. I wish I could take a picture."

"You seemed happy being in charge before."

"I was. But that's not my ideal. That's not the way I want it anymore. Maybe there's a domineering inconsiderate creep buried deep inside you that's just waiting to come out and do stuff to me."

"I'm not against giving anything a good try," I told her. "But you don't think I can. You're betting against me, aren't you?"

"Surprise me. I want you to keep surprising me."

She got up to take a shower, picking a few of her clothes up off the floor on her way. When I heard the water running I called Christina and asked her to suggest someplace to take Claire for that late drink.

"Try that place all the way west on Eleventh Street," she said.

"Oh yeah. I haven't been there yet." I wanted to tell Christina about Claire's little innocent bedtime request, I wanted to run this new angle by her, but I didn't. Instead she had some news of her own.

"I couldn't go into it while you were at the office," she said, "but I'm leaving for Europe with Susan the day after tomorrow."

"That's great. What for?"

"She and David are taking Miles on a tour. Cologne, Paris, Milan, and some stops in between. We're positioning him for *Documenta* and the Venice Biennale."

"Positioning?"

"Yes, I mean quietly promoting him for the European market. I've set up interviews, and we'll be having dinner with the important curators. It's all so last-minute, I didn't even know I was going until this morning."

"How long will you be gone?"

"Four days."

"Anyone else going?"

"Todd's going too."

"It's pretty shameless. I mean all this effort at celebrity making. Miles Levy is quickly becoming someone else's creation."

"Thanks for your enthusiasm. I'm getting a huge opportunity, and all I get is your usual bullshit. Can't you just be happy and spare me the decline-of-Western-art speech?"

"I'm sorry. I am happy for you. It's just that I recoil whenever I get exposed to the mechanics of this stuff."

"You know how things work just as well as anyone. You're right, Miles is becoming the creation of the agency, but at least there's pride of authorship. This is just the latest kind of performance art."

"P.R. as performance art? Maybe you're right. The process is what gets celebrated, the process is what's admired now. What happened? Before you had nothing but bad things to say about Susan. Now you're in love with her."

"She's still no saint, but I'm getting real breaks, opportunities to go places and do things."

"What are you going to do over there anyway, carry her luggage? Help unpack her Chanel?"

"Go to hell. I don't do that stuff anymore."

I lowered my voice. "When I was with Kohlman the other day we were talking about Miles and everything else. He thinks all these people are full of shit, all style, no substance. He's right. Maybe you and I are getting sucked in."

"Oh, *please*."

"He thinks I should write about Miles, one of those process-revealing, fly-on-the-wall articles that Susan hates. I'd have to do it under false pretenses. Then she'd put me on her blacklist."

"Kohlman treats you like you're some precious genius, and you're starting to believe it. I'm sorry we can't all be as pure and principled as you two."

"That's such an undergraduate observation."

"Undergraduate?" she said, raising her voice. "Is that supposed to be insulting? Stuart, you're the biggest fucking snob I know. All you can do is criticize. You put down Miles even before you met him."

"I'm smart enough to know when I'm being fooled, and you should be too." Here it comes, I thought.

"It must be such a burden being so smart, always knowing when you're being fooled, always the most honest and perceptive person in the room," she said right on cue. "You're always so sure of yourself. Where do you get this confidence of judgment? Oh, make way, here comes the specialist with his opinion. Well, life isn't just some Old Master drawing to be attributed and categorized and appraised. Quit appraising everything. There's a whole world out there beyond your museum and Kohlman; it's filled with well-intentioned people trying to make something new, trying to do more than just reference the past. Don't resent them for trying."

She stopped finally, and I said nothing. She must have had a strong sense of my silence because she tried to backpedal, sounding regretful and apologetic for having come down on me all of a sudden, and I wanted to tell her that she needn't be.

twelve

I TOOK CLAIRE to the movies on the night Miles Levy and company left for Frankfurt or Cologne or wherever it was they were off to. It was one of those films filled with well-trained English actors and tasteful countryside locations. They should have stopped making these things as soon as they ran out of E. M. Forster novels. Claire kept taking hold of my wrist to look at the time elapsed on my watch, and the minute the credits began to roll she nudged me up to leave.

"It's a myth," she said in front of the theater.

"What is?"

"British charm. Americans think it lends a bit of class and intelligence to everything, so they're always hiring Brits to run things."

"Only Jews of great wealth do that. Makes them more secure. Something about needing the approval of the old nobility."

"It's so misguided," she said. "My boss at the auction house is a perfect example. You have to keep in mind there are more soccer hooligans than butlers over there."

"You don't get along with your boss?"

"Who, the Ice Queen? No, she's *lovely*," said Claire, then she hailed a taxi without even telling me where we were off to.

After enduring a harrowing ride we arrived at a small narrow bar on an impossibly hidden West Village street. It was dimly lit and crowded, with little round marble-topped tables and cast iron chairs. Somehow she was able to secure seating for us, and I remember wedging a couple of matchbooks underneath one leg of our wobbly table to stabilize it. She looked at me after I did this, grinning.

"What?"

"You're just funny," she said, leaning in to kiss me. We sat close, almost adjacent, and I was surprised how comfortable I felt being in the middle of this clamor, a thick swirl of nicotine, alcohol, and voguish conversation.

"I'll bet I'm the only guy you've ever slept with who's had work published in an academic journal," I said.

She took a long moment to think about it before answering and then shook her head. "No, I'm afraid not."

"So you seduced some poor professor along the way, some Clair Quilty figure?"

"I would venture at least one," she said. "I'm always with older men. I haven't been with anyone my age since I was eighteen."

"Makes this seem more of a challenge. Miles looks like he's got fifteen years on you."

She said nothing and inspected one of the stylish little matchbooks left on our table, then looked at me. "Stay at the loft with me."

"The loft? But we've got my place. There's nothing wrong with my apartment, is there?"

"No, I just think it would be a thrill. The whole place is empty now."

I thought about it. "We can use all his cool stuff. We'll

142

raid that big freezer and fire up the Viking range," I said. "Maybe we'll take that old Triumph out for a spin. What else? Am I forgetting anything?"

"Stop. So he has a few toys. Big deal."

"Tell me how you got involved with Miles and David and all of them?"

She shifted in her chair and thought about it, tossing her hair about. "I was doing odd jobs for a photographer, and one day there was this shoot for a *Vogue* article about some hot new artist, and I didn't think much of it. Of course it was Miles. At that time I had no idea who he was, but when he came in with his friends, I thought they were the coolest, hippest thing." She shook her head. "You have to remember I was just sweeping the floors and shucking film when Miles made this huge impression on me. Before I knew it we were going out three days later. I don't really remember a lot of it, since it was just a whirlwind of people and restaurants and clubs and everything. You can imagine what it was like." I nodded. "He was well funded, let's put it that way. That was just when everybody was starting to write about him.

"So one night at the Odeon," she continued, "after one of his big gallery openings, he introduced me to David. A few months later David said he needed someone at the gallery. I quickly worked my way up from sandwich getter to archivist. That's the thing about David—he saw that I was more than just one of Miles's girls."

"What do you mean?"

"He gave me a shot to do interesting work. I turned those breaks into so much more than they seemed at first. Others my age with the same opportunities couldn't make it past sandwich getter. I used the gallery's resources to educate myself on contemporary art to the point where people in the field respected me. I spent hours every day in David's library, hours with him learning the market. When the auction house offered me this position, I took it. It felt good, you know, to get something like that on my own. Look, I know I did it myself. But I worry that everyone thinks it's all built on a precarious system of lucky breaks and people who know other people."

"Who cares? What's important is that you know how it happened," I said.

"I know what you're thinking. You're thinking none of the other sandwich getters at David's gallery were sleeping with the star artist, so of course they didn't make it any further."

"That's not what I'm thinking. Not at all, trust me."

"You don't know how much I hate that, how much I resent it," she said.

"I promise I never thought that." I got close and looked at her. "You believe me?"

She nodded and I kissed her. "I never know what people think," she said.

"Forget what people think."

"It's more than that. It's Miles saying I owe him big, it's him hinting that I'll have regrets."

"He says that? He says you owe him?"

She shook her head. "Every time I move an inch away from him, he lays it on me. You've got him all crazy, he doesn't know what the fuck to do about you because you're not what he's used to."

"What's he used to?"

"He's used to, well, like these—"

"What? Like a faster crowd?"

"What I mean is, he has trouble dealing with you, you intimidate him a bit."

"I don't follow."

"Look, he knows you're smart, and he's afraid he doesn't have all your references, he's afraid you'll make him look bad. Other guys he's seen me with were never like you. He could always come across as the big shot, the star. But you make him insecure because he knows you don't operate on that level, he knows you don't give a shit about that stuff. To him, you're the goddamn academy." She took a sip from her glass. "So now he's full of these veiled, childish threats."

"And that's why you're afraid to leave him?"

She looked down at her glass. "Sort of. It's complicated, Stuart. It's terribly, hopelessly complicated."

"Tell me," I said.

She said nothing.

"You can tell me, you know. I just want to do what I can to help."

She smiled the smile of someone who knows more than you, of someone who had long ago lost her optimism. "That's sweet," she said, "but I don't want to think about it anymore. Can't we be together for five minutes without Miles's name coming up?"

Claire had several friends in the room that night, and I remember one in particular. Her first name was Diana, but I never got the last one. She came to our table and sat next to me, placing her hand on my leg. She had dark frizzy hair and wore a delicate rayon jacket buttoned at the bottom, with nothing underneath but a black bra, a bit of which was visible between the jacket's graceful lapels. Claire knew Diana from school, she said. They had been hanging out since running into each other a few months before at some acid-jazz night at the Knitting Factory.

"You're the one who was in the *Times* with Claire," said Diana.

"That party shot? I'm afraid so."

"We were all wondering who that guy was."

"You could wallpaper my bathroom with all the paparazzi shots that Miles gets," I said. Then I remembered Claire's prohibition on talk of him.

145

"You know I don't even check anymore," said Diana. "The trick is to just poke your head into the frame of the camera and smile." She kept ordering drinks and became more talkative with each round. Every time she began to say something she would place that hand of hers back on my leg and look at me all glassy-eyed with a permanent smile.

"So what do you do?" I asked her.

Surprised, she paused for a moment, as if to think it over, as if trying to recall, as if this was not a question one would ever be expected to have to answer.

"Well, lately I've been reading poetry at KGB over on Fourth Street."

"Oh," I said, the rest of the English language fleeing my consciousness.

"Diana's father invented the intermittent wiper," explained Claire.

"I see."

There is something about the American Dream that inevitably leads to indolence. Why was this always the fate of the children of prominent people? Why was the next generation always doomed to lead directionless lives of leisure? Diana might have had a publicist, I thought. For all I knew she might have even been one of Susan's clients. I didn't want to be an expert at recognizing this stuff, but now I was slowly becoming one and there seemed little I could do about it. When Diana introduced me to her friend Juliet, I felt desperate to wake up from this dream. It was Juliet Wilcox, the woman Christina was pushing on some magazine when I had gone to visit her at the agency. Her career was a concept I had trouble grasping that day, but now I somehow got it, noticing that she looked better in person than in that agency head shot. Juliet said she had just landed a bit part in an independent film.

"What's it about?" I asked.

"All I know is it's a very cool crime film," she said, hardly containing her excitement. "It's filled with stylish violence. I get to use this big silver gun. It's huge!"

"I'm so fucking jealous," said Diana, still flirting and as drunk as ever.

At a certain hour a very low-frequency bass began to tremor up through the floor. A few people began slowly migrating down a creaky wooden staircase to join the music. Before we left I quickly visited the men's room, which was just off the stairs leading down there. On my way out I stopped to look at the scene, a cramped space of exposed brick lit blue and red. It was a crowd dancing to what was basically soul music. I spotted Diana moving skillfully at the center of the floor and watched her for a moment. She wasn't with anyone in particular, just floating among bodies like a free agent. As I watched, a man about my age stopped me along the stairs.

"Stuart Finley," he said, breaking my stare.

"Yes," I said, not recognizing him. "Don't tell me, we met at an opening, right?"

"No, I write for the *Observer*. I'm doing an article about Harry Vogel, and I happen to know you're one of his tenants."

"You're writing about Vogel?"

"Yes, about his new project."

"But how do you know me? How do you know he's my landlord, or even what I look like?"

"I ran a Nexis search on a list of tenants. The only thing your name turned up was some art criticism and the caption for a photograph of you at some party." We exchanged numbers, and he said he would call me as his article took shape. Claire and I left the place, and I began to contemplate the fact that my name was now in the Nexis database. Anyone could simply type my name into a computer at a library, and there would appear that damn photograph of Claire and me from the party page. I wasn't comfortable with the idea that someone could sketch out my life from the results of a Nexis search, that great tributary to the culture of celebrity. I was now indexed, logged, sorted, digitized, and listed in cyberspace, the modern card catalogue of public life.

Piloting the elevator up to the loft was almost as difficult as the last time I had tried. Claire pulled the gate back and opened the door when we reached the landing. The vast space was completely quiet and dark. As we walked around, I felt we were trespassing on Miles's privacy. Everything he had, from the significant to the mundane, was laid out bare, from the works in progress in his studio to the clothes in his bedroom to the disks left in his CD changer. The answers to whatever mystery there might have remained about Miles Levy were now available to me in that loft. The trick was to find them without losing my own sanity, which I now know would prove impossible.

I looked at a few half-finished canvases. "Do you ever wonder about the guy's thought process?" I asked.

"What do you mean?"

"Don't you want to know what goes on in his head?"

"I used to, but not anymore."

"Why, have you got him figured out?"

"It's not that complicated," she said, walking over to a worktable. She picked up a black leather-bound notebook. It had a wide rubber band around it with a thick fountain pen wedged in between.

"What is it?" I asked.

"It's the *cahier*."

"The what?"

"The *cahier*, his legendary idea book where all of his inspiration is jotted down and worked out. He usually carries it with him wherever he goes. I don't know why he left it here. It's attained a certain notoriety as a document of the creative mind or something. No one's ever seen its pages, but of course everybody, *tout le monde,* wants to know what's in this little black book."

She held the book out toward me, smiling, her thin, beautifully shaped eyebrows raised. I looked at her and shook my head. "What are you proposing?" I said. She said nothing and quickly tossed the notebook at me. I caught it with one hand, surprised at the force she put into it.

"Open it."

I hesitated.

"It's just a notebook, for Christ's sake," she said.

I pulled off the rubber band. "I always thought Miles used one of those Apple PowerBooks."

"That was just for a magazine ad."

I flipped through a few pages and saw nothing but scribbled numbers and figures and then realized they were stock tips, letter symbols with exchanges next to them: NYSE, AMEX, NASDAQ. There were numbers of shares written next to prices, as in a log of trades. He had written little notes to himself in the margins next to the symbols: *Grossman says earnings to disappoint. Call E. Scharf before market open.* Another: *Buyout at $45? Call Grossman in* A.M. *to spread word, dump at 40.* It went on like this for pages and pages.

"What do you think?" asked Claire.

"Have you seen it?"

"I've given it a glance. I wonder what future scholars of the late twentieth century will say when they turn this one up in an archive. Don't you want to see the looks on their faces?"

"It will be an easy verdict," I said. "All they'll have to do is tally up the total return on investment. I mean it looks like he's beating the S&P by far."

We went up to Claire's bedroom, and she started to get ready for bed. She kissed me and went into her bathroom, shutting the door. The sound of running water was the only noise in the entire place as I sat on her bed and looked at the books she had. The worn French paperbacks had their titles written from bottom to top along the spines as if in stubborn defiance of English literary convention. She took her time, and I got up to look for another bathroom.

Down the hall I glanced into Miles's bedroom. I walked in and looked around, contemplating going through his stuff, wondering what I might find. I briefly considered being good and touching nothing, but the weight of my feelings was never behind that choice. On the floor by the bed was a messy pile of magazines, a mass of perfect-bound coated paper. Fashion, shelter, celebrity monthlies, youthful downtown rags, hip cyberspace manuals. English, French, Italian, German. On the night table sat a thick biography of Jackson Pollock. I picked it up and turned to a marked page. It was a passage concerning the famous drip paintings, telling how the artist's inspiration for the technique was a memory of his father urinating on a tree.

Discreet stock market plays, slick magazines, tagged biographies—everything was proving such a rich cache of Miles's hopes and fears that I couldn't stop myself. I casually opened a few dresser drawers, poked through a wire basket, peered inside a cookie jar purchased at the Warhol estate auction sitting by the bed. I went into his closet, which could have been another bedroom, and marveled at the expert carpentry of its built-ins. I looked through hangers carrying linen shirts and wool jackets, counted all the pairs of shoes and boots fitted on cedar trees, checked out all his black cashmere-wear and held up a pair of leather jeans to see if they might fit. Miles didn't disappoint. Everything was exactly the way I would have expected, maybe even more perfect, only there were no paint-spattered clothes, no work pants or stained smocks. But then, everything must have had its place. The work was downstairs, the living was upstairs, as Miles had told me that day I first visited.

I decided then not to touch another thing, feeling almost exhausted. I sat in a chair, a gorgeous Giacometti, its pitted metal green with oxidation. It was remarkably uncomfortable, but somehow I didn't care. Near me, along the row of windows, sat a small grouping of sculpture. Among the works I recognized were two tin cans with string by Joseph Beuys, a Donald Judd steel rectangle, a Joseph Cornell windowed box, and one of Louise Nevelson's black painted wood towers. I thought I knew that Nevelson from somewhere and wondered why, since they all looked the same. I got closer to inspect the five-foot-tall piece and then realized I had seen it a couple of years before at an auction preview. The sale catalogue indicated that it had a hinge and a hidden door. Back then I tried to open it, but an angry guard stopped me. There seemed no way I could leave without playing with it this time.

I gently pushed and pulled at a few places to learn the trick, and it opened. Inside were several old spiral notebooks, diaries—*real* diaries, not that inane book of stock tips, but something to leave for posterity, something to help those biographers get the details right. Miles must have thought he was being so smart keeping them there. Not many people would have known the Nevelson sculpture could be opened that way, and fewer still would have thought to touch such a valuable piece. I felt as if I had outwitted him in some way.

February 28. Spent the whole day arguing with the Whitney people about my installation. I told them it was too hidden, that people would miss it. Some young helper kept asking me what it meant. I hate that. I never have a good answer ready. I have to work on a few sound bites, a few smart little phrases to drop on opening night.

April 20. DL introduced me to this kid Todd Bryce at Barocco. I thought he looked like his ambition in life was to work in the Barneys sportswear department. Get paid to cruise the floor. But DL assured me he was smart, that he could help us. I'm learning to trust DL, even when I think he's lost his mind.

July 6. Drove back to the city from Amagansett. I'm all burned. Claire never burns, just tans beautifully. We got home to find the loft was broken into. It freaked me out. They took a lot, no paintings though, just the stereo, VCR etc. Called the cops and insurance. I couldn't sleep.

September 11. The fucking NYT! Gave my show at Griffin a tiny little review. Said it was overwrought. What does that mean? They gave Kiki Smith more column inches than me.
Todd came over. Gave us some of his new score. It was the best I've had so far. Claire went crazy, begged me to do a lot of weird stuff. I'm bored with it though.

September 14. Some kid at Chris's party said she knew my work. She said her name was Jess. I didn't want to ask how old she was, but she couldn't have been seventeen. She was cute and very funny. Somehow she got in my cab and ended up staying over. We got high and she showed me what a double-jointed acrobat she was. It's nice to be interested in sex again. Little gift to myself for that fucking Times review.

These diaries were almost two years old. The latest ones were missing. He must have traveled with them. A lot of it was mundane, but from the few pages I read it seemed Miles was feeling a sense of boredom, a lack of interest. He was looking for new thrills. That's what happens when you get everything you've ever wanted, I thought, flipping the pages recklessly to find more mentions of Claire. Suddenly I froze up. The sound in the loft had changed, and it startled me. Claire must have turned the water off in her bathroom. It brought me back for a second, made me realize where I was, what I was doing. I hated it.

Not wanting Claire to see me reading his diaries—did she even know they existed?—I walked into Miles's bathroom, a large, sumptuous space with different marble-tiled areas, one for the stall shower, another for the deep round tub, and so forth. The late Romans would have been comfortable here, I thought. I washed my hands and then looked into his medicine cabinet for some mouthwash. He had an unending collection of personal-care and grooming products. It was a laboratory of sophisticated marketing and product packaging. Shaving cream, face scrub, face peel, skin texture lotion, blister ointment, moisturizer, oil-free, wet-look styling gel, organic baking soda granulated teeth whitener, astringent impregnated cotton swabs. It looked as if Miles had some kind of contract to test products for *Consumer Reports*.

All I wanted was general-purpose mouthwash. I finally found some in the back, behind a phalanx of little plastic amber bottles of prescription drugs—Valium, codeine, and Xanax among the labels I bothered to read. There was a tin Band-Aid box, empty except for a dozen or so small glassine envelopes, each one containing a measured amount of off-white powder. Todd had said his particular brand of heroin was known on the street as Daydreamer. My curiosity was still at work when I flinched at the touch of a cold hand against my back. "Christ," I said, turning around as Claire stood behind me laughing.

"Sorry, I didn't think I'd startle you like that."

"Sure you didn't."

She looked at the crowded shelves of the medicine cabinet. "Every man needs a good moisturizer," she said.

"Maybe one or two, but six?"

"You've been snooping around, haven't you?"

"You started it by showing me his notebook."

She came close and put her arms around me. "Oh yes, I'm a very bad influence on you," she said in a low voice. "You were such a nice innocent boy before you ran into me."

"A gentleman and a scholar," I whispered.

Without saying a word, she showed me how to use the powder Miles kept stashed in that Band-Aid box, emptying the contents of two glassine envelopes onto the cover of a thick September *Harper's Bazaar*. It was more coarse, more crystalline than I expected. But the biggest surprise was the way I didn't resist, the way it felt so natural. She was such a warm, generous hand holder. She went first, taking in a neat but tiny pile right off of Linda Evangelista's chin. Mine was near the features list, just above the words BRILLIANT SHADES FOR FALL.

I led us toward Miles's bed, its parchment-colored comforter looking so inviting. "Wait," she said. "Let's go back to my room."

"Why? We're here now."

She pointed to the bed. "You don't know what goes on in there."

Claire's room suited our needs just as well. She put on some Brazilian music, which she said was her favorite, and all I remember was the feeling that everything had slowed down, that everything was waiting for me if I wanted it.

thirteen

I AWOKE NOT in my own bed for the first time in months. Claire had these big, fluffy down pillows, which paralyzed us with laziness. I was up early as the sun came right into the room through the old tall factory windows and shined off of Claire's perfectly smooth bare back. She didn't seem to mind, breathing away peacefully in sleep. I got out of the bed carefully, uncoupling one leg of mine from between both of hers, to which she shifted slightly without completely waking. But I quickly felt sorry to have left the soft press of her firm, cool skin. I had been woken several times during the night by sharp stomach pain and thought for sure I would vomit, waiting quietly over the toilet while Claire slept, but it never got that bad. I wanted to know if I had done the things Claire had asked for, if I had succeeded in making those changes of nuance she had so gingerly suggested, but I couldn't remember a thing. This would be my last and only time with any of Miles's drugs, I decided.

I walked downstairs barefoot into the empty studio and looked around at the artist's supplies. Everything was so clean, each tube of paint in its proper color order and the brushes grouped perfectly by size. All of them called out for use, begging to be thrown around, violently pressed, extruded, scraped, thinned, and mixed in the service of reckless creativity. But instead they just sat dormant on their neat clean shelves and in their spotless jars.

Below, the streets of SoHo were already awake with the sound of heavy trucks and the intestinal rattle of their idling diesel engines. Car alarms were still going strong, having remained constant throughout the night. Those pointless devices had become a signal that everything was fine, that all was normal on the street. If suddenly they stopped for some reason, if suddenly all I heard was silence, then I would go to the window thinking something was wrong, thinking something terribly illicit must be taking place. Calmed and reassured by their blaring freakish whistling, I went back up to Miles's bedroom and took out those diaries of his.

January 3. Just got back from Miami. Except for one or two spots, the scene is beat, overrun now by the kind of frightening people who wait on line to get into theme restaurants. I've decided we're no longer evolving as a species. Instead we're splitting up, we're getting fucking tribal. It's us and them. I declared South Beach officially dead to that guy from the Voice *and he put it in his column (lead item!). Life is like a theme restaurant. We invest a little money. We're there on opening night. Then we run for our lives, never to return, pulling up the gates behind us on our way out. Although we make sure to collect a few pennies off every T-shirt from far far away.*

January 19. Just got asked to write an article about my visit to Cy Twombly's home in Italy. It should be a useful association. His paintings are getting the right kind of respect.

March 5. Lately Claire keeps putting this Brazilian music on when we make love, it's so fucking annoying. But I can't tell her. I'm relying on her in other ways, though. When I showed her what I had written for the Twombly article she said it was too much travelogue, too much name-dropping. She was right. She totally rewrote it for me. She's always saving me now.

For pages it seemed Miles wasn't impressed by sex with her anymore, although he was still obsessed with her life, obsessed with what she was doing, where she went out, who she was with. With success and notoriety, his desires began to mutate. Finding pleasure had become a challenge that now required new people, new places, more money. Scattered pages filled out a picture that included sleeping with young men and crazy trips to Las Vegas where huge amounts of cash were blown. These aimless ordeals were interrupted only by phone calls from New York, David making sure Miles wasn't killing himself. The artist was always off somewhere, and it was hard to find a stretch of more than three or four weeks when he would just stay in New York. Milan, Aspen, Los Angeles, Paris for the shows, then L.A. again, then Telluride, and Vegas again. The casino town seemed such an odd destination for him. He was so disdainful in these pages, never turning down an opportunity to remark on how middlebrow it was. Perhaps he received some pleasure or sense of security from what one finds there. The coastal elites—the overclass—must need their own kind of zoo, their own kind of natural-history exhibit, a scary theme park of thrills and amusements, a freak show to make home back at the big comfortable loft, with its central air conditioning, its six cable boxes, its Giacometti chairs, feel truly closer to heaven.

Miles seemed so removed from the day to day, safe from any kind of grind. There were no chores in his life, nothing to be done, no lines to wait on, no civil servants to deal with. I tried to imagine what it would have been like for him to renew his driver's license, get stamps at the post office, attend jury duty, *God forbid.* I wanted to see him stuck in a six-hour line at the passport office, surrounded by crying babies and dozens of worried resident aliens who spoke no English. It would have been enough to force a nervous breakdown. The truth was that these were the kinds of things that get *taken care of.* People like Miles somehow manage to never interface with bureaucracy, never assume the specific burdens of citizenship, as if the sacrifice of their tax bracket should be enough, *Goddamn it*!

Flipping through random pages, my eye caught several lines of verse written in a quick, casual scrawl:

> *Paint as theater,*
> *turn up your nose.*

> *Find a dealer,*
> *wear fine clothes.*

> *Lips together,*
> *teeth apart.*

> *Call your dealer,*
> *exit art.*

When Claire awoke she made breakfast in the huge, spotless kitchen. It was filled with all sorts of expensive culinary toys and seemed such a waste for a guy who ate out every night. Claire took two steel pans, the heavy kind with their handles welded on by two bolts, and whipped up the best apricot jam–filled crepes I had ever tasted. She had both pans going at once, pouring the batter perfectly and forming the crepe with just the right hand motion. We ate them quickly, leaning against the counter.

"I like all the stuff you know," I said, dabbing at the sides of my mouth with a napkin.

"What stuff?"

"Everything. You always know what to do. I don't know where to begin."

She put another morsel in her mouth and shook her head. "You're crazy," she said, her mouth half full. "Your eyes are trained, you have real expertise. I'm jealous of that, I'm attracted to it."

"God knows why. It's all so esoteric, it's really fucking useless. I'm sick of what I know." I looked at her standing there in just a man's white oxford shirt and nothing else. "I want to know the things you know."

"Then we'll make a trade."

We spent the day walking around, and I gave her my guided tour of the neighborhood's cast iron gems. Worn cobblestones and loading docks were the only things left behind by nineteenth-century industry. I wondered what this era, with the leisure of its microchip office and the complexity of its paper profits, might leave behind. Miles Levy's paintings, of course.

I laughed out loud when I heard Pied Noir had lost its reservation book. That tall and pretty black hostess looked slightly agitated as we arrived but put on a beaming wide-eyed smile when she recognized Claire, and the two of them kissed on both cheeks. Claire made a point to introduce me, and the hostess nodded discreetly as if from then on my face would be enough to get a table. I remember feeling uncomfortable with this weird ritual of approval.

"Someone stole the reservation book," she said to us.

"Why would anyone want it?" I asked, trying to contain my laughter.

She was not amused. "Some kid walked off with it."

"Maybe it was just a prank," said Claire.

"Perhaps a disgruntled would-be customer," I added.

"They've got all our reserved tables through New Year's Eve. Now we have to reconstruct it, and there's a bit of a panic going on. No one remembers what was booked."

Knowing what to expect now from Claire's alluring wardrobe, I kept an unofficial count of all the turning heads as we walked through the crowded room. She had left the loft that night wearing a silk shirt tucked into a pair of black pants. It was casually open near the neck and shimmering like dull mercury, but then came down to hug her sides, its buttons ready to burst open if she took too deep a breath. I predicted the strained necks and wandering eyes. What I had not anticipated was the equal number of women and men who stopped chewing to look at her.

The service there had always been aloof, but now I sensed a newfound friendliness, as if they knew their days were numbered and would soon have to draw customers simply on the merits of the place, the inevitable fate of all momentarily fashionable spots. One of the waiters even gained my sympathy after a man sitting at the table next to us sent his potato leek soup back to the kitchen.

"Is something wrong with it?" the server asked.

"It lacks a certain cohesion," said the man.

Later we met Claire's friend Diana again. She was alone at the bar and came to our table just as the check arrived. I remember Diana remarking that Miles's loft is so much fun when he's not around, to which Claire agreed.

"All that space," said Claire. "It's got everything you need, you could spend several weeks there without ever having to leave."

"It needs a roof garden," said Diana. "Then it would be complete."

"Miles considered buying the floor above him to get direct access to the roof."

"Why didn't he?" I asked.

"He'd have to fix it up or else his insurance premiums would skyrocket."

"Liability?"

Claire nodded. "You see how many people trample through there on the average day. If someone so much as slips on a tube of acrylic, it would all be over."

"How many other artists live in that building?" I asked.

"None," said Claire. "It's all lawyers and investment bankers with false artist certification."

Diana got up to settle her tab at the bar, and Claire began to tell me about her. "She's a lot to handle. She was always crazy in school, got thrown out before graduation."

"What for?"

"Had an affair with one of the teachers."

"Tell me more," I said.

"She's got a good heart, but she's still kind of crazy."

"Did you get expelled too?"

"No. I just hung out with her. I wanted to be a regular old American kid. I was good at that."

Diana tagged along as we left Pied Noir for some club near Greenwich Street. She jumped into our cab at the last minute, swinging closed its creaking door before our manic-looking driver plunged his foot on the accelerator to get to a nearby red light.

The first thing I wanted was fresh air. The club was warm, its space intimate and crowded. It was an eclectic group, all commingled and moving dexterously to remixed soul music. The youngest ones were wrapped in tight little pink T-shirts and six-button vests, the women showing a lot of midriff or thigh, the men with hair so short, just a few wisps and curves ending above the forehead. The older patrons had on stepped-out garb with interesting hardware: a pair of silver-buckled ankle boots here, a zippered black pullover there, anything to give some zing, some flair. I realized too late how clear it would be to Claire and Diana, not to mention the entire crowd, that rhythm had never been one of my stronger skills. But now there was no way around the featured activity.

Claire looked at me, leaning in close so that I could hear her. "Just do what I do," she said. How sweet of her to notice my condition. She took me by the hand and led me into a crowd of sexualized bodies undulating to the bluesy riffs of the soul music. I looked at her movements, at first just a simple shuffle of the feet that seemed easy enough to copy. But the real trick was how she moved every other part of her body. Her head rolled around as if she were moaning pleasurably, her shoulders thrown back, her arms in a slow, controlled flail. Her waist and chest went in seemingly different directions as her whole midriff bent and shifted marvelously to the bass line of the music. The arms I could do, the head sort of, the shoulders maybe. It was enough to feel halfway competent. She smiled as I lost my inhibitions and then came close to kiss me.

"I'm cutting in," said Diana. She had found her way toward us from across the room. I was a bit confused. Did she mean to take Claire's place or mine? Besides, the whole room was just a big mix of people, no one was really dancing with just one other person. But Diana stepped in front of me, facing Claire, and they began to move together like old pros. I left them there to watch from the bar. I remember noticing how completely in synch their bodies were, and it was at that point, between sips of overpriced vodka, that I realized Diana would turn out to be one more uninvited houseguest at Miles Levy's that night.

I remember Claire and I were making espressos in the kitchen of the loft. Diana had followed us back home and was downstairs putting on Claire's favorite Brazilian music. I was beginning to love that kitchen, all stainless steel and polished black granite. I was starting to understand why it was so important to Miles to have the *right* stove, even if he never lit all eight burners. I thought about making love to Claire on one of the countertops. Next to the instant hot-water spigot? By the big blue Kitchen Aid mixer that looked as if it had never been used? No, clearly the center island was the best choice, with its wide-open expanse. While the granite might have felt too cold against her skin, it would have made for easy cleanup. Yes, I *was* beginning to understand this kitchen, its thoughtful design and loving, if unreasonable expense.

"Why are you so quiet?" Claire said. "What are you thinking?"

"Nothing. Why aren't we having decaf?"

"Because then what would be the point?"

"Fine, fine."

She smiled and whispered, "You're attracted to Diana, aren't you?"

I said nothing for a moment, then looked at her. "I think the question is, *are you* attracted to Diana?"

"I am."

I swallowed loudly and tried to play this as cool as possible, choosing my words carefully. "And, uh, how well do you, like, know each other?"

"Quite well."

"I see." Now we were both wearing wide grins, and I didn't know what to say. I fidgeted with the coffeemaker. "You think she likes me?"

"She loves you." She turned to walk out of the kitchen, holding her little espresso cup. "You know," she said furtively, "you could learn a lot from watching two women together."

"Shall I take notes?"

"Definitely."

fourteen

K OHLMAN RETURNED to work the following week, seeming a little older and a bit thinner. The department was preparing that big show of Raphael drawings for the spring, and he had to finish writing the catalogue quickly, leaving a lot of the organizational work to others. He would often throw me a few sections of his books to work on, letting me write certain historical or biographical portraits that he found tedious. He was so behind schedule on this one, though, that he asked me to do most of the work. I became a kind of ghostwriter for him, and he trusted me to keep that fact concealed from everyone else. We developed a routine whereby I would show him the work I had done and he would sign off on it, initialing the top of every approved page. Sometimes I would have to go back and rewrite; more often he would just make a few notes in the margin.

Kohlman also had a small consulting business operating quietly out of his apartment on 71st Street, even though the museum forbade any of its curatorial staff from charging for outside work. Like a few others I knew, I had spread word through friends that I was always willing to make a house call. What I loved about appraisal was the opportunity to glimpse other people's lives, to see the objects, the people who owned them and the places they lived. For me the money was small-time; I thought of it more as a hobby. Kohlman, by contrast, had a full schedule of appointments at his apartment, where private dealers used him to certify the authorship of Old Master paintings and drawings that needed special expert appraisal. His opinion carried great weight, and he could radically change the value of a given work of art by simply altering its attribution. But now, fatigued by the medicine he was taking, he couldn't keep up and asked me to do one for him. It was a small oil thought to be by the Dutch painter Van Goyen, a dark strip of landscape rendered under an expansive cloud-filled grayish blue sky. He let me have this one, since the Dutch had been the focus of my graduate work.

It was a very good picture, for sure, but I doubted its direct attribution to the artist for several stylistic reasons. Those reasons seemed fairly obvious, and they revealed themselves to me from almost the minute I laid eyes on the picture. I asked Kohlman to take a look at it to confirm what I saw, and he said he would. In the morning on the day the owner was scheduled to pick up his picture, I typed out a written opinion with a new attribution: "Studio of Van Goyen." This meant that the work was probably by an unknown hand in the studio of the named artist and was not necessarily executed under the artist's direction. Of course what it really meant in terms of the market was that the painting had effectively been downgraded. Attribution was a tricky business, a subjective exercise intended only to answer the technical question of authorship. It was not criticism, it was not a comment on whether the work was good, bad, or mediocre. To me the painting was still just as nice; I would have been more than happy to have it in my home whether Van Goyen had done it or not.

At the very last minute Kohlman signed his name to the letter. "Did you see it?" I asked him.

He seemed distracted. "Sure."

"So you agree," I said, watching carefully for his reaction.

"Yes, of course."

There was something about the way he answered that bothered me, and when I got to his apartment to meet the owner, letting myself in with a set of keys, the first thing I did was take another look at the painting, which I had left on a table in the study. I had carefully draped a linen pillowcase over it to keep dust and sunlight off, and it seemed untouched. I doubted then that Kohlman had ever even bothered to look at it. I was on my own with this one.

The owner arrived, a well-dressed dealer who said he split his time between London and New York. I viewed him as simply a momentary caretaker in the 350-year life of the fine work. "The light is all wrong," I said. "It doesn't have the light of Van Goyen. The sky is luminous, but not in the right way. The highlights on the clouds are too blunt to be Van Goyen. Also, the way these figures have been painted over suggests some reworking by another hand. But it's a very nice picture nonetheless."

He looked at me, stunned. I handed him the letter, but he refused to take it. Finally I just shrugged and said, "I'm terribly sorry, but the light just isn't there."

"*The light just isn't there?* What in God's name do you mean—how can you say for sure?"

I shifted my weight uncomfortably. "Well, of course, no one can say for sure, but we do get paid to make these judgments."

I sensed panic in his voice. "Couldn't you take another look?"

"It wouldn't change anything."

"You don't understand," he said. "This picture is as good as sold. You see, my buyer is only waiting for this opinion."

"I'm sorry, but this is our conclusion."

He threw up his hands and grunted in disgust. "Now, look here, young man, I didn't come here to have the value of this picture cut in half, you understand?" He looked like a man about to lose a great deal of money, sweat beginning to form on his brow, blood rushing to his head. I thought it would blow off and steam would come rushing out. He put his finger between his neck and the high, tight collar on his shirt to get some fresh air in there. "Do you realize this opinion is the only thing standing between me and my client's checkbook? I need that check. If I don't make this sale, I'm broke, that's it, finished. You understand? *Finished!*"

"So I guess you don't need this," I said, holding up the letter.

"Who are you exactly? When can I speak with Dr. Kohlman?"

"He's not available until next week," I said.

"How old are you, *fourteen*?"

"Twenty-eight, if you need to know."

"You little prick!" he fumed. "Where do you get the balls to pull a fucking stunt like this?"

It turns out that a lot of these art and antiques dealers, half-brogued Savile Row types, can swear like Nixon. When I calmly and confidently offered to make a more scientific examination, using X rays, cross-sectional paint chip analysis, and the latest in autoradiography and infrared imaging, he started yelling something about a lawsuit. Then he took the small painting, turned to leave, and said, "I'm sure I'll have no trouble finding someone a bit more—cooperative."

Claire was even busier, getting ready for the season's big contemporary art auction. She called me at the museum after that perfect long weekend we had spent together, and I told her how much I appreciated everything. But the pleasure, she said, was all hers. Later the sound of concern flattened out her words when the talk turned to Miles Levy.

"Something happened while they were away, Stuart," she said.

"Something did happen while they were away. You and I really fell for each other."

"I don't mean that. Something changed with them."

"Changed with who?"

"Miles, Todd, and David. They were all in a bad way when they got back from Europe. Everyone is tense, they haven't stopped arguing since they got here. Have you talked to your sister yet?"

"We spoke briefly, she said the trip went well."

"I don't think it did." Then she told me that one of Miles's paintings was going to be in the Sotheby's sale. "David couldn't get his hands on it. They're holding their breath on this one."

"They think they can control everything, don't they? David can't carefully place every one of the bodies like a child up for adoption."

"He called me up, kept saying I let him get blindsided. I mean, I only found out yesterday, there was nothing I could do. This one came in under his radar, and he just got totally unhinged."

"Was he rude?"

"He can come down on you like a ton of bricks sometimes."

"Claire, why would you take that? You don't work for him anymore. You should've hung up on him. They can't expect you to intervene for them."

"They like to call in debts," she said, sounding upset.

"You should have told him to fuck off."

"Will you stay at the loft tonight?"

"Why? You can stay with me."

"I just want you to come over. I can't stand being there alone when everybody's like this, it's uncomfortable."

"Why should we both be uncomfortable?"

"I mean just stay the night. We can go out and then crash in my room."

"But Miles is back now. I don't understand, Claire. I thought he said he didn't want to see you with me."

"I want to know if he really means it."

It felt strange to be in Miles's loft again after living there with Claire for several days and nights. It was as if I were back in high school. I had buried the condoms and their bright red packaging deep in the trash and made sure to put back in its place everything that was not mine—a terrycloth robe, various CD's and remote controls, and of course, those notebooks of his. It was just after eleven at night, and I walked in from the old elevator. The downstairs studio was dark, so I went up to the living area and found Miles sitting at the edge of one of his beige sofas thumbing through the Zagat restaurant guide. A copy of the *New York Times Book Review* was lying open on his lap. I noticed a little silver bracelet that Diana had taken off; it was peering out from under that sofa like she had left it behind to mark territory.

"Ah, Finley," he said, getting up and putting his hand out to shake. He gripped hard, harder than seemed appropriate. He looked tired and was not shaven.

"Hello, Miles, how was your trip?"

He sighed and picked up a glass of what looked like whiskey. "Four cities in four days. You must know what that's like."

"I can imagine."

"I guess you had a hell of a time here," he said with just enough sarcasm to make me uneasy.

"Here? Sure, I mean the weather was good."

"The weather?" He laughed and looked at me. "She's a beautiful woman, Finley."

This was exactly why I had tried to avoid going down there that night. I said nothing for a moment, then attempted to change the subject. "When will you start painting again?" I asked.

"So where did you fuck her?"

"Jesus, Miles."

"It's a big place, isn't it? There are lots of interesting choices."

"What?"

"Yes, I mean that's what you spent your time doing, wasn't it?" He had always annoyed me, and now I was a bit disgusted.

"Don't worry," I said, "not in your bed."

"You're such a gentleman."

"Miles, come on. I just think we should try to—"

"Oh, yes, a gentleman and a scholar, I forgot. By the way, did she introduce you to any of her friends? She has lots of friends, you know. Very good friends."

"Look, I am not going to have this conversation."

"Why not? You find it crass? Tasteless?"

"Try pointless."

He paused, looking a bit spent, and I thought he must have been on his third or fourth glass. Then he picked up the *Book Review.* "You know, you're right. I guess it is pointless. It's all pointless." He ignored me and began turning the pages.

"I'll just check and see if Claire's ready," I said, then left him there. I walked to Claire's bedroom, pushing open the door. She was sitting on the floor with papers scattered around her.

"What are you doing?"

"Paying bills," she answered. I sat beside her to look more closely, and she turned to kiss me. "Thanks for coming." She was barefoot and had on a pair of old ripped jeans and a white cotton T-shirt.

"You don't look ready to go out."

"I'm tired. Why don't we just stay in?" she said.

"I guess it is kind of late."

"Did you stop to talk to Miles?"

"We exchanged pleasantries."

"I'll bet you did."

"He's in a real mood. I think he's rather drunk."

"By this hour he's either falling asleep with the bottle in his hand or on a drunken rampage. At least there's enough space out there for him to get sloppy. I told you, everyone is so damn gloomy around here now."

"What happened?"

"It's just business, I don't want to bore you. So what did he have to say?"

"Not much. He was reading the *Book Review* and the Zagat guide *at the same time.*"

"He loves the review. It's such a great cheat sheet for him. You don't want to be caught without an opinion about the opinions."

"What about the Zagat guide?"

"They're both tools of social planning. One tells him what restaurants to go to, the other tells him what to talk about over dinner. They're perfect complements."

"He must read a few real books."

"He reads by using indexes. You know, flipping to the pages with the names he wants to know about."

"What about that stash?"

"The Band-Aid box?"

I nodded.

"He said he gave it up. It was always Todd's drug. He's

around somewhere contemplating the universe. But Miles is through with it."

"What do you mean?"

"He said he had a bad experience. He said it wasn't fun anymore. He'll move on to something else, then he can be like, 'been there, done that.' But Todd's a big user. The guy isn't in a sane state of mind, and it's turned Miles off. Now one of them is shit-faced and the other is going through heroin euphoria." At that moment I wished I had insisted we stay at my place.

"All I remember is feeling sick," I said. "I almost threw up."

"You never said anything."

"I didn't feel like going into the details."

She shook her head. "I'm sorry."

"Don't be."

"Look, we were there, it was easy. I'm sorry, Stuart. It was stupid."

"I'm perfectly responsible for my own actions, Claire. I was in a curious mood that night. I was a bit caught up." She moved a few of her papers aside to get closer, and we kissed. She was so easy to get undressed—barefoot, no bra, her jeans quickly unbuttoning and the loose T-shirt sliding up over her head. But I had shoes to deal with, the laces tightly double-knotted, troublesome dress socks, a belt, a wrist-watch, a tucked-in button-down shirt.

She laughed at me. "You've got so much to undo. You're like a gift with too much wrapping paper."

I thought of Miles in the other room just down the hall from Claire's door, and there was a slight thrill in the risk of detection. We played on the floor for a while, and after a few different games of bodily exploration, I got up. "I want to make sure the door is closed all the way," I said. I pushed on the door and heard the sound of the catch entering the doorjamb, then turned back toward Claire. She was sitting up, reaching behind her telephone answering machine.

"I'm not taking any calls right now," she said, holding the phone's coiled white cord out toward me. *What did she have in mind*? "Here," she said, "tie my hands."

Her little pushes and nudges, her softly spoken requests had been heading in this direction for a while now, and I had trained myself not to act surprised. But this was clearly moving beyond the realm of nuance. I imagined Miles bursting in and finding Claire with rope burns on her wrists, something destined to cause a severe escalation of tension. The thought was almost too much to bear, but in the end she got her way, although I jumped when we heard Miles call out from the hallway a bit later.

"Claire?" he kept calling. I froze. She looked at me with her hands behind her back and said nothing. He called out again for an answer, and she made a shush sound to keep me from opening my mouth. "Claire? Claire," he said again. After a little while he seemed to give up. I must have looked a bit nervous, because she made a point to calm my mind about all the classic confrontational ex-boyfriend possibilities.

"Don't worry, he probably thinks we're gone," she whispered. "I told him I was going out. He doesn't even know which way is up." I began to relax, trusting her, and we heard nothing else until much later.

I could tell Claire was close to falling asleep. It was just past one-thirty, and I was scratching her back, watching her. Events that rouse you out of bed are the worst because they catch you when you are least able to respond with anything approaching good judgment. There's no sharp decision making after your dreams have started. Claire opened her eyes and whispered, "Listen."

"What is it?" I asked. Suddenly she had the alertness of a German shepherd just before some seismic activity.

"Do you hear them?"

"Who?"

"Miles and Todd. They're arguing again." I listened and heard their raised voices echoing through the loft. It was a lot of angry shouting, Miles's voice mostly. I could hear Todd only during the lulls.

"Maybe we should have gone to my place," I said.

She seemed so unnerved. "I hate this."

I tried to listen to what all the fuss was about, but everything was diffused by the echo. I tensed up as we heard books falling, glass breaking, and then a loud slam, like a heavy table had been pushed over. Claire and I didn't move, hardly even breathing. I was no longer thinking of this as an interruption, no longer considering taking Claire to my apartment, since the last thing I wanted to do now was step outside that door. I was fixed only on what Miles and Todd were up to. Did they argue like this often? Why was Claire so still? What was it she feared? I wanted to roll over and put my arms around her and just pull the covers over us, but I couldn't move. It must have become more physical as some grunting could be heard and then a trample down the stairs.

The sound of their voices became more faint as it moved farther away from us, and I figured I had to go out there.

It seemed clear someone needed help, but which one? They were both bigger than me. Neither one was in any condition to be thinking clearly, acting rationally. Showing my face might have just antagonized them. I got up anyway. "Where are you going?" Claire asked.

"To see what the fuck is going on."

I put on pants and walked out barefoot. I could hear them down below as I slowly and quietly made my way to the top of the stairs and looked down. It was dark, the only light coming in off the street. The two of them were near Miles's motorcycle, the restored vintage Triumph by the elevator. Todd was walking backward, awkwardly, while Miles hovered over him. "I'm leaving," Todd said. "I'm leaving it all. I just, I just wanted to make a stand, I mean, we were partners."

"Listen to you. You make no sense."

"I swear. I swear, Miles. I'm going. I'm going to—to do something else, you know? You know what I mean? I, I'm going."

"So go. *Get the fuck out already.*"

Todd looked like he needed help. He seemed disoriented, and he kept touching a bleeding lip. His clothes and hair were all messy. He was having trouble getting the words out and kept repeating himself. "Miles, I just, I just—oh God, let me just get going. Help me go."

"Look at you wasting away. You're so fucked up. You don't know what you had. You don't know what you're throwing away by doing this. You're nobody, you'll never be anybody."

"You leave me no choice. I don't want to do this."

"You don't understand, Todd. Your interests are my interests. If I go down, you go down with me."

Something was not quite right with Todd. He looked sick, like he was tripping badly. "I want—I want what I know is fair. You know it is. You know it's fair," said Todd, breathing hard and talking in stops and starts. He grabbed onto the front fork of the motorcycle to keep himself from collapsing, but Miles forced him back toward the elevator door, then opened it, swinging it around to reveal the empty shaft beyond.

"Get out, then," said Miles. "Leave. You're no longer welcome here."

Todd was just feeling his way around the darkness, as if

he had no perception of depth or space, no focus on where he was or even what was happening to him.

"Did you hear me?"

Todd didn't answer.

"You are really pathetic. You haven't got a chance without all this. You're spoiled now."

Todd closed his eyes and put his hand on his head as if he were in some kind of pain. "I don't care about all that," he said.

"Leave. Go already," said Miles.

"Miles, you know this is business. I mean, I know it's business, all right? Don't, don't do this, 'cause I'm leaving."

"What the fuck are you babbling? Just go. *Leave.*"

"Wait, wait. I gotta sit down. You know, just pull myself together."

"I thought you said you were leaving."

"Miles. Oh God, oh God. Shit." Todd had his back facing the open shaftway, his arm leaning against the doorjamb.

"So what are you going to do?"

"I'm going to leave. I'm leaving right now. Right now." Miles must have been aware of the danger of Todd's next step. I wanted to go down there and show them to the stairs, to help Todd get himself together, but I didn't. The whole thing seemed so bizarre and confused that I just stood there silently.

"Just get away from me," said Todd.

"Here," said Miles putting out his hand.

Todd flinched. "*I said get away.*"

"Okay, okay," said Miles with his arms up. Miles watched Todd for a moment as he struggled to pull himself together. Then he got a bit closer to him and abruptly put his hand out once more. "Here, let me help you," Miles said.

"Get away," said Todd, one step from the edge. He must have thought Miles was going to hit him or something, since he reacted by turning away every time Miles made a move.

"Jesus, look at you," Miles said. Todd was too far gone to be any kind of fair opponent, and I thought that Miles was calling off the fight, ending the little game. But Todd's eyes were still unfocused, and rather than explain to him that the elevator wasn't there, Miles kept causing him to flinch. "Come here," said Miles, going to grab him again, but Todd pulled away, moving closer to his last step.

"Don't touch me," he said.

"Come on, Todd." Miles went to grab him again, but Todd jerked back, scared.

He fell in an instant. The only thing to remember him by was the sight of limbs reaching for the air. He was in too much of a daze to even make a sound. Miles, however, called his name out in a sharp scream and then just kept repeating, "Oh my God. Oh my God."

fifteen

I LOOKED DOWN over the edge and saw the body spread out at the bottom, the head made almost unrecognizable from the impact. Todd Brycc, I thought to myself, the kid who had arrived hoping to be a model and instead became something else. Where in that short, eventful path had he gone wrong? He was the only one in that whole place, oddly enough, who really knew something about art as far as I could tell, the only one who had ever expressed any kind of passion for the stuff. I could make out the body's outline in the darkness, but what caused me to turn away suddenly, what I found so horrifying, was the spray of blood that rose almost a full story onto the walls of the shaft. He had left a kind of aesthetic mark, the energy of his impact expressed by those perfectly arrayed pinpoint droplets like a frozen moment in time. Claire was shaking, unable to really speak, and I remember wanting to cry with her, wanting to just hold her and cry, but we were too stunned to do anything.

"It was an accident, I swear it was an accident," said Miles, breathing hard and frightened. "I had no idea you guys were still here." He told us how Todd was having a ter-

rible drug reaction. Todd, he explained, thought he was getting onto the elevator when he tripped and fell into the dark
empty shaftway, not realizing the car wasn't there. Miles didn't
know we were home until Claire came running down to see
what was wrong. For several minutes Miles disappeared. We
thought he had run down to check the body. Instead, watching him from the window, I saw him use a pay phone out on
the street. Then he came back upstairs and told us that
David and Susan were on their way. Not until about twenty
minutes later did he dial 911 to get an ambulance, this time
from his own phone. It was just enough time for David to
arrive, with Susan following soon after.

Their efforts at damage control began instantly. I
watched David make several cellular calls that I suspected he
did not want chronicled on Miles's phone bill. "It doesn't
look like that to me," he said into the thin little phone. He
nodded several times and then said, "What about involuntary manslaughter?" He nodded some more. "Even so, there
could be some civil action, I mean the family, we need to
prepare for a wrongful death suit. . . . Yes, I have copies of
the policy in my vault. . . . I'll call you back in a few hours."

He hung up and told Miles to drink some mouthwash to
get the smell of alcohol off his breath. I figured they had very
little time to clean up any signs of altercation, but they
worked quickly. Claire and I watched as the broken glass
was swept away, the rug straightened and the books
returned to their shelves. I remember how much I didn't
want to be there, and I even considered leaving, but I couldn't
make up my mind fast enough when Miles and David looked
at me. They were trying to turn the big heavy cupboard back
up but couldn't get it to budge. I was afraid they might ask
me to help, and I prayed for them to just leave me alone.

"Come on, give us a hand," said David.

I so clearly hesitated that I could see them beginning to

hate me by the second. "We've been good to you this whole time, now help us out here," read their faces. The problem was that I knew Miles had a few of the details in his story wrong, terribly wrong, yet somehow the events had left his hands clean. I considered walking out of there, running down the stairs and out the door, never to return or something along those lines. But that was just a fantasy. There was no way I could leave. To be fair, I had no right to leave, no right to claim that I had no business there. I couldn't pretend to be a spectator anymore, I couldn't simply observe amused and detached as I had in David's gallery or as I had done upon first visiting Miles's loft. For the first time I understood that my association with Claire had made me another character of that place, and maybe even part of whatever might have transpired there that night. I could never have said no to them and still expect to be welcome. Besides, I didn't want to look weak.

"Stuart, for Christ's sake, just help us get this thing up," Miles said finally.

I acquiesced, lifting the tall French provincial piece along with the two of them. We raised it, and I was uneasy about the whole thing, feeling very involved now. I'm not sure why I suddenly participated in their machinations, but I did. Maybe it was because they struck me just then as such winners, certain to succeed. The way they handled themselves, the way they instinctively knew what steps to take, made it all seem okay, risk-free. How could they lose when everything was approached as a manageable process, when everything in their lives was arranged to their advantage? Luck, I realized just then, is a commodity that can be manufactured. They had all the confidence, determination, and strong will it required, and there was a contagious quality to their brio that was impossible to fight off.

Miles sat down with his two handlers to go over their

story just as I heard the siren of an ambulance pull up outside. When the police arrived, they asked David if anything had been moved or touched. "No, nothing," said the dealer with remarkable cool. Other tenants were woken by the activity and came up the building's stairwell to see what had happened. One man identified himself to the police as the president of the co-op board. He said he was an emergingmarket debt specialist, and he did nothing but look around disapprovingly, as if thinking he should have never allowed these artistic types to move in. *You idiot*, I thought, *you're the one to be kept out*, since it was a building zoned only for working artists.

David and Susan were both trying to manage everything and protect their investment, acting like Miles's mommy and daddy. The seasoned New York cops kept telling them to sit down and wait as each of us was questioned one by one. Miles went first, then Claire, and then me. David made the split-second decision that Miles agree to be questioned without a lawyer present, since to have done otherwise might have made things more complicated. It was done in the kitchen, and as I sat outside waiting my turn Claire came out and looked at me.

"What did you say?" I asked.

"I told them we were sleeping upstairs, that we didn't know what was going on."

"That's all?"

"What else is there?"

I went into the kitchen and was greeted by two uniformed officers and a plainclothes detective named Chaffee, a man in his forties with a look of hardened experience that made me nervous. He asked me to sit down and tell him what I was doing at the time of the accident and what I thought had happened. I told him that I was in bed with the door closed and that I was concentrating on something else at the time.

"Did you hear anything?" he asked me.

"Well, yes, I did."

"Whaddya hear exactly?" I thought about it for almost a whole minute before answering, realizing that I had never had any real contact with the police for anything. I loved New York cops, always imagining them as easygoing and pudgy, sensitive to the Bill of Rights. If L.A. cops were Nazi storm troopers, then New York cops had to be the Weimar police.

I looked up at the industrial rack where all the pots and pans hung and remembered eating those crepes Claire had made. I hoped I might get to taste them again. The detective asked me once more. "You said you heard something. *Whaddya* hear?"

"It was just a bunch of echoes. I really don't know what I heard."

"Echoes like what? Like shouting?"

I had to think too fast, with too many different emotions going on inside me and not enough time to synthesize it all. I envied the way Claire had emerged from this same spot with such a clear head, as if it were no big deal, like she had just had her teeth cleaned and was admiring their new smoothness with her tongue on the way out of the hygienist's office.

I lied. "No. Nothing like that at all," I said.

"You didn't hear anything else, Mr. Finley?"

"That was it. Then we heard a scream and went running out there. It was dark. I guess Todd had overdosed and was disoriented. Look, I really wasn't there. We were upstairs the whole time." I thought then that the problem with being less than candid is that once you begin down that course there's no way to change direction no matter how hard you want to.

"All right, thanks. You can get going."

"That's it?"

"That's it." He started to walk away, then turned back toward me. "Wait. One last thing before you go. Did he ever tell you the street name? If it was a lethal purity, we could track it down and maybe prevent something like this from happening again."

"The street name?"

"Yeah. The brand, the tag."

"Daydreamer," I said. He looked at the uniformed officer, who noted it, and then thanked me for my time.

sixteen

I CAN REMEMBER reading about it in the *Post*. I had never made a habit of buying the tabs, but after you spend time with a flack like Susan you learn how to discreetly keep an eye on these *lesser organs*. It was a small item several pages inside, the headline just a few simple words and fairly tame:

MAN FALLS FOUR STORIES, DIES

And then in smaller type: "Downtown Art World Figures Questioned After Accident." A day later the *Times* picked up the story, again short and buried in the Metro section, reporting that Miles Levy had been cleared of any suspicion. With no forensic evidence or witnesses to suggest otherwise, the death was declared accidental, and a small fine was charged to Levy for violating the city building code on elevator doors that open directly into a loft space. As expected, Todd's family put the wheels of a lawsuit in motion, charging that wrongful death had resulted from this negligent building-code violation. Miles and his insurance company quickly settled out of court, however, and the rural northern

Florida family, who hadn't cared to speak to their son for almost five years anyway, readily agreed not to disclose the amount of money they received or even talk publicly about the affair.

"That's what I love about those big umbrella policies," David told me when I had called the loft. I wanted Claire, and I was surprised he answered. "They write the check no questions asked," he said. "You just let them know how much. Hell, I used to complain about how those premiums were like ransom money. Now they look like a bargain."

The few public details had proved to be the perfect little bit of publicity, nicely sharpening Miles Levy's image of avant-garde edginess. The story wrote itself, and Susan didn't have to lift a finger or even expose the fact that Miles was ; client. Miles had the best representation in Susan and Davi they were so good at spin, so skilled at putting him where needed to be. My sister was right when she called it a ; formance. The two of them were masters, and I marvele the tidiness of it all.

Despite everyone's hasty return to normality, I replaying the events of that night in my head, kept try understand the decisions Miles had made. And the were the decisions I made. Why had I chosen to do at the crucial moment when Todd seemed so in need to think there might have been an instant, standing of that floating white staircase, when Todd and I i made eye contact, a split second where he looked ognized who I was and what I might do for him. days I pushed this thought out, content that i guilty delusion. I no longer trusted my detailed b confused memory of the whole thing. It was the parts but could no longer place them in th But the people who came to believe Miles Le version of events, those paramedics who fir

scene, the cops, the cub reporters assigned to police-scanner duty, even the hopelessly intimidated small-town lawyer for Todd's mother and father, none of them knew there had been a heated argument. That bit of information would have changed everything, and anyone who might have even suspected this could never hope to establish it without more cooperation. No one had to tell me that it would have opened up troublesome new legal questions.

I was at a birthday party filled with children in a brownstone apartment somewhere uptown. Claire and I had stopped there to pick up her niece, Lisbeth. The children were all grouped in well-behaved cliques of conversation. This was surprising, given the potent mix of sugar available. At one table I saw a little brown-haired boy take a bite of fluffy white iced birthday cake, pop a handful of M&M's like pills from a bottle, and then wash it all down with a Dixie cup full of Coca-Cola as if it were a shot of tequila.

"That kid will be the first of his friends to experiment with drugs," said Claire.

"You think he'll start by stealing his mom's Valium?"

"It's always the first step, usually around age fourteen."

When little Lisbeth saw us she came over to give her aunt a kiss and a big hug. "I remember you," she said, pointing at me. "You're the museum guard." She laughed and did her best impression of a guard, standing up straight with her hands stiffly at her side, and said, "Don't touch the art!" I became insecure at this ironic insight, wondering if she meant to say in her own wry, intelligent way that I was too stiff and buttoned-down. Could this cute little kid have had me figured out from the start?

"You're a perceptive girl," I said, uneasy at the knowing smile she was shining back at me. She turned to Claire to say she wasn't ready to leave the birthday party just yet, and the

two of them negotiated in French. Then she left to be with her friends, promising to return in "five more minutes."

"Everyone's been asking about you," said Claire as we watched the little girl from the window.

"Everyone?"

"David said he wanted to speak to you about something."

"What about? I just spoke to him the other day."

"He didn't say. They'll all be at the loft for brunch."

"It's amazing, nobody seems to have missed a beat," I said.

"The service at Grace Church was packed."

"At least they went through the motions." I had stayed away from the service, knowing how uncomfortable I would have been there. I gave some lame excuse about work and sent my donation to DIFFA in lieu of flowers, as requested.

"I think Miles made a very nice speech."

"I'm sure he did. I guess that makes everything fine, right?"

She said nothing and leaned against me. I rubbed her back and then placed my hands around her waist. She felt warm. "Sometimes I think about Todd," I said.

"We all do."

"No, I mean I have this distinct image of his face. Look, I didn't really know him very well. The truth is, I hardly knew him at all. But there was something about the way he looked when I saw him last that I just can't shake."

"What did you see?"

"I saw a lot of things—despair mostly."

She said nothing.

"Claire, tell me what was going on between them. I mean, with business and everything."

She pulled away from my grasp and then turned around to face me. "A lover's quarrel, if you need the details."

"Miles and Todd?"

She nodded. "Todd was upset, he was always jealous of

me, he couldn't stand the fact that I still lived at the loft." I said nothing and just let the news settle. "I didn't think you'd be surprised," she said.

"I guess I should have figured it out."

"The two of them were always discreet. Miles has never officially *come out*. But a lot of people knew they were together. Somehow they managed to keep people from writing about it."

"I thought you said it was business trouble, things went bad in Europe or something."

She paused. "You need to know one more detail," she said.

"What? Tell me."

"Todd did all of the work."

"How do you mean?"

"He did everything—all the conceptual work, all the canvases and the sculptures. Not just the execution, I mean he even came up with the ideas. Miles and David paid him for the work. They had an arrangement. It was all Todd's work. It has been for years. After a while there really was no Miles Levy. Todd Bryce had become Miles Levy."

"I don't understand. The guy just stopped working?"

"It goes back a long way to when David first took Miles in. It was a huge break to be at Griffin—they had all the influence, the magazines in their pocket, David could get people to buy anything. But Miles spent so much time just cultivating his persona as this hot new discovery that he needed an assistant. He started hiring different people. He went through a lot of them before finding Todd."

I listened closely to Claire's words, afraid to miss one detail of the story. "Todd was a popular kid, everyone knew him from the clubs," she went on. "David liked Todd's ideas, so he convinced Miles to hire him. Everything worked out well. Todd got his hands on the work sometimes, even doing a whole piece here and there. As he did more and more work, Miles got lazy, more interested in spending money than in painting or designing installations. He said he had lost his touch. He would walk around the loft saying he was dried up, that he was blocked. David sent him to every shrink and New Age guru he could find, and nothing helped. But it was all just an act to make up for his laziness. Meanwhile, Todd kept producing and David went right on selling the work."

"As genuine?"

"No one ever bothered to say anything. They figured Miles would get back to working soon and no one would ever notice. But after a while his block, or whatever you want to call it, became fixed. He couldn't even bring himself to prime a canvas. He had spent so much time away from the work that he was afraid to try and paint again. It was like some kind of neurosis. But David's gallery still needed feeding, and Miles's lifestyle was only getting more expensive, so they all worked out an arrangement. Todd did the work and Miles just signed off on things, and for the past couple of years he hasn't picked up a brush or mixed a single color."

"But Miles showed me works in progress all around the studio," I said.

"But you never saw him working on them. All that stuff was produced at another site, some warehouse west of Varick. The pieces were brought over in different stages of completion to give the appearance of works in progress."

"How elaborate."

"Less elaborate than you think. It was really quite easy. That was the problem: It was too easy, Miles got so complacent."

"How many people knew?" I asked.

"Just the three of them and Susan."

"And you."

"And me," she said.

"Why didn't Todd just go out on his own if he was doing all these works himself?"

"It went on for too long. Everyone knew the style as that of Miles Levy. Nobody was ever going to be interested in Todd Bryce's work."

"The irony is, *they were* interested, but they didn't know it," I said.

"I don't think it bothered him. It was his only real opportunity."

"A very lucrative opportunity. But you said they weren't getting along."

"Not lately," she said. "Everything was going so well for so long that they were surprised when Todd began asking for a lot more money. He had them in a bind, and I guess while they were in Europe he threatened to walk away from it all if they didn't pay him more and if Miles didn't make me leave."

"So they were lovers," I said. "That's why the guy warmed up to me. He figured I was taking you away from Miles." I shook my head. "So what will they all do now?"

"There's enough new work to last them a year or so. After that, who knows, maybe Miles will start working again. They'll send out a press release calling it a new period or a new direction. They could even have one of those friendly critics write a book documenting the evolution of the work."

"They're so good at that stuff," I said. "You still say Miles had nothing to do with the accident?"

"They were both on Mars. They misjudged the edge or something."

"You don't care who was responsible?"

"What are you getting at, that Miles wanted him to fall? What would have been his motive?"

"I know it makes no sense. But then why didn't he help him?"

"Miles would have never meant to hurt him."

"So we'll bump it down to involuntary manslaughter."

"The police made their inquiry."

"I doubt those cops were following the intricacies of the art market," I said. "They never even knew there had been an argument after David and Susan did their magic."

"It was an accident, a tragic accident. Whatever they did only made things easier for everyone. Look, Miles never meant to hurt him."

"Maybe Miles never meant to take things that far, but he was ultimately responsible. I watched him, and maybe I'm crazy, but Miles knew Todd was going to take that step. He knew it."

"How do you know? Were you reading his mind?"

"Look, Claire, he let things get out of hand, and now he doesn't have to deal with the consequences, since we all lied for him."

"There's nothing anyone can do now." She lowered her voice. "They put a top criminal defense attorney on retainer for about forty-eight hours until it was clear how things were going to play out. I knew they wouldn't need him."

"They got lucky. That's the kind of luck that runs out, you know. I guess I can't swallow this as easily as you people."

She lowered her voice even more, though managing somehow to increase its intensity, the breaths of her whisper sounding almost harsh. "Yes," she said, "they were protecting Miles's viability. Is that what you want me to say? Are you satisfied now?" She kept her eyes on little Lisbeth across the room. "I don't want to talk about it anymore," she said. "I just want Miles to get through this."

"I'm sure he'll pick up right where he left off," I said, and she shrugged. "What do you see in him? I mean what else

191

besides the opportunity, what else besides the cheap rent?"

"I don't know," she said, sounding bothered by the question. "Me and Miles really had something once."

"Had what? A nice little game of control?"

She turned and looked at me. "What?"

"Isn't that what you always want?"

"Go to hell," she said, more annoyed than I had ever seen her. "You did some of the tying, as I recall."

"I'm not the one who's compared the relative qualities of phone wire to those of an extension cord."

"You're being such an asshole. You're making so much more of it than it is."

"Am I? What about those debts? Why do you always complain about how they own you, and then you do nothing when it threatens you? You protest about their control, but then you always end up toeing the line, don't you? You *really are* a submissive, Claire, only it's not as subtle as you first made it out to be. No, it's very fucked up, isn't it? And it's everything. It's Miles, it's the loft, it's David and the business. You're addicted."

She was red. Her eyes glassy, welling up. "Fuck off," she said. "I don't need your cut-rate psychology."

"Think about it; it's true."

"You're full of shit. You were right, the only things you really know are useless and esoteric."

"Maybe, but I know you. I know finally why you've made certain choices, and I know why you keep making the same mistakes."

"The truth is, I've learned a lot from Miles, all right? He has a kind of confidence you could never hope to know."

"You told me once you were afraid to be in his reach, afraid he would take your career away, which sounds pretty pathological to me. Now you sound so admiring and forgiving."

She looked at Lisbeth and seemed lost in a long stare.

"Maybe I don't want to be out of his reach," she said. "Maybe I belong in his sphere. Maybe the rewards are greater than I ever thought." I wanted so badly to know how long she had felt this way, to know at what moment she had decided, but I said nothing else, almost afraid to hear anymore.

On our way over to Lisbeth's plain, almost humble way-east home, I thought it odd how her school, her friends and playmates all seemed from a more affluent milieu, more west of Lex than east of Third. These shades of difference, these absurd fractional distinctions were endlessly tied up in the Manhattan esoterica of buildings and schools, locations and connections. I hated having such sensitive antennae for these things, but I still couldn't place the girl or her parents in this picture, and I was curious as to the details of their story. When we left her in front of the tenement-style building, she asked us to come upstairs and visit. Claire declined, saying she didn't want to impose, and I remember thinking that this was one of the few thoroughly adult concepts that the girl did not yet understand.

We arrived at the loft a bit later. I walked up the stairwell, not wanting to deal with the groaning moodiness of that old elevator. Claire took it right up, however, and then disappeared into her room. I remember having the feeling that I might not see her again for a while. The place was crowded with members of Miles's entourage and various people I recognized from the art magazines and the Griffin Gallery. David and Susan were skillfully mixing with their clientele. The only one missing, of course, was Todd. The big fall auctions, eagerly anticipated bellwethers of the art market, were only a couple of weeks away, and the people in that loft weren't going to let any incident, no matter how unfortunate, interrupt the general excitement. Claire had told me how David was holding his breath to see how one of Miles's pieces would fare at the sale, a piece he couldn't totally control. David may have been concerned, but no one else seemed to be. The season was advancing with all its familiar social vigor, with openings almost nightly and all those performances and benefits to go to. Signs of a robust economy had everyone hopeful that the general prosperity might spread to contemporary art. "This could be our best season in years so long as the Fed keeps from raising interest rates," I overheard someone say. But then, there was never a shortage of optimism at that time of year.

Standing conspicuously alone was a young woman I recognized from David's gallery, an assistant working there on the day I watched him sell to that Silicon Valley wunderkind in the killing room. She was the one who had ordered only a muffin when all her other young colleagues were eating expensive sandwiches. I walked over to introduce myself, and she said her name was Rebecca.

"I've been there for almost six months," she said.

"How's it going?" I asked.

She looked around the room. "It's been all right. I mean, I like it, so far."

"You don't sound too enthusiastic."

"No, I'm very happy to be there, really."

"Don't worry, I'm not going to report you."

"And why should I be so sure?" After I told her that I worked at the museum, she opened up. "I would love to be there," she said. "I want to be at a museum or a nonprofit space. This gallery thing just isn't for me. After I first interviewed with Griffin, they told me I didn't get the job. Then this guy I met at a bar who used to work there told me how they knew I was more than qualified to answer their phones, but the positions were reserved for the children of clients. They're like favors."

"I hope that wasn't news to you."

"Okay, so I was a bit naive."

"But you ended up with the job somehow."

"They called me back after one of the other girls they had hired got mugged walking down Crosby Street. Her parents made her come home. That mugging was my lucky break."

"I hope she wasn't hurt," I said.

"She didn't get hurt, just real shook up. She was so distraught after the mugger had run off with her Prada bag."

"She'll probably never come back to New York."

"We should only be so lucky," said Rebecca. "They should give the guy a medal; he's a local hero."

I wondered what could possibly cause such cynicism in someone so young. Then she told me all about her charming two-hundred-square-foot basement apartment in Alphabet City, about her crack-dealing neighbors, about how her air conditioner had been ripped right out of the window in the middle of July. She talked about her huge college loans, her tiny after-tax paycheck, and the clothes everyone at work expected her to wear but that she could never hope to afford. She told me about some guy she had dated who rode a motorcycle, how one night at the end of a meal he excused himself from the table and stepped out of the restaurant to warm up his bike, only he never returned to pay the check and she hadn't heard from him since. "At least we never slept together," she said. By the end of her confession I was surprised she hadn't gone on an angry, resentment-filled SoHo killing spree, perched high above lower Broadway with an assault rifle and a Prada bag full of ammo.

"Things are going well for this guy," she said, pointing across the room to Miles. "He just won some prestigious European prize, and everyone is so excited about his new house," she said.

"What new house?"

"Didn't you hear? Miles just purchased a beach house *with a history* somewhere along the eastern end of Long Island. He rented it last summer and had such a grand time that he bought it. He did everything out there, even playing in that benefit softball game. He played shortstop and got hit in the head by a Mort Zuckerman line drive. He was all swollen, and he wore the injury around like a badge of honor. He couldn't wait for people to ask him about it at dinner and everything. He got more mileage out of that proud injury than anything he had done in years."

"Who's the guy over there?" I asked her. "He looks familiar."

"You mean that dandy sitting next to the brunette?" I nodded. "That's their lawyer," she said.

"You think his collar is high enough?"

"Maybe for Lloyd's of London. Look at the knot on his tie. I thought that was a lost art."

Entertained, I looked at her. "You would be a valued source of gossip on Miles Levy and company," I said.

"Oh, I talk to everyone. I'm their worst nightmare, an anonymous disgruntled employee. You remember that item last month about how the gallery was being audited by the IRS?"

"No, I must have missed it."

"Well, I was the one who leaked it."

"Why are you telling me this?"

"I don't know. You don't look like you fit in here, so it doesn't seem like much of a risk. Besides, what are they going to do, take away my health insurance? Maybe *if I had* health insurance." It struck me how she was the only sane person there, and yet in some terrible subversive way the place was driving her crazy, making her leak gossip items, making her aware of all the frivolity, making her play their games with their rules. "If you stick around here long enough, you'll never be yourself again," she said. Incredibly, I thought I had finally found it: the one thing David and Susan couldn't manipulate to their advantage, the one loose cog in their wheel; and she wasn't even on their radar screen. Her kind was the most threatening, since she wasn't vested in any way. She had decided there was nothing to lose, nothing to be afraid of anymore. Rebecca was what Claire should have been—but then Rebecca didn't know everything about what went on there, at least not the most important details.

I found David standing at the balcony looking down at the studio. "Stuart," he said, "I wonder if I could have a moment with you." He had on his uniform: fine white shirt buttoned to the top, a pair of black jeans, and comfortable loafers. He affected a casual style meant to put people at ease, but for me it did the opposite, since I found it so carefully calculated.

"You know my daughter Fiona, right?" He pointed her out in the crowd.

"No, I haven't had the pleasure."

"She's at Warner's, one of those development girls. She's getting married next month."

"Congratulations. Who's the lucky groom?"

"A young Hollywood agent, represents a lot of TV writers."

"Is that right?"

"I wanted to have Barbara Kruger do the invitations to the wedding, you know, in that signature block type of hers." He held up his hands as if laying type. "I thought it could say something like: Marriage, Union, Bondage."

"Sure, that would have been great," I said.

"Yeah, but it never worked out, she was busy at the time." He took a sip from his glass and then looked over at his daughter and seemed contemplative. "She's beautiful, isn't she?"

"Very nice," I said. "Good luck with her."

"My son Josh just made partner at Goldman, the youngest ever."

"That's great."

"Yeah, but it doesn't mean what it used to," he said.

"So what did you want to talk to me about?" I asked, getting edgy.

"I wanted to run an idea by you. I'm about to start an Old Master prints-and-drawings division of the Griffin Gallery. How would you like to run it for me, I mean, really be in charge? Look, I'm well established in the contemporary field. What I need is someone with your background and expertise to give this venture some instant credibility."

I guessed that this was what he had always been after. It certainly explained his welcoming me into his gallery to watch him sell. It also struck me as his attempt to keep me on the right side. "I appreciate the recognition, really, especially coming from you. But I already work in a curator's wet dream. It would take a lot to make me leave the museum."

"Everyone knows you're Kohlman's protégé. He's a great figure, a real legend, but someday you'll have to break out on your own. I'm planning this operation with a big budget. You can travel the world and buy anything you think we should have. We'll rent space on Fifty-seventh Street. Prime space with big windows and a sun-filled library with shelves made of polished maple. If you think the museum is a wet dream, I will make this the best sex you ever had."

"How about a leggy receptionist with a curt phone manner and a cute young assistant named Whitney?"

He laughed. "I know just the girl. You see, you could get into this. I knew you could."

"I'm only joking. I just don't see myself contributing to the brain drain of academics who go to work for private dealers."

"It's a false distinction. You'll learn that one day."

"We try hard to keep art in the hands of the public."

"The public? How often does the public really have access to the stuff you guys keep in that vault? As much as you'd like to think of yourself as a public servant, what you really are is a person of a different kind of privilege. You get to see and appreciate these things every day, while the public has to wait for you to determine what it can see and what it cannot. The public only gets to see a trickle of art that is tightly controlled, more tightly than in private collections, if you want the truth."

"Well, then, if it's such a privilege, why change?"

"This is a hell of an opportunity, Stuart. Look, go home and think about it. My endeavors tend to be very successful, and my associates are always generously compensated. Miles just closed on a summer house," he said, as if to prove the point.

"I heard."

He looked surprised. "Who told you?"

"I don't remember offhand."

"Six acres on Georgica Pond," he said, putting his hand on my shoulder. "The renovation should be done by Memorial Day. I hope we'll see you out there." Then he came close, his head near mine, his eyes looking past me, and said in a low voice, "By the way, the other night, I know you did the right thing."

I decided to leave and walked down the stairs to the studio, where I saw Christina standing with her arms folded and looking at one of the big canvases. "What the hell are you doing here?" I asked her.

"This is my job," she returned. "What the hell *are you* doing here?"

"I don't even know anymore."

"Well, I'm getting a lot out of this place."

"Chrissie, you should really think long and hard about that."

199

"What's your problem?"

"I'm very confused at the moment."

"You look it."

"Do I really?"

"I've been thinking about what you said, about how this art is political. I think you're wrong about it. I mean, you know that piece against violence that got so much attention?"

"What about it?"

"It was powerful. Makes me feel good about promoting this stuff."

"Chrissie, if you only knew."

"Don't give me this 'Chrissie' bullshit."

"Tell me this, how many card-carrying members of the National Rifle Association attended the Whitney Biennial? How many serial rapists? Two? Three? It's not the hardest thing in the world to be against violence. But it is hard to be eloquent about it, and that piece was so clumsily conceived. But that's not even the beginning of its complete dishonesty."

"I think you're really out of touch, I think you've just completely lost it. You and Hilton Kramer."

"Hilton Kramer? That's not fair. I gave this stuff a chance. I was never against Miles's work, never just opposed to it no matter what. But now I know there's fraud going on here."

She sighed in disgust. "What are you talking about? You're going out of your mind, Stuart. You're so unbearably earnest about everything, not to mention totally paranoid. Just leave me alone, go back uptown to Kohlman and your sleepy little world of Old Master worship. Isn't that where you belong?"

"I wish I knew. At least you know what you want. At least you're content," I said, then went home.

seventeen

IT LOOKED as if someone had turned my apartment upside down and shaken it violently. Everything was on the floor—clothes, photographs; the shelves of my medicine cabinet were wiped out, the lamps knocked over. My books were everywhere, an old copy of *The Death and Life of Great American Cities* by Jane Jacobs lying facedown by the window. A few things were missing: my family's antique watches, the VCR, and a small, modest piece of Greek pottery, the only antiquity I had ever owned. But the most curious thing about this burglary was how the intruders had deliberately broken my protomodern chairs. They were smashed, the wood split into small pieces and left in a pile near the bookcase.

I had never felt unsafe in that old building, even then, after the landlord had convinced everyone else to move out and the entire place was empty. Maybe it was because I had never been the victim of anything like this. I had never been mugged, assaulted, or burglarized. I lived my life as if those things happened to other people, not me. I never thought twice about dark streets or late-night subways, and I hoped this wouldn't change that. For several days there had been a pattern of curious coincidences that I attributed to the landlord. My mailbox was pried open several times, my phone line made an odd clicking noise every time I placed a call, the gas for the stove was suddenly turned off, and regulating the hot water had become a touch-and-go experience every morning. I had been doing well in my stubborn defiance of these tactics, proud that I could frustrate any effort to reverse my entrenchment. But this break-in made me terribly uneasy; it seemed such a Sicilian Mafia–like message. I called Christina later to tell her.

"Are you all right?"

"Yes, although I feel a little violated. They got in through the window."

"They? You think it was more than one?"

"There were cigarette butts left all over. I counted at least three different brands. Maybe it was Vogel's people."

"Yeah, right. Be serious."

"He wants me out desperately. Last week he started screwing with the hot water, this week there's no gas for the stove."

"You're paranoid. It was probably just a couple of thieves, crack addicts."

"Why would they break the chairs? What were they, thieves with a dislike for Mackintosh and Rietveld? Some burglars who just happened to be violently opposed to Modernism?"

"Don't be ridiculous, Stuart. He's a big developer with a legitimate reputation."

"A legitimate businessman? You really are becoming a good flack. You're starting to sound like Susan, spinning everything with perfectly formed sound bites. Why don't you go work for the Vogel Development Corporation?"

"Look, you can stay at my place if you need to."

"I'll be all right. But thanks."

Christina was right: It couldn't have been Vogel. Part of me wanted to be able to pin everything on him. It would have been convenient, and a good boost for my morale as well.

But I realized how illogical it was as I settled in to clean the place. I didn't care about what was taken. What I minded was the knowledge that someone had been going through my stuff. At least I had the decency to put everything back when I had done it.

Jenny from the museum called just as I was considering whether to arrange my books by size or by subject. I remember what a difficult time she had breaking the news to me, her words disjointed, her voice soft. She wasn't making much sense until she decided to be simple and direct. "Harlan passed away," she said finally. "He suffered a heart attack in his sleep. The maid found him this morning. I'm so sorry, Stuart."

I wished at that moment that I could have had one last day with Kohlman because I knew he still had more to teach. But just one more day would have never done. What would I have asked him had I been given the chance? Something about the nature of creativity? Definitely not. It would have been much more mundane: What was that tobacco blend he sometimes smoked in little carefully rolled cigarettes? And wine. He always promised to give me a quick course about wine. I know he thought California reds were a joke, and I wanted to know about all those French labels that were always at the tip of his tongue. And there were a few great stories he had. He once told me of meeting Piet Mondrian near the end of his life, just when the artist had painted *Broadway Boogie-Woogie*. Kohlman used to talk about knowing Mies van der Rohe in the late forties, about how Mies had shown him how to make the perfect martini, demonstrating his famous attention to detail. I wanted to hear those stories once more, and maybe even write them down.

I wanted to know all Kohlman knew, to have all of his abilities, all his style and judgment transferred to me as if they were pieces of his estate. But more than that, I realized how much I would miss him, his spirit and wit, his calm, confident criticism. Kohlman had been my safety net, a place to run to whenever I found the real world troublesome. I'm not sure how long I expected him to live, since I never thought about those things. He always seemed the same age to me. I had known him only at the end of his long life, and he had always just been an old man, not on his deathbed, but simply a white-haired citizen, with just as much life in him as the next person. Everyone was aware of his chronic heart trouble. When he had gone in for surgery a year earlier, the museum allowed a rare change in an exhibition schedule so he could curate it after his recuperation. He assured everyone he would come through fine, as if he were giving them his word of honor. He came back sharper than ever. Not this time, though. Now he wasn't coming back, and at that point I still felt lucky to have known him.

I had a specific memory of being a student of his in graduate school. There were about a dozen of us waiting to get back our papers on the iconography of the Counter-Reformation, and we were all tense because he had hinted that there were problems with everybody's work. Everybody but one, it turned out. One day around that time he took me aside into his office, sat me down, and reached into his old leather case. I was surprised when he brought out all the other students' papers and began showing them to me. He held up examples of faulty research and wrongheaded opinions that he found humorous. He never bothered to hide the names as he made fun of them. He could be rude that way:

In private, when he trusted you, he would sometimes let down those good manners. I realized just then what a weakness this was of his. At the time I thought he was such a great guy to be letting me in on this, to be confiding in me like that, and I was grateful. But now, recalling the incident for no particular reason after hearing the news of his death, I finally understood how all the other students had suffered so unfairly from these private moments we had.

I screened my calls as messages piled up from those expressing their concern. The news spread quickly, and I never knew so many people were aware of how close Kohlman and I had been. I tried calling Claire. There was no answer at the loft, so I tried the auction house and she picked up. "So what's going on?" she said quickly and with disinterest. For some reason I decided not to tell her about Kohlman. Had she answered the phone differently, I might have.

"Nothing, I just wanted to talk."

"The big auction is next week. We're so busy."

"Will it be a good sale?" I didn't know what else to say. I just wanted to hear her voice.

"It's hard to tell. Everyone's on edge. We're all hoping the big money shows up and is willing to spend. By the way, do you want a ticket to the evening sale? We're sending them out tomorrow. I can add your name to the list."

"Sure," I said, even though I didn't care.

"I have to go, I'm really busy with everything, but we'll talk soon, I promise."

"Claire, wait." I had a change of heart. "Harlan Kohlman died over the weekend. He had a heart attack."

"Oh my God, Stuart. I'm so sorry." She paused and I said nothing. "I know how close you were," she said. "I envied you for that, really I did. It would be so nice to have a great coach like that. My boss makes me ill. It's too bad it wasn't my boss," she said, and I laughed subtly. I surprised myself. It felt like the first time I had laughed in days. She laughed along with me. It was brief but wonderful relief for a moment. I was glad I had called her, glad I had forced her to stay on the line at the last minute.

"It's good to hear your voice," I said.

"You sound like you're okay."

"I don't know yet. I hope so."

There was something positive in seeing Kohlman's obituary above the fold. Going through the paper at my desk at work, I found it on page B9. It was written by the *Times*'s chief art critic and was accompanied by an old photograph of Kohlman from 1981. Why didn't they have anything more recent?

I did my best to keep everything inside, to not show a lot of emotion at work that day. There was no real reason, it just seemed the easiest course. The phone calls I needed to make got made, the writing I needed to do got done, the people I needed to meet with were met with. I was getting through my day with a kind of cold productivity. In the afternoon I oversaw the hanging of a group of drawings, and everything rushed to the surface when a colleague disagreed with me about the placement of a frame.

"It shouldn't go there," she said. "Maybe more to the left."

"No," I said. "It's fine where it is."

"There's a terrible glare. Why not move it to the left, Stuart?"

"The frames should have equal distance between them."

"It's more important to cut down on glare than to worry about symmetry," she said.

I raised my voice. "I'll decide what's more important, all right?" The people around me were silent for a beat.

"Gee, take it easy," said one of them.

I felt terrible for yelling at her. "I'm sorry," I said, shaking my head. "I'm sorry, Liz. I don't know what's wrong with me."

"Don't worry. We're all a little under right now," she said kindly. I looked at the wall of drawings for a moment, embarrassed.

"You're right. The glare is bad right there. You're a much better hanger than I am. You always were." Unable to concentrate on the work, I excused myself and went to my office, shaking. I put my head down on the desk and tried to think about nothing.

I took the next day off and went up to visit my mother. Ever since her divorce she had lived just off Riverside Drive way up in the Nineties. Riding up there on the subway I saw an old man sitting at the end of the car who reminded me of Kohlman for just an instant, but then I realized how they looked nothing like each other. It was on that loud, speeding subway car, sitting in comfortable New York anonymity, that I felt unsure about what lay ahead for the first time in years.

My mother had lived in that building long enough to see all the doormen change, along with many of the old windows, for newer, sharper-looking ones. The one thing that could never change, however, was the slight, ever-present odor of food cooking. The result of years of simmering chicken soup, the ghost of fried onions past, it had somehow managed to soak itself into the walls of the hallways on every floor. I always found the subtle smell, so common in buildings of that age, to be reassuring.

"They're tearing up Columbus Avenue again," she said as I walked into her living room. She always looked good for her age. She wore very little makeup, and her naturally dark hair was tied back. She was a kind, sometimes neurotic woman who read a lot of Holocaust fiction and attended community board meetings to speak out against developers like Harry Vogel. I guess I was very much her son in this last regard.

"They've been working on it forever, that's just the way it is," I told her.

"But why do they need to tear it up every six months? Just fix everything once, and then leave it alone," she said, exasperated.

I noticed a dog-eared paperback sitting on the table. "Are you reading this Cynthia Ozick novel again?"

"I was only showing it to a friend."

"I don't believe you."

"Fine, don't believe me," she said.

"You're reading it again, aren't you?"

"So what if I am?"

"How many times are you going to read it, six million?"

"That's not funny."

We walked into the kitchen, and I took a slice of zucchini bread she had baked.

"Use the knife," she told me. "Who's this girl your sister tells me about?"

"Who?" I said with a full mouth.

"Come on, Stuart, I know about her."

"Well then, if you know all about her, why do I need to tell you?" I said smiling, but not looking at her.

"Christina only tells me a little."

"Her name's Claire. I've known her maybe a month at the most. But it's nothing really, I mean, I think we've stopped seeing each other."

"What do you mean, 'you think'?"

I picked at the bread right off the cutting board. "All I know is it's not going anywhere." I never liked to talk about these things with her because it took so long just to get her up to speed: the where did you meet her, what does she do, where's she from, where does she live, and all that. And then when I do explain everything I always end up feeling guilty that I didn't let her know more all along.

"So, what will happen now?"

"With what?" I asked.

"At the museum. Will you take Kohlman's place?"

"Of course not, Mom. I can't take his place. I don't have the reputation or the experience. It has to go to a much older person, a well-known figure."

"So you'll have to work for someone new."

"Yeah, probably someone I don't even know."

"What about teaching? Herb Bloom told me that Columbia is looking for some art-history faculty."

"I don't want to teach. I haven't got the patience. Besides, there isn't any good art up at Columbia. I need to be near the drawings. I can't imagine what I'd do without those drawings. And the Dutch painting, I can't live without those paintings."

"It's not like the Vermeers won't be there anymore." She laughed. "I mean, you can always go and visit."

"You don't know what it means just to be able to walk around them during my lunch hour," I said.

"I don't want you to be static. It would be too easy to spend the rest of your life there if you're not careful," she said. None of this had much credibility coming from her, but I also knew she was right.

Standing there in the kitchen, I remembered being about twelve years old and sitting at a small dinner party with my parents. My mother had several friends over that night, and my sister was eating at another table with her friends, away from the adults. But my mother never expected me to sit with the other kids; she seemed to enjoy the fact that I wanted to be at the big table. That I related to adults with more ease than I did with people my own age felt like such an advantage back then. Everyone welcomed me to keep up with the conversation. I remember one man who said he was a journalist got to talking with me on some subject that I can't recall, but he never treated me as a twelve-year-old kid, taking everything I said with seriousness and respect, as if I were his peer. I was enjoying the treatment so much that it was a long time before I noticed everyone watching me, even the kids at the smaller table. I didn't know whether they thought something was seriously wrong with me or had simply been amused, but I'll never forget the way my sister's friends looked at me, every one of them so curious and confused by my behavior.

My mother stopped me at the door before I left her that afternoon. "Before you go, Stuart, take your coat."

"What coat?"

She pulled an old winter coat of mine from out of a nearby closet. "It's getting cold now. You have a coat here you should wear."

"Mom, I don't fit into this thing anymore. I've got plenty of coats."

"Warm like this?"

"It must be ten years old. Why do you still have it lying around?"

I had to leave before she might offer me her Channel 13 membership tote bag, or maybe ask me to go with her to see Fran Lebowitz at the 92nd Street Y. "I'll see you soon, I promise."

eighteen

On the day there was to be a service for Kohlman, an article about him appeared in the *Times* with revelations about his past that had escaped that comprehensive obituary. An author researching art stolen in Europe during the Second World War had unearthed documents that linked Kohlman to the looting that took place in occupied France. The article maintained that his signature appeared over and over on recently discovered German cargo and shipping documents. It talked of cattle cars filled with Renoirs and Monets and Rubenses and Rembrandts. There were also long inventory lists of artworks confiscated from wealthy Jewish homes, many of which had Kohlman's name attached to them. The author, who was to publish her book the following year, made her findings public after reading of Kohlman's death. The article quoted several people who remembered him as a young scholar in his twenties. They said he was pressed by the Nazis to select and catalogue the work. Most of it was shipped to Berlin, and not all of it has been accounted for over the years.

Incredibly, a small portrait of a ballerina by Degas that

hung in Kohlman's apartment was being inspected by authorities to see if it was in fact from one of these looted French collections. I read the article over several times. Each time I finished it, each time I came to the end of the last paragraph, I would go back up to the top and read it again, hoping to find something I had missed, something that might change the facts.

At first I refused to believe what I was reading. They must have the wrong man, I thought, a different person with the same name. None of the timing fit the few stories he had told me. He always said he was running from the war. But there was no denying the great wealth of disgusting evidence. It all stunned me, and I was at such a loss to explain so much of what I had believed, of what I had been taught by the man and learned so well. Now part of me wanted to unlearn it all, to never have been associated with him, to wash it all out and start over. The truth about Kohlman was not only bizarre but painful. For days I could think of nothing else, and from then on his name would fill me with anger, anger that he had lied to me, anger that he could have been so flawed, and also anger at myself for having put so much stock in him. He never knew those other European expatriates. As vivid as those details about meeting Mondrian and Mies were, they had to have been lies, part of his cover.

There were too many open questions. Had he sympathized with the fascists? Did he know that some of the works came from Jewish families? Was he aware of the fate of those families? Even if Kohlman had been forced to do what he did, even if he was not an anti-Semite, even if he hated his orders and believed, falsely, that he was saving the art from destruction in the war, he had still lied. He had covered up the embarrassing episode and now might even turn out to have been a crook, if that Degas proved to be a *souvenir*. Part of me thought it all quite absurd. I pictured Kohlman sitting in his apartment off Fifth Avenue with the looted painting and telling friends how little he had paid for it at a fire sale, or something like that. But it hurt much more than it amused. It hurt because I thought he was a believer in the standards that I cherished. I wanted to still believe in those standards, even if for him they had been a sham.

As a student I had learned from him a certain way to look at the world, a theory of art, a system for comparing various acts of creative expression and building out of that analysis a history of art that could be passed down. All of that was in pieces now. The only way to continue would be to pick up the broken shards and make from them a new system I might call my own.

Kohlman's funeral was, predictably, awkward. The service was held just one block from the museum, at the Frank E. Campbell funeral home, and I remember the terrible feeling that everyone was looking at me. Even Jenny, who had always been so warm and whom I had worked closely with, seemed to have made a point of not sitting next to me. Later she said she wasn't feeling well and didn't want me to catch her cold, and I do remember her severe cough, *but still.* When the short service was over, I left there not knowing how difficult it would be to return to work. Before, I could try to suppress emotion and continue on in the knowledge that what I was doing had the man's grace, his spirit still attached. Now I didn't want that association. At work the department of drawings was more quiet than usual, which meant that it was silent. The search for a new head was under way, and everyone was trying to figure out how Kohlman had been able to hide his secrets for so long. Although no one had been more closely identified with him than myself, I was unconcerned that anyone might ever hold it against me. Maybe it was just my belief that merit would always prevail, or maybe I assumed that people would understand how I had been fooled just like everyone else. The only thing I knew how to do was go on with my work and wait and see how people would react. But within a matter of days it was impossible to ignore how these revelations about Kohlman's life had quickly become the buzz of the art world, not to mention the entire museum and cultural community.

A reporter called at work asking me to comment on the matter, and I remember thinking that what Kohlman really could have used was some advice from Über-publicist Susan Edelman. I was sure that she would have found a way to turn the story around, some way to make Kohlman look like a victim. Sitting at my desk with the reporter on the phone, I imagined her pitching the Nuremberg defendants as clients in that edgy staccato manner of hers: *All you guys really need is some good spin. And you, Speer, get your face at the right parties, be seen at the runway shows, and everything else will follow. We'll give new meaning to the word* rehabilitation.

"Did he ever tell you about those years before he came to New York?" asked the reporter, who said his name was Garcia.

"No," I answered, still in a daze. "He rarely discussed it. He once told me that he came over as a refugee, said that he found work at the New School and then at Columbia. Maybe you should ask them what they knew."

"But surely he must have confided in you something of his past. I'm told that you were very close to him."

"Told by whom?"

"Michelle White at the Getty Museum. She told me all about how you were his protégé."

That bitch. "I wouldn't go that far," I said.

"So, then, you knew nothing?"

"Right, he never spoke of it. I'm as shocked as anyone. He used to talk about befriending certain figures of the period. But it was all self-serving." Then he asked me about Kohlman's politics, about his opinions on art, what kind of critic he was.

"Is it possible to see him as a Paul de Man–like figure?"

"I guess it's possible."

"You think people he criticized might use this as some kind of vindication?"

"I guess there's always that risk," I said, only hoping he would quote me accurately.

I called Claire again at the auction house but with no luck. I left three messages, one in the morning, one at noon, and then another at the end of the day. I tried her again for three straight days as I left for lunch, each time from the bank of pay phones at the monumental entrance to the museum. I resigned myself to the fact that she was avoiding me. Was it because of Miles? The accident? Even Kohlman perhaps? I decided to go and watch her one afternoon at a place where I knew she would be.

I stood inside the doorway to one of the townhouses on 72nd Street and watched the uniformed children in front of the school across the street. After several minutes I saw little Lisbeth waiting at the curb for her Aunt Claire. The girl looked prettier than I had remembered and was in animated conversation with a crowd of young friends. Then Claire came to meet her, walking quickly, her legs pulling on the narrow wrap of her skirt as she stepped. She smiled and knelt down to straighten the girl's clothes and lightly brush her hair. There was something about the way Claire looked at Lisbeth that made me sad. Maybe I saw sadness in Claire's eyes or maybe it was the way she seemed to be so affected by the presence of the little girl.

I wanted to step out from my hiding place to cross the street and be with them, but I stayed where I was for a moment. Then it was too late. Lisbeth said good-bye to her friends and took Claire's hand as the pair walked toward the avenue and out of my view. I remembered the time I first saw Claire at that party before we even knew each other, where she walked off with one of those nice books and I figured, wrongly, that I could write her off. Now it felt as if she were someone I still needed to be introduced to, as if she had never known me, as if her life had resumed almost uninterrupted by our brief time together. I realized then that she too was hiding something, she too had a little surprise to spring, and I understood exactly what it was. Lisbeth meant a whole lot more to her than I had ever imagined.

nineteen

I THOUGHT FOURTEEN times was a bit extreme. That's how much my rent would increase, according to a letter from the Vogel people that was left at my door. They now claimed that I had to pay the "market rate" for my apartment because my aunt had not been married to my uncle during the years she had lived there and was therefore not a legal family link in the transfer of a rent-controlled apartment. I couldn't begin to understand how they had come to know this arcane detail, nineteen years after the fact. I imagined them paying teams of private investigators, researchers, archivists, and genealogists to dig up anything that might allow them to win. At that point I admitted to myself just how much I was wearying of all this. At one time I had looked forward to years of long, drawn-out litigation as a fine opportunity to educate myself in the subtleties of real estate law. But I wasn't sure I still had the passion to go on with this, the steely patience it would require. Maybe there was something in Todd's death, something in seeing his life cut so short, that made me want to live life a little more quickly. I felt as if I were way too young to be holding out, to be lingering like this.

After reading the letter from my clever, tenacious adversaries, I thought about that dealer who had come to Kohlman's apartment to get his Dutch landscape painting appraised. I had downgraded his property, gutted its value, taken away his sale. I remember how upset he was, not just with the opinion, but with me, with all my false righteousness, my unbearable, self-satisfied precocity. There was something about the almost total subjectivity of connoisseurship that only now began to bother me. It was like those Dutchmen of the dreaded Rembrandt Research Project who had been traveling the world to take the master's name off half the works attributed to him. Those for whom "circle of" was not good enough were never moved by the art in the first place, only the name. But if Rembrandt's imitators were once good enough to hang under one name, why not another? And if he could be so widely imitated, then what was so unique about him in the first place? But you couldn't start asking those questions, you couldn't begin down that road, because then everything would start to unravel.

In my business, from where Kohlman and I stood, doubt ruled, doubt was the mode of operation, doubt was our currency, our language. There had been too much of it, though, and what I needed then was a little faith. For Miles and David and Susan, faith was the essential commodity. They had a monopoly on faith, and they used it to raise mountains, build bridges, and live their lives. That English dealer with the questionable Van Goyen had been wronged in some way. Kohlman never looked at his painting, and yet he signed his name to my attribution as if it were his own. I was misrepresenting the work I had done. It wasn't just a few letters; I had ghostwritten whole articles and countless pages of catalogue copy for him. It was just like Todd doing the work for Miles, and the artist simply signing off on things as Claire had described it. We were guilty of the same kinds of sins, and we didn't even know it.

* * *

For the first time I could remember, the museum no longer interested me. I spent long afternoons in front of highly important drawings and priceless seventeenth-century artist's sketchbooks and failed to be impressed by the privilege. These objects now struck me as irrelevant. I could only picture Claire and Miles living at the loft. I even thought about the rising price of a Miles Levy canvas and of my little sister peddling his myth. I found myself drawn back to the loft, of course, as everything about that place still intrigued me. Perhaps it bothered me that I did not feel missed, more likely I just needed to be with Claire, but a strong and odd attraction to Miles's world and his accomplices led me back there again despite my better judgment.

Several nights after receiving that letter from my landlord I walked down to Mercer Street. I rang the buzzer marked 4 and hoped so much that Claire would answer. Instead, as usual, I was allowed in without anyone ever asking who it was. Given what a big, dangerous city New York is and considering the vulnerability of a wealthy home like Miles's, I admired the casual risk that this small detail implied. After my own experience with burglary, it seemed positively heroic. Perhaps so many different people came and went there that Miles had simply tired of the formality of asking who it was. Maybe it was all just part of his carefully cultivated persona. There was no way to ever know for sure. This time I felt competent at running that manual elevator, and I walked into the loft after bringing the car to a perfect landing.

"Come to see Claire?" said Miles, looking down at me from the edge of the balcony. "Well, she's not here. She hasn't been home before midnight in days." He walked down the stairs toward me.

"Where is she?"

"The auction, you know. She's practically never here." Then he looked at me. "Sorry about Kohlman. I always knew that guy was a fascist."

"I'm learning that not everything is always as it seems."

"The sooner you learn that, the better off you'll be."

I shook my head. "It's all so bizarre."

"I hate to say this to you, but his rhetoric just got watered down after the war. Instead of railing against degenerate art, he started talking about standards. It's the same thing."

"We don't know all of the details."

"Don't start with denial now." He lit a cigarette and then blew smoke. "Mind if I smoke?"

"Funny, you never asked before," I said.

"I forgot that you don't like smoke. We had that little war of wits at Pied Noir over it, remember? Anyway, you want one?"

"Sure." I took one out of the attractive blue package and lit it with his polished silver lighter. Then I tried not to show how much I was enjoying it.

"Look," he said, "the problem with critics, or for that matter anyone with an opinion, is that everything boils down to two camps. It's either old fuddy-duddy conservatism like Kohlman, or it's this 'let's bring down the academy' foolishness. Everyone in between is a phony because they'll always end up gravitating toward one extreme or the other. The trick is to find your natural gravitational pull."

"It doesn't strike me as much of a choice," I said.

"You just have to figure out where you belong."

He got up to look for an ashtray near one of his worktables and after not finding one decided to tip his ashes onto a palette that looked brand-new. "I never did thank you for covering me," he said. "I mean, I realize you must have had a hard time figuring out what to do after the accident, and I want you to know that I appreciate your—" he searched for the right word, "discretion."

"The strange thing is, I don't know why I did it. I don't even know why I'm here."

"You did it because it felt right, and you're here because you want to be. Sometimes things are just that simple." He looked at me and smiled. "Come over here, I want to show you something."

I followed him to a long, gray metal flat file, and from the bottom drawer he pulled out a large black portfolio.

"What is it?"

"Drawings," he said, opening the dust-filled cover to reveal an exquisitely rendered portrait of a nude woman's backside, her head turned toward the viewer. It was a powerfully dark take on the human form, filled with a lot of troubling psychology. Miles lifted the thick page, its image drawn in pencil and charcoal, to show me dozens of figurative drawings. There were so many that at one point he was lifting and turning them over so fast I had trouble seeing what they were of.

"They're very good. Who did them?" I asked.

"I did them."

I looked at him. "When?"

"Years ago, when I was just out of school."

I looked back at all the drawings and then laughed, a short, quiet hiss of a laugh.

"You're surprised, aren't you?" he said.

"Honestly, yes. Although I see why it makes perfect sense now."

He gave a smile of satisfaction, the way a teacher does when his student grasps a concept. "I remember how you said it's the ability to recognize irony that separates us from all other animals."

"I said that?"

"You did, one night when we were at Pied Noir." He began to put the drawings away. "I've always loved these," he said. "But no one makes a living with figurative drawing anymore. Not this living anyway. They're not commercial. This stuff was so out of fashion when I was breaking in that they stopped teaching it. I learned it all myself. Someone once said that you need to learn the rules before you can break them. I believe that. I have always believed that."

"You went on to break them, all right. Why are you showing me these, anyway?"

"Because I knew you would appreciate them," he said. "I thought of them when I read about Kohlman. Something about people reinventing themselves, perhaps?"

"But these drawings are very good, I mean, really skillful."

"I still draw bodies," he said. "Although now they're very different. I try to make them awkward, wrongly proportioned, not true to life. You see, to me there was always something elitist about this kind of skill."

"That's not a bad thing," I said. "We like virtuoso performance, we respond well to it. It's part of our nature. People cheered Willie Mays because he was good at what he did, he was an elite. There's nothing wrong with virtuosity."

He shrugged. "Why is it that everything to you is either competent or incompetent? How did you ever get to see the world that way?"

"I wish I knew. I hate it. I don't want to see things that way anymore."

"When I started out I wanted to be pure and just make art for myself," he said. "I never cared to be in fashion, I never thought I would sell out, and I was determined not to bend. But then slowly I changed my art, I changed it so much to become a success that by the end it was no longer even my art. Everyone goes through a similar experience, albeit on a different level. But it's the same. There's no difference between compromising a little bit and totally selling out. No one was ever better than me at totally selling out. I just took it over the top, to a new level, to its logical conclusion. That's where I became a real virtuoso." He looked at me for a moment, then asked, "Did you know about Kohlman? I mean, did he ever tell you anything?"

"Everything he ever said about his past was a lie."

"He was a mythic figure. You thought he was pure, but he represented something that was never real."

"Only as fake as some of the works you've tried to pass off. I mean the works that were never really yours, all that work Todd did for you."

"Quit resisting. I showed you those drawings so that you could reevaluate my technical ability. But now you know that I suppressed that stuff for something more commercially viable. Call me a media-hyped sellout, call me anything you want, but understand at least that purity does not exist, that everyone is partially corruptible and that we all choose our moments of honesty with great care." He kept his eyes on me, waiting for my reaction. "Look at you," he went on. "You live in a fucking rent-controlled apartment. You're being subsidized by every other New Yorker for no good reason."

"It's not the money. It's the broader point."

"Oh, yes, *preservation*. Finley, you and I both know the only thing being preserved is your disposable income," he said and laughed.

I said nothing and walked over to one of the large canvases, a work that I now knew had been created by Todd. I inspected it up close and then took it in from several feet away.

"I don't know," Miles said. "Maybe one day we'll wake up to find that it's all gone, the gig will be over. I'll no longer be considered important. No one will buy anymore, no more groupies hanging around the place, no more young artists coming up to me in restaurants to pay their respects." He shook his head, "Poor SOBs, every one of them. You know, I think about that day."

"I'm sure you do."

"Yeah, but I've been pretty good at putting that day off. The fact is, I've become a master at putting that day off."

The two of us stood there looking at the painting in silence, and something from him came through to me at that moment, something so simple and clear and perfect. I understood then that his art was only partly on that canvas; the rest was in the compromises. The genius was in the compromises.

"You know, Miles," I said finally, "what you have really become is just a different kind of elite, and I think you're right, this *is* virtuoso performance."

A bit later he offered me a drink, I asked for another cigarette, and the two of us talked all night. I remember him bringing out a couple of large glasses and a bottle of bourbon with a silver horse atop its cork that looked like an elegant hood ornament. He poured a generous amount into each glass and then handed me one of them and said, "Let's get lit."

"Wouldn't this be better on the rocks?" I asked.

"No way," he said. "What should we drink to?"

"Whatever you like."

"How about to the New York School, to Pollock and Motherwell and Rothko and Clement Greenberg."

"Why are you so obsessed with them?"

"Because they were the real thing," he said as he turned the glass up at his lips.

I had hardly recovered from the system shock of that first drink before he poured another. "Barneys just asked me to do one of their Christmas windows," he said. "I have to come up with something by the end of next week. But I have no idea what to do for it. What do you think? Give me some ideas."

"I can't tell you what to do."

"Why not?"

"Because," I said.

"It's easy. Just try it."

I thought about it for a moment. What would it take? What would something like this require exactly? I had studied works of art all my life, and yet I had never made one, never even tried, if you didn't include grade school. My first instinct was to think of a work in its various parts, build one just like it, only different. Reverse-engineer something, then slap a new face on it. What was a Warhol silkscreen but a photo of Marilyn Monroe? What were Duchamp's urinals but commercial ceramic? What were Jenny Holzer's blinking signs but cheap LEDs spitting out slogans? Of course each of these was much more than the sum of its parts, and as I sat there trying to suggest something to Miles for this project— to be placed in a Barneys Christmas window, perhaps even alongside a gabardine wool suit and a nice pair of brown buckskin shoes—I couldn't come up with a single thing. He waited patiently, with a smile, as if he knew I would draw a blank. "Well, I mean, I'm sure I could come up with something," I said.

"Like what? Give me *one* idea."

I still had nothing.

"All you need are three things," he said, as if about to reveal the source of cheap, clean, reusable energy. "It has to be clever, with real smart-ass wit. It also has to be original, something no one's done yet."

"What's the third thing?"

"Meaning. It has to be meaningful. But that's the easy

part—that can be finessed. From my experience it's best if others fill that in for you. People buy meaning on faith, as long as you sound like you've given it a little thought. So the hard part is the joke, the clever concept."

"Why not something political? The rain forest, the homeless, fur, anything."

"No way, political art is out now," he said. "There's a new estheticism going on. I have to get on top of that, I have to stay relevant. They say sensuousness is the new buzzword. I want my work to be sensuous."

I shook my head. "Forget it," I said, realizing how Goddamned difficult this was—at this late date, after all that had come before. Were painting and sculpture dead? Was art dead? Had all the good jokes been made? Of course not. There was an endless supply. You just had to be able to *do it*, and I couldn't.

"I'll come up with something at the last minute," he said finally.

"You *really are* making this up as you go along."

He shrugged. "I think film is the next step. I went to that Sundance thing last year and caught the bug. Filmmakers are getting all the attention now, not painters. Susan says it might be the right time to change direction." I took another sip and asked him where he was from.

"I'm from Woodmere, Long Island," he said. "It's a nice normal affluent Jewish suburb, thirty minutes from midtown, with no traffic."

"So you were never that naive midwesterner who came to New York with big dreams, never that anonymous young man struggling to get recognition?"

"Are you kidding? That sounds like something Susan would dream up for a press release. No, I was a sharp kid with well-connected parents who knew exactly what he wanted and how to get it."

"You never went to school?"

He squinted slightly as he gulped the drink and then took his time answering. "I went to school, but dropped out after one semester."

"Where?"

"Cal Arts," he said, pouring himself another. "I think an MFA is a piece of crap," he said loudly. "Do you know how many they turn out every year? Hopeless! Who was it that said art school is very good at preparing you for a life of poverty?" He raised his glass to a toast. "Well, I want that on my tombstone."

Then Miles said something that convinced me that he now either trusted me completely or was just too drunk to know better. He filled my glass again, handed it to me, and admitted his long-held secret desire that after his death he be buried at the Green River Cemetery in Springs, Long Island. To the uninitiated it might have sounded like any old shady resting place. It was, instead, a small, classy, much revered burial ground of the East Coast cognoscenti, filled with art-world figures from the charmed 1950s. People like Jackson Pollock and Lee Krasner, Stuart Davis and Ad Reinhardt, Elaine de Kooning and Frank O'Hara. Every summer a new generation of students, art groupies, and assorted romantics would make pilgrimages to Springs to leave flowers and Camel cigarettes at the Pollock grave, where a natural, uncut rock serves as the headstone and a facsimile of the painter's signature is cast onto its greenish copper plaque. Expecting to have your own plot there is nothing less than hubris. "I'm going to reserve a space," he said. "I'll be just a few feet from Pollock. And maybe we can even get you in there too, a nice little plot next to Frank O'Hara, how does that sound? It can be arranged, you know."

I thought to myself that all of this had to be a joke. But then I realized he wasn't kidding, and that of all the things he had been able to pull off, this would be the easiest. Even though he had no right to be near the great figures who were buried at Green River, I sensed how he did not regard the admission of this strange, obsessive desire to be interred there as revealing of some bald, hollow ambition. Instead it was part of the whole plan, something that would follow logically, fittingly. Hell, by then, if all went well, he might even deserve it, and I never doubted that he would always get exactly what he wanted.

I took another sinus-clearing swallow from my glass and then looked at him. "Is that what you think about, death?"

"Yes," he said. "I want people to be feuding over my estate, arguing as to my intentions. I'm going to leave all the money with a ridiculously ambiguous mandate. People will ask, 'What exactly did he mean by *give grants to further the visual arts?*' No one will win. All the money will be perfectly squandered, every drop siphoned off by lawyers, armies of artistically disinclined lawyers. You know, it's the only way to go."

"You mean we'll still have to endure your name appearing in the gossip columns long after you're dead and buried at Green River?"

"That's right, the ultimate legacy." He raised his glass again. "Here's to my posthumous press clips!" He swallowed, then looked out over his grand loft and said in complete contentment, "I'll always be considered *a good item*."

I got up to leave a bit later, moving slowly, thinking only of going to bed and not at all looking forward to operating that old elevator. "I met Lisbeth, by the way. I think I finally know who she is," I said as I searched for the sleeve openings inside my wool jacket. I only wanted confirmation of what I had come to believe: that the girl was Claire's.

He looked up at me. "She told you?" I said nothing at

first, hoping to draw him out. Then he shook his head and sighed.

"It's your kid, isn't it?"

"And what if it is?"

"Look, I'm not making a judgment here—"

"How refreshing."

"What happened between you and Claire, Miles?"

"What happened? What happened was that little girl, that adorable little girl, that's what happened."

"But she's got a whole other home, I mean, Claire says the girl's her niece."

"It's not her niece. Claire was like twenty-three. Both of us were kind of crazy, a little careless."

"But she didn't have to have the kid."

"Of course not. I mean, this is no home for a child, so the choice seemed pretty obvious. She would have never brought the baby to term except her brother's wife couldn't have children. The woman had some kind of operation and afterward the doctors told her she had, like, a one-in-a-hundred chance of ever bearing a healthy child. Claire said she couldn't end her pregnancy in the face of that. I tried to convince her otherwise, that it would be awkward for everyone. But she had seen them try so many times to have children, only to have their hearts broken." He shook his head. "Miscarriages, the works. Claire was right, though. That kid changed their lives. It was the best thing anyone could ever give them."

"So they adopted her?"

"Right, and I help them. They want the girl to have a bilingual education—you know, the French have this thing about their culture." He rolled his eyes. "I said I would pay for tuition at that fucking French school. Then it was doctor's bills and clothing and whatever else. That's fine, I don't mind paying. They don't have any real money, and God knows I have more than I know what to do with. It's like my good works, you know? Maybe it'll get me into heaven. But I wish I hadn't used it as some kind of leverage over Claire. I don't know why I did, I guess it seemed easy. Claire fell into all my traps, almost willingly."

I walked up the stairs to Claire's bedroom before leaving. The room had always felt temporary to me, as if she had been ready to pick up and leave at any moment, as if she was afraid to put down roots, afraid to get too attached in anticipation of that very day. Her answering machine was blinking with messages, one of them surely mine. She had a miniature leather backpack on the bed, lying open, its contents spilled out from the top: matches, Certs, a health-club photo ID. There was a folded newspaper clipping among the items. I could tell from the way it was folded that it was the party shot of the two of us from that Sunday *Times*. I never expected her to hold on to something like that; I was surprised she, of all people, would think it worth keeping. She was supposed to be too jaded to clip and save any of those shots, and it made me glad to know she was secretly cherishing this one, maybe even taking it out every once in a while to think of me.

I sat on that bed in silence and tried to remember what life had been like before I ever met Miles Levy, when all I knew of him was what they wrote in the newspapers, when I used to come across his picture in a magazine or on *Page Six*, when I spent all my time cooped up in the museum cleaning old drawings, devoted to Kohlman, and Miles Levy was just a symbol of the hothouse world he inhabited. It seemed impossible to put myself back in that old mindset, and it was frustrating not to be able to perceive things through that lens anymore. It was like bad eyesight: The more I strained or tried to correct it, the worse it got.

twenty

I STOOD FIXED, taking in the view from the offices of the Vogel Development Corporation high above 57th Street. Waiting in the reception area for my meeting to begin, I looked out over the city with my hands pressed against the window, a clean wall of plate glass. Clean except for my palm prints. The air above the city had a brownish ozone haze, and from behind the sealed glass wall I could hear none of the street sounds, only the hum of the building's ventilation system working hard to filter out the many urban carcinogens. The view north was unobstructed, and I looked down at Central Park, a rectangle of fall foliage thinned out by the November winds. At the park's edge was a cluster of short attached buildings that made up the various sprawling wings of the Metropolitan Museum of Art, and from where I stood now, that all seemed so far away. That I had finally been persuaded to end my holdout was not the result of any of Vogel's duplicitous ploys, not the emptiness of the building, not the loss of decent plumbing nor the darkness of the unlit hallways. It was not even the inelegant burglary or the stolen mail. In the end there was only one person who could ever convince me, who could deliver the message I needed to hear, who knew all about the curious nobility in selling out. It would have been much too easy to think of Miles as simply cynical. Instead, I now thought of him as a misunderstood hopeless romantic.

When the time for my meeting arrived, I was shown into a large office filled with men in suits, all of them sitting around a coffee table in busy discussion. Here were the men responsible for those insipid white brick boxes. If only there could be an international tribunal to bring them to justice, I thought.

"Ah, Finley," said Harry Vogel. "Good to meet you once and for all. Have a seat, we'll be right with you." I nodded and took my place around the coffee table. He was a big man, and I thought his suits must have been custom-made, not because he cared about taste (since he had none), but because garments that big didn't come off the rack.

His aides were explaining something to him as they pointed to a bunch of charts and blueprints. They seemed afraid of him, looking at one another before speaking and then watching for his reaction.

"There's a bit of bad news," said one of them meekly.

"What now? We've had so many delays, the bankers are breathing down my neck. I was really hoping there wouldn't be any bad news," said Vogel. He was a heavy breather, and the words just kind of slid from his lips as if exiting from the mouth of a big lizard.

The aide swallowed hard and shuffled his papers. "Our suppliers on the Eighth Avenue project are giving us hell. The brick was delivered yesterday, but it's the wrong shade of brown."

"I don't care, use it anyway."

"Fine, but the prefabricated steel trusses for floors nine through twenty-seven haven't arrived at the site yet."

"Where are they?" demanded Vogel. "This little delay is gonna push my interest payments way up. *What the fuck are we gonna do?*"

The aide looked uncomfortable as he shuffled more papers. "Well, we could make up the cost by using some left-over tile on the exterior of the mezzanine rather than the pink granite." He uncurled a big blueprint. "Or we could eliminate the costly stone detailing here at the entrance."

Vogel quickly weighed in with his decision. "Get rid of that granite, use the tile."

"But the community board is gonna scream bloody murder."

"Fuck 'em." He looked at me and smiled. "God, I love cutting corners."

The phone made a high-pitched whirring noise just then, and he answered it. "Yes? Put him through . . . Hello, Sol . . . No, not those fucking Municipal Arts Society people. Don't they have anything better to do? I mean, Jackie O. is dead . . . Tell them we'll promise to refurbish the Seventy-second Street subway station . . . We'll just slap a coat of paint on it . . . What do you mean the mayor won't go along? What the fuck was all that money for? . . . Environmental impact study my ass . . . *Do something,* Sol. Get them off my back."

He hung up the phone, and there was an unbearable silence in the room. Every one of those suits sitting near me had been chilled by ten degrees. Then he turned to me. "So, Stuart, how's the hot water?"

I remember glancing at the other end of that spacious office where there was a scale model of the luxury tower to be built after the demolition of my old rent-controlled apartment. It was worse than I had ever imagined: a tall and bulky structure clad in custard-colored brick, with dark-tinted glass and poured-concrete balconies. Of course I had prepared myself for some hard, smart bargaining, reading up on basic negotiating tactics (I had a *first offer* and a *maximum position*), but now, after laying eyes on this urban affliction masquerading as architecture, I felt I had to make them pay through the nose.

When I walked out of 9 West 57th Street, it was already dark and rush hour had begun. Even though it was getting late, there was one more stop to make. It was that hour of terrible, crawling traffic, trucks and buses moving inch by inch and punching their pedals. Brakes, gas, brakes, gas. Every intersection was a mess of sharply squealing axles, blowing horns, and idle exhaust fumes. It was beginning to rain now. I looked for a cab, but every beat-up yellow sedan in the vicinity had a fare. So I began to walk, and after a while I gave up on catching a taxi, picking up my pace among the workers who were pouring out of their office towers. I made a left at Park Avenue and headed uptown in a hurry, often crossing on the red, challenging frustrated drivers and leading other brazen pedestrians along with me. After a dozen or so wet blocks I turned east and started along 72nd Street toward the river.

The grayish granite of Sotheby's auction house came into view, and I slowed a bit to regain my breath and straighten myself out. The evening sale of important contemporary art was already well under way, and the place was ringed with empty waiting luxury cars. I could tell the car-service drivers from the private salaried ones: The latter were reading copies of the *Post*, and many of the former were eating falafels.

Just inside the door I was stopped by one of those Sotheby's women. "This is ticket-only," she said, ready to block my advance.

"I lost it."

"Sorry, but you must have a ticket to get in."

"But I'm with the Met. I was caught up in traffic, and I have to get inside to advise on our bid before the lot comes up." I pulled from out of my wallet my yellow museum identification card. "Assistant curator," I announced, "twentieth-century art." If I had said Baroque drawing, she would have sent me packing.

"You'll have to stand," she said. I was shown up the stairs, past a crowded auxiliary room where the proceedings could only be watched on closed-circuit television. None of the power brokers could be found among these unlucky souls sitting in row after row viewing the event on a big-screen TV as if it were a prize fight. Turning a corner, I quietly slipped into the real saleroom, standing at the back to watch the theater unfold as each work of art went on the block.

The large space was packed with both spectators and participants, most of the men in dark suits and French cuffs, the women in smart little dresses. There was an overflow crowd, and I stood among many gallery kids and other young hangers-on at the fringe of this herd. The auctioneer conducted the scene from a large mahogany podium, his voice projecting in a singsong rhythm and coaxing buyers to bid. His accent was difficult to place. He looked European for sure, not necessarily Italian or French or German, but supranational in an almost aristocratic way, as if he might have been comfortable in six languages and had blood ties to every one of them. His gavel was a small round piece of wood that he fit between his thumb and index finger and slammed down sharply on the podium to signal the close of a sale. As he carefully watched the room for signs of potential bidders, perhaps ten busy men and women stood to his left and right, some on the phone with overseas buyers, others spotting discreet bids from the floor. Among these was Claire, her hand clutching a sleek, thin telephone receiver as if it were the old hot line to the Kremlin. I could tell she was concentrating and a bit tense, switching hands to write something down as the phone's cord wrapped around her smartly fitted suit. Her job was to bid for the party at the other end of that phone and to relay the events in the room to the caller. There were no casual pauses, no backing up, no slowing down, and everyone looked pumped, focused. The woman standing next to Claire must have been her boss, I guessed. She had an icy, clipped middle-aged manner, just as Claire had once described, and her clothes were the perfect mix of business and sex.

I recognized David and Susan sitting together toward the front of the audience, the powerful dealer holding close his copy of the glossy sale catalogue. Mounted high overhead was a currency conversion board. An electronic scoreboard of sorts, it listed the current lot number and that moment's highest bid. As the dollar amount changed, so too did the amount in yen, pounds, francs, and deutsch marks. Susan couldn't stop looking around the room, even checking out the row of glassed-in sky boxes on the second level. Those windows were shining serious VIP glare back down to the crowd.

Lot number 49, coming near the end of the sale, was a familiar Miles Levy canvas from the series of "painted collage fallacies." With its estimated selling price of $80,000–$100,000, it was by no means a star of the evening. Important works by such artists as Rothko, Stella, Judd, Lichtenstein, and Jasper Johns had already gone under the gavel for many times that. These artists were huge figures, and the inclusion of the more recently trendy Miles Levy was a way to keep the sale current, up-to-date. But for David and Susan the fate of Lot 49 was an unwanted test of Miles's strength following Todd's untimely death, a test of their damage control and of the health of their creation.

The auctioneer, moving along with a rigid swiftness, gave the briefest of descriptions. "Lot number forty-nine, Miles Levy, untitled oil on canvas from 1987," he said. "We have fifty thousand dollars to start, at fifty now, fifty thousand." Several seconds passed without a bid until a single paddle was raised toward the right side of the room. Bids from the audience were signaled by the raising of numbered paddles, and after this opening salvo only one other paddle was raised. "At sixty thousand dollars now, sixty, I have sixty thousand for it," he continued, "say sixty-five." But nothing more came. Another long, silent moment passed, and the auctioneer turned to the phones for help, but still nothing. Thirty seconds felt like an eternity in such a drought. I glanced at David, expecting his face to be full of concern, but instead he wore a slight smile and sat in a confident recline, as if he knew something no one else did.

The painting had a reserve, a minimum bid sought by the seller without which the work would go unsold, and I doubted that this level had even been reached yet. It was beginning to look like crash-and-burn. But at last a new bidder standing at the rear of the room raised his paddle, perhaps a bottom-fisher hoping to walk out with a bargain. The auctioneer tried to prod the room into going one better. If the painting failed to reach the reserve, then it would be "bought in" and the auctioneer would simply say "passed," quickly moving on to the next lot so as not to lose momentum. That is exactly what would have happened had Claire not suddenly intervened. She motioned toward the podium signaling a new bid from her phone. The man in back, tall and dressed in a suit of finely woven material, bid again. Claire relayed this to her caller and then bid once more.

They were at $80,000 now, the low estimate, which meant the price was now at or above the reserve. But the man bidding against Claire's caller seemed determined and followed her even higher. The two of them went on like this for almost a full minute, back and forth in a perfect volley. What had only seconds earlier looked like a disaster was now a resounding success at $190,000. The volley continued as everyone in the room watched the duel. Each time I felt sure the last bid would go unanswered, another followed.

There seemed no stopping them as the auctioneer rang out the numbers with such efficiency. "Two hundred and twenty-five, two-fifty, two seventy-five, three hundred and twenty-five. Three-fifty, on the phone. Three seventy-five, far back now, *say four.*"

The bidder in the room had nodded at $375,000, tying the record for a work by Miles Levy. Claire's caller would have to set the new record in order to be successful now. The audience watched as Claire spoke into the phone and waited for a reply. I had never felt seconds take so long to pass. "To you, on the phone," said the auctioneer. When at last she received the instructions from the other end, she looked at the podium and nodded in the affirmative; her caller wanted it for the record. "Four hundred now," he said. "Against you now, with four hundred thousand on the phone. Against the room now at four hundred, say four twenty-five." The man at the back waved him off. "Fair warning now, I have four hundred on the phone. Four hundred is bid. All done? Sold for four hundred thousand dollars to the bidder on the phone." With that came the short sharp blast of the gavel hitting wood.

Claire read the client number to the auctioneer, and a few in the room broke into applause. It was applause, ostensibly, to honor the price, applause in admiration of someone's ability to bid the highest, as if this required some kind of skill, some unique talent to be admired and celebrated. But it struck me then that nobody had applauded when the painting was made, no one applauded when it was exhibited, nor when it was hanging on a living room wall in Brentwood or East Hampton or TriBeCa. No event in the entire life of that work of art had ever warranted applause until now. But they were applauding a virtuoso performance of the highest art, a skillful exploitation of their fears and insecurities. They had been entertained and at the same time needfully reassured. The setting of record prices served to confirm both their faith in the entire enterprise and the wisdom of their actions, to confirm the viability of their investments and the purpose in their lives.

I thought of all the curious relationships in the room at that moment. How perfect that Claire be the one to push Miles into the stratosphere like that, how nice that David and Susan could watch from a comfortable distance, and that I could look upon the event in typically clean, amused detachment. There was always a bit of mystery around a phoned-in bid. Was it a man or a woman? From L.A. or Paris? A collector or museum buyer? To this day I have a recurring dream, or more likely a fantasy, that it was Miles himself, calling from the safety and anonymity of the pay phone just down the street from his loft, as he did the night of the accident, and waiting on the line with Claire in case his career might require a little propping up.

Later that night, after all the pretty people had filed out and into their waiting cars and hailed their taxicabs, Claire's boss and her staff would stay behind for a small informal press conference, giving useful quotes for the wire services and tomorrow morning's *Times*. It would be something like, "Miles Levy showed strength, a new record for him. We're all very pleased." But for now the room simply felt the glow of success, not yet interested in the next morning's papers but only relieved that for at least one more day the gig, as Miles had put it, could continue. He and David and Susan could rest easy at least for now. The day when we would wake up and it would all be over—the day Miles might no longer be seen as important—was nowhere near and, as I now understood so well, postponed not by a stroke of luck or scheme but by skill.

Would Miles's work endure through the ages? Would future scholars devote their efforts to his paintings? I predict it will go one of two ways. Either they will see it as uninteresting and ignore it, like all that tiresome nineteenth-century academic painting, or it will be read like the Rosetta stone of its day. At that moment, in the middle of that sale, I actually stopped caring which way it would turn out. Maybe that guy who teaches oil painting on TV will endure. Perhaps there is something in all those thirty-minute landscapes, all those palette-knife pine trees and perfectly reflective lakes that might get discovered one day as the ultimate expression of the 500-channel nation. What the TV oil painter and Miles had in common was their message about what it takes to fulfill the American dream: a large and reliable audience.

I looked over at Claire standing up front near the phones and realized that she was watching me. Somehow she had picked me out of the crowd, and despite all that was going on around her, she froze for a moment. I observed a smile gradually define itself clearly across her face. Eyes bright and wide, she gave me all her attention in that moment even as the room moved on to the next lot, and finally she mouthed the words "Wait for me."

twenty-one

SEVERAL MONTHS have passed. With Vogel's money I moved into a loft on Wooster Street, just around the corner from Miles and, it turns out, directly across the street from the Griffin Gallery. When the broker first showed me the place, I noticed how, if you craned your neck, you could see right into David's office from the bedroom window. But in the end it was the new automatic elevator that sold me. I was surprised to get the place after offering low in a sealed bid. The board was no problem. David and Susan furnished me with impeccable references.

I recently resigned my post at the museum to become the director of Griffin Prints and Drawings, David's new high-profile venture. He and Susan have enlisted me to write the copy for an admiring and lavishly illustrated coffee-table book on the work of Miles Levy. "We're going to do a book," was the way Susan phrased it. I think she has my sister already planning the party. There will be a perverse thrill in seeing all those heavy copies of Miles's book piled high at Rizzoli with the simple words "Text by Stuart Finley" written along the bottom. David and Miles have both been giving me pointers on how to affect the mind-numbing language of contemporary art criticism. "The trick," according to David, "is to reference everything in a learned way while managing to say absolutely nothing."

As expected, Miles has started to paint again, proving that nothing will clear a creative block quite like the piling up of bills. There is something about New York living expenses that can suddenly bring everything powerfully into focus. For a time Miles was even in negotiations with the Museum of Modern Art for a retrospective of his work, but he pulled out after a bitter disagreement over the space they had promised him. Two weeks later the Guggenheim announced it would mount its own show with the artist's cooperation. I suspect he was always just holding out for Wright's famous rotunda, and that his "shocking" break with MoMA (leaked to the *Times*, of course) was his way of raising the bar for jaw-dropping stunts, establishing the new high-water mark of hubris, as if to say to his peers: *Top this.*

Meanwhile, I'm settling comfortably into my new role as dealer and gallery director. Navigating the market with all the curious enthusiasm of a kid who just got his driver's license, I want to go everywhere. I had always prized my museum perquisites—the unlimited access, the private staff dining room, the endless openings—and for a while I feared missing them. But now I understand just how modest they were. David has introduced me to two new wonderful concepts: the clothing allowance and the voucher car. Susan even asked me last week whether I wanted a spare ticket to one of the fashion shows in Bryant Park. "Sure, why not," I told her, recalling Miles's admonishment to quit resisting.

Walking up West Broadway on this remarkably clear day—you can always gauge the smog level by checking the color of the midtown horizon—I run into Christina sitting outdoors at one of those bistros at the corner of Grand. She

is eating lunch with several friends and tells me, from behind
a pair of big dark sunglasses, that Pied Noir is over. When I
ask her why, she says the scene died the day *New York* magazine got wind of it.

"I did notice they were getting friendlier over there," I
say.

"Yeah, that's always a bad sign," she tells me. But not to
worry, she adds, since there's a new spot emerging called
Nivôse. Very subtle. No published phone number yet. "It's
on one of those corners in TriBeCa that uptown people can
never find. But it's easy if you just remember to take Varick,"
she says. This being Christina's world, I have to ask her what
Nivôse means.

"It's the fourth month of the year in the old French rev-
olutionary calendar," she says.

"Ah, how perfectly esoteric. You're always up on these
things, Chrissie."

I leave them eating their mixed-green salads and mineral
water to walk to my newish home, arriving to find Claire sitting on the floor in the middle of the loft because I don't
have any furniture yet. She is on the phone, and sections of
the newspaper are spread around her like random floor cov-
erings. She has taken well to a new pair of reading glasses,
delicate faux-antique frames made of etched metal. They're
sitting on top of the real estate section, which will go unread
by me for the first time in years. I'm content here, very content. I think back to the first time we made love, when right
afterward she looked at me and said how glad she was that
I turned out to be more than just an Old Masters expert.
Well, I don't have to fool her anymore.

When I had once asked her what she saw in Miles Levy,
she couldn't quite put her finger on it, she couldn't explain
the attraction to his sphere except to say that the rewards
were greater than she ever thought. I have no illusions about

why she's still with me, and I know we're not in love. I may have made the choices that suited her, but I made them because they suited me. I've come, finally, to know Claire as a woman attracted to accomplishment, to the comfort of a man who is in some way established. For her, there must be some confirmation of potency, some way, I believe, in which her man's life must develop with a kind of social and professional forward momentum that will ultimately, although still years from now, perhaps a decade or more, supersede her expectation for the sexual ideal. I fear she just wants someone to take care of her, and at this moment I don't like to think of myself as that kind of insurance against menopause.

Miles, his self-worship notwithstanding, was always the perfect match for her. As an artist he could pretend to be avant-garde, he could play his hip nonconformist role while the whole time being truly conventional, almost boringly so. The bad-boy artist wasn't much of a bad boy, because in the end he couldn't be. Nobody *drops out* the way they did twenty-five years ago; nobody turns their back on ambition. That's not cool anymore. It hasn't been for years. I'm sure Miles realized this back when he was in school. In the last decade the money men came to town to seal the fate of those quaint, almost naive days forever. Miles's success, his affluence, insured a thoroughly well-appointed life, eliminating the risks of his more edgy activities. He knew there was no longer any romance in self-destruction, another foolish notion cast aside by those years. For the artist, like everyone else at millennium, the romance was now in self-preservation, self-promotion. Tragic lives don't get *discovered* anymore, they just get buried. No one wants to know about them. Todd couldn't understand this. Todd let his drugs take over. Miles knew when to stop: the moment it threatened his control, his attention to the details. Todd had become a loser

in this game. What he had lost was his grasp of the big picture, and Miles had told him as much moments before he died. Todd had missed Miles's point, which was this: You play only for effect, only until you can stop and still understand how to keep the checks coming in. Even Rembrandt, who had died broken and bankrupt after a very bourgeois life, was never able to balance it all the way Miles has.

There was a point in my life when I would have obsessed about whether Claire would still be with me in two months, one month, a week. The truth is, I don't give us much time, since the forces that brought us together are no longer at work. She needed to get some of her life back from Miles—not much, but enough to feel like her own person again. Being with me was a kind of statement for her to make, a way to gain some distance without losing everything. For me too much has changed to make a neat, clean list. It's enough to say only that at this moment everything seems to feel right, although I'm anxious to know if over time I'll be grateful.

Acknowledgments

THE TRICK of first fiction, Gore Vidal once wrote, is to disguise your ignorance and make a virtue of your limitations. He should have added something about seeking the kindness and advice of others. Without the constant support of family and friends, I would never have been able to write this book. A thanks goes out to every one of you.

I owe a special debt to ICM's very cool Suzanne Gluck, whose hard work and enthusiasm may have surpassed my own at times. She's the sharpest co-conspirator a writer could ever want. Also, I am grateful to Neal Karlen, who provided his generosity at a crucial moment, and to Eric Steel, who kindly gave this book a home, guiding the manuscript through its final stage with intelligence and taste.